A DREAM OF STARS AND DARKNESS

Queen of All Fae, Book 1

Madeleine Eliot

Copyright © 2022 Madeleine Eliot

All rights reserved

The characters and events portrayed in this book are fictitious. Any similarity to real persons, living or dead, is coincidental and not intended by the author.

No part of this book may be reproduced, or stored in a retrieval system, or transmitted in any form or by any means, electronic, mechanical, photocopying, recording, or otherwise, without express written permission of the publisher.

ISBN: 9798363277993

Cover design by: Madeleine Eliot
Printed in the United States of America

To all the authors who never thought they would be.

CONTENTS

Title Page
Copyright
Dedication
Chapter 1   1
Chapter 2   14
Chapter 3   30
Chapter 4   42
Chapter 5   50
Chapter 6   63
Chapter 7   75
Chapter 8   89
Chapter 9   98
Chapter 10   116
Chapter 11   125
Chapter 12   136
Chapter 13   150
Chapter 14   161
Chapter 15   170

Chapter 16	179
Chapter 17	187
Chapter 18	196
Chapter 19	204
Chapter 20	215
Chapter 21	225
Chapter 22	238
Chapter 23	246
Chapter 24	258
Chapter 25	267
Chapter 26	275
Chapter 27	285
Chapter 28	294
Chapter 29	305
Chapter 30	314
Epilogue	323
Acknowledgement	327
About The Author	329

CHAPTER 1

A ball was the last place I wished to be at this particular moment. Rather than checking my supply cabinet, grinding up healing herbs, or spinning spider silk into suturing, I was here, surrounded by the most inane company I could possibly imagine.

The Fae nobility were known for raucous parties and flowing Faerie wine, but not even the charms of the lanterns bobbing overhead under a ceiling of stars could make me forget who these Fae truly were.

Traitors.

Gliding between the noble Fae lords and ladies, I pricked my pointed ears for the telltale sounds of useful gossip. The trick, I had found, in discovering secrets of any importance, was to seem demure and pretty and completely unintelligent, and to find the most overconfident, pompous males I could to surround myself with. I became the shadow on the wall behind them, a pretty ornament to decorate their arms and listen to their whispers, and maybe someday warm their beds.

As if.

"All of His Majesty's men will be slaughtered by those savage rebels," came a booming voice from my left.

I joined the party of Unseelie males who had converged around a fountain of Faerie wine to listen. Any discussion of the rebels could be important. Leaning on the edge of the fountain and pretending to adjust my silk slipper, I tilted my head to try to catch something valuable. I was so focused on the conversation that I didn't sense the approaching presence until it was directly behind me.

My best friend surprised me with a hug from behind, and I jumped, almost toppling over in surprise and taking her with me. The males turned toward the commotion as we righted ourselves and I grimaced. Aurelia looked radiant in lilac silk, her golden hair crowned with orchid blossoms, and her eyes glamoured to match their violet hue. I scowled at her.

"You startled me," I hissed, as I hooked my friend by the elbow and squeezed her arm, possibly with a little more pressure than was absolutely necessary.

"And you cost me my next mark," I added when we were far enough away for the males to lose interest in us.

"Oh please," snorted Aurelia, giving me a knowing look. "Those males knew nothing of importance. I heard them bragging a full half hour ago about the cost of their weekly wine shipments. They care more for money than strategy, and I doubt anyone would trust them with vital information."

I humphed. Aurelia was usually right about reading her marks, but I was still annoyed. Her job was to seduce our targets into spilling their secrets. Her willowy frame and shining blond hair was perfect for this work, and males usually told her whatever she wanted to know before she ever had to bed or threaten them.

I was not willowy or blonde or generally as lovely, so my job was to lurk in the shadows and let the secrets come to me.

I sighed morosely. Now I'd have to mingle and make pointless, unintelligent small talk for another hour or more in the hopes of learning something that probably wouldn't even prove to be useful. I was tired and starting to feel the effects of the Faerie wine, and I desperately wanted to be in my infirmary, cataloging mushrooms, instead of here, attempting espionage.

"Oh don't make that face," said Aurelia, seeing my scowl. "I promise I'll make it up to you." Aurelia's eyes gleamed violet in the starlight. In a singsong voice she added, "I hear there's going to be a very important guest arriving any minute."

I smiled despite my annoyance and let my friend lead me across the room to a quieter corner. Aurelia had been my best friend and closest confidante since we were infants. Having had no siblings, Aurelia was like a sister to me, and we were partners in all things, crime or otherwise.

"Fine, Aurelia, tell me about this *very important* guest," I said, whisking another glass of Faerie wine off a floating tray as we walked through the crowd. If I was going to be stuck here all night, I might as well try to have some fun.

Aurelia waggled her eyebrows at me and took a sip of her wine, throwing a shield of air around us so we wouldn't be overheard.

I felt a twinge of jealousy at the small magic. My powers were basically nonexistent and limited to coaxing plants into growing ever so slightly taller or faster. A mostly useless skill, it was the only magical talent that had ever manifested in me, and I could never shake the envy I felt for my friend's much more useful, if still small, magic.

Since the Great Fae War, which had raged for over two centuries and ended just before my birth, Seelie powers had faded to almost nothing. Prior to the death of the Seelie Queen, the Seelie Fae had been healers, spellbinders, fire wielders, and all manner of other gifts associated with life.

After her death and the failure of a new Queen to emerge, the Unseelie reigned over both realms through fear, cruelty, and wicked magic of impressive strength. They wielded darkness, decay, withering, and death, and the Seelie Fae had been either forced to bow and retain some small scrap of power, or be cast out entirely into the Wilds without any power to speak of.

Still, better to be cast out than bow like my wretch of an uncle.

Try as I might to tap into any hidden depth of power, it was quite clear by the end of my second decade that I was almost powerless. I knew now that my only perceived value, in the eyes of my uncle and his traitorous friends at least, was my noble blood and pretty face. My magic was nothing to speak of.

I was pulled from my reverie by a pinch on my bare

upper arm.

"Are you even listening to me?" snapped Aurelia, now scowling fiercely. "Ember?"

"Sorry," I started, with a little shake. "I promise I'm listening now."

Aurelia rolled her eyes and, exasperated, said, "I was saying that Prince Hadrian will be here. Tonight. In person."

I laughed at the joke, then frowned at my friend's face when I realized she was not laughing with me.

"You're serious?" I asked incredulously.

"Deadly serious," said Aurelia, glancing around at the crowd through the still-in-tact air bubble. "I heard from several noble ladies hoping to marry off their daughters that he will be there with several nobles from his court. This is the mark we have been waiting for!"

Aurelia's eyes gleamed with hopeful promise, but I frowned. This could indeed be a boon, if we could actually pry anything out of the fearsome Unseelie Prince. But it would also be incredibly dangerous.

The Unseelie Prince had a reputation for cruelty that rivaled even his father's. After the war, the Unseelie King and his merciless son had rained terror on the Seelie Fae, driving most into hiding and forcing the rest to kneel to their will. Some, like my uncle, had knelt more readily than others, happy to sell out others in exchange for royal favor, including his own wife.

I knew how important any information the Prince might betray could be, but I wasn't sure it was worth risking myself or my dearest friend without knowing for certain that we would be successful.

"You are either drunk or mad," I hissed as we left the protective bubble to seek more information on the

Prince's arrival. "Or possibly both."

Aurelia laughed, and my anxiety grew. Aurelia was aggressively fearless and dangerously bold, and I knew she was reckless enough to do anything for valuable information.

"Please," I spun to grab Aurelia's hands and pleaded. "The Prince will gut you if he learns who you are, and use your entrails to feed his horses."

Aurelia's gaze softened as she saw the concern in my eyes. She took my hands in hers and smiled gently.

"Don't worry, Em," she said, giving my hands a little squeeze. "I know how to take care of myself." She linked arms with me again and continued steering us around the room.

"Plus," she added in a conspiratorial whisper, "I'll keep my dagger on me the whole time." Aurelia pulled away and winked. "See you in an hour."

I watched as Aurelia waltzed off between noble lords and ladies to listen for more gossip. We had a standing policy of checking in every hour at events like these, unless we were actively working a mark, but I couldn't shake the ball of anxiety that had settled in my stomach.

I knew Aurelia was smart and capable, and that she could wield a dagger as well as any male, if not better, but this was too far, even for her reckless self-confidence. I prayed to the stars that the Prince's appearance was only a rumor, and nothing more.

For another forty minutes, I glided between guests, a few favored Unseelie noble families, Seelie loyalists, and many Unseelie interlopers who had stolen Seelie lands at the end of the war. Both were glamoured to appear more beautiful and powerful than they really were. I caught little snippets of conversation here and there, interspersed with tinkling Seelie laughter and more cruel Unseelie mirth, but not enough to merit actually listening and playing the role of vapid noble lady.

Just as I was about to give up and find yet another glass of sparkling Faerie wine, I heard something that caught my attention.

"Yes, he'll be here shortly," came the nasal voice of a tall, slightly built Seelie male with golden curls, surrounded by fluttering nobles with awed expressions. I recognized Lord Thorn standing in a small crowd of nobles, and grimaced. The oily lord was my uncle's cousin, and a frequent visitor at my uncle's estate. He was a lord of some fortune and lands at the border between the Unseelie and Seelie realms, and based on his lecherous appraisal of my figure whenever he dined with us, I knew it was only a matter of time until he asked my uncle to consent to make me his bride.

I shuddered at the thought. Lord Thorn was the worst kind of Seelie, selling out his so-called allies long before the Unseelie king had officially conquered Seelie lands. He was a well known informant for the Unseelie king, and he had always unsettled me. He looked too long and too intently at certain of my features, and his tongue was always laced with sweet sounding poison. Moreover, while dalliances were common among the unmarried noble lords and ladies of both courts, I had heard stories of how he treated the females who warmed his bed.

I kept my attention trained on Lord Thorn and his group as I moved slightly closer, hoping to hear something useful without being noticed. Lord Thorn had lowered his voice a fraction in an imitation of a conspiratorial whisper.

"I hear he has been tasked with finding himself a Seelie bride before the next new moon." He looked up and said in a loud carrying voice, "Ah, there he is now. Your highness!"

The room grew unnaturally quiet as the music from the Faerie fiddles and the tinkling of glasses and chatter of conversation came to an abrupt halt. Darkness seemed to seep in from the corners of the room and a chill filled the air as all eyes turned toward the towering form of the Unseelie Prince.

Built like a warrior more than a politician, the Prince emanated malice and danger. He strode into the room, polished boots clicking across the ballroom floor in the absolute silence of the crowd who had stopped to watch his movements.

Dressed in black armor from his head to his boots, he looked more fit to be in battle than at a social gathering. On his shoulders, pauldrons ended in black spikes that curved halfway down his arms. The symbol of the Unseelie king, a two headed raven representing death and decay, was embossed on his breastplate, ruby eyes gleaming against the darkness. A crown of spiked black obsidian, so sharp it could draw blood, rested in his short, dark hair. It framed his pale face, chiseled jaw and cheekbones standing out in stark relief, almost making him look sickly.

As he moved through the room, shadows swirled around him. I couldn't tell if the dark aura was his power or a glamour, but it was unsettling. His gaze cut across the room as if counting enemies and checking for exits.

Belatedly, the assembly remembered to bow. I

dropped to my knees with the rest of the crowd, noting that the Prince brought a small entourage, just one Unseelie male and one female, both who looked just as wicked and menacing as he did. They wore the same black armor and ferocious looking daggers. The female's silver braid swung down her back as she marched after her prince. I arose as the Prince passed me and anxiously began seeking my friend from beneath lowered lashes.

"Your Highness, so glad you could come," came the wheedling voice of the lord. "I assure you, only the most loyal of our Seelie allies are here. You honor us with your presence."

The Prince said nothing, but glared darkly around the room as several noblemen and women began attempting to subtly corral their daughters toward him to make introductions. He greeted a few with a slight nod of his head, tight lipped and unsmiling at the simpering ladies. Clearly, he had not come to make friends with the Seelie nobility tonight, and I sincerely doubted he was here in search of a bride.

I hovered a short distance away from the Prince, wondering how Lord Thorn had gained his favor. My uncle and Thorn corresponded regularly, and I made a mental note to slip into his study later when he was asleep to check his messages.

Hearing about the Prince and his dark power was one thing, but finally seeing it in person was far more terrifying, and I knew I couldn't let Aurelia go through with her mad plan. I followed at some distance, hoping to intercept Aurelia before her recklessness got her killed.

The Prince seemed disinclined to dance or socialize,

and leaned against a gilded pillar scowling at the room in general and oozing disdain while Lord Thorn made introductions and prattled on at great length about the roads and the weather and the guests. As if made uneasy by his menacing aura, the guests mostly gave the Prince a wide berth, gathering some distance away to gossip and cast speculating looks in his direction after each introduction. I kept my distance, hovering by a table of Faerie wine and inspecting myself surreptitiously in a gilded mirror.

My face had gone paler than its usual warm tan, and I tried to pinch some color into my cheeks. My auburn hair, which was usually pulled back in a messy braid, was woven in an intricate bun atop my head and adorned with honeysuckle blossoms. The dress I had chosen for tonight was a midnight blue, with a skirt that flared out to disguise my larger than average hips and waist. It was more modest than most of the ladies around me, but my goal was to go as unnoticed as possible, and drawing attention with flashes of skin would defeat my purpose. I had to wear a glamour to blend in with the crowd, but I kept it as minimal as I could: a faint glow in my eyes and cheeks, a slight trimming of my waistline. Any more than that taxed my meager powers too much to sustain for an entire ball.

Finally, I spotted Aurelia behind me in the mirror, beginning to inch toward the Prince. I moved to intercept her as slowly as I could force myself to go, to avoid drawing attention.

"We do have some strikingly pretty females here," I heard Lord Thorn say to the Prince as I tried to glide past unnoticed. "Some have remarkable talents and grace.

Others" my neck prickled as I felt the lord's eyes on me "not so much."

I tried to keep walking as I felt a shiver travel up my back. Turning slightly, I met the Prince's gaze, something electric passing between us. He was possibly the most handsome male I had ever seen, despite the sickly pallor, and definitely the most dangerous. His eyes were gray, but something in them flashed silver as he looked at me. My stomach flipped.

"Ah, Lady Ember!" Damn the stars and the goddess and Lord Thorn. There was no way to pretend I hadn't heard that. Before I could force myself to move, his hand gripped my forearm firmly and dragged me before the Prince. I dropped into a deep curtsy before them, panic blooming in my chest.

While I knew this might be an opportunity to gain some very useful information, I did not feel up to the task after four glasses of Faerie wine. Also, Aurelia would skin me alive for stealing her mark, regardless of whether I had intended it or not.

I kept my gaze trained on the floor as I heard the oily voice of the lord. "Your most royal highness, Allow me to present Lady Ember of the Seelie Court." Lord Thorn pulled me to stand, and I brought my face up to meet the gaze of the Prince.

His eyes met mine, and I felt that electric charge again. Then he looked to where Lord Thorn was gripping my arm. Darkness seemed to pulse around him as he glared at Thorn, and he quickly dropped my arm.

"A pleasure, my lady," the Prince purred. The corner of his lips quirked upward as he held my gaze, and my heart sped up slightly. Tendrils of darkness had begun curling around my ankles and snaking up my calves. I shivered at the sensation, surprised that I felt more drawn to the Prince than terrified of him, and wondering how to draw information from this impassable wall of a male. Stars, I needed to get away from this terrifying, alluring male as soon as possible

"Lady Ember has no more than very small magic," continued Lord Thorn, gaze sweeping over my form with a lecherous gleam. "But she is a fair dancer, your Highness," he continued. "You would honor her uncle's house if you would consent to dance with her."

"Small magic?" asked the Prince skeptically. He looked me over with a raised brow and my ire rankled at being appraised like a mare for breeding.

"Unfortunately yes, your Highness," I said, bowing my head and trying to sound demure while simmering with anger. Lord Thorn was a bastard, but he had given me the perfect excuse to start a conversation with the Prince that would not draw suspicion. I was a good enough spy to recognize the opportunity.

The Prince gave me another appraising look, smile twisting into a grimace.

"I have no time for small magic, or insincere humility," he said coldly as he turned on his heel.

I blinked in surprise at the sudden rudeness. That the Prince would be imperious and cold didn't surprise me, but that he would be so brazen about ignoring the courtesies expected in an assembly of Fae was unexpected. And that he would snub me so suddenly and publicly was going to cause a stir among the gossips of court.

Sure enough, ladies leaned toward each other and tittered behind their hands, and I felt my face grow warm with the embarrassment of being so publicly humiliated.

Lord Thorn scowled at me as if the Prince's rudeness was somehow my fault.

"Your uncle will hear of this," he hissed, and he jogged after the Prince, resuming his unending description of the court and their festivities. I took a steadying breath as Aurelia finally joined me, violet eyes wide in shock.

"What happened? What did he say to you?" asked Aurelia, grabbing my hand and leading me outside to fresh air and a clear, starry night sky.

I gave a humorless laugh.

"That he has no time to dance with powerless Fae" I snarled, feeling anger replace my embarrassment.

Aurelia frowned. "The ass," she said quietly, resting against the railing of the balcony and removing her heeled slippers. "If he asks to dance with you another time, you should refuse. Let him feel the pain of being snubbed."

I raised my eyebrow at her.

"And then I can sweep in and seduce information from him," she added with a mischievous grin, twirling prettily on her now bare feet.

I laughed again and said, voice dripping with antipathy, "I think I can safely promise you that I will *never* dance with the Prince."

CHAPTER 2

The dream was always the same.

I sat on a cold rock under a sky full of stars. Magic hummed in my veins, stretching deep into the earth until I was aware of every root and earthworm, and reaching high overhead to touch every star and particle in the night sky.

I felt more alive than ever before, but I was also incredibly sad. I felt a loss of some kind, like something vital had been taken from me, but I couldn't remember what.

As I looked up, the stars began to wink out one by one. The night sky darkened, and cold dread replaced my sadness as every star was banished from the sky. I could no longer feel the humming of the earth and the heavens.

My fear and dread intensified as darkness blotted out my vision.

It always ended the same way, except this time I woke with a terrible headache from the intense emotion, and probably also excessive consumption of Faerie wine.

At breakfast, I sipped chamomile tea in merciful quiet, the only disruption coming from the flick of papers as my uncle read the morning reports.

The quiet never lasted long.

"My Lord," a messenger came scurrying up to my uncle and handed him a sealed envelope. "From Lord Thorn, my lord."

I grimaced. If Lord Thorn was writing to my uncle this early in the morning, he would almost certainly be stopping by at some point during the day. I intended to not be present whenever he arrived.

"Lord Thorn says you were snubbed by the Prince last night," said my uncle without looking up from the letter.

"I didn't care for him much either, Uncle," I said calmly as I sipped my tea. My uncle glanced up at me and pursed his lips before returning to the missive. I reminded myself to find and copy the letter later in case it had any strategically important information aside from my inability to find a husband.

While the Great Fae War had been officially over for more than two decades, factions of Seelie resistance had never stopped opposing the Unseelie king and his conquest of the Seelie court. After murdering the Seelie Queen, the Unseelie King had declared himself King of All Fae, and many Seelie nobles bent the knee rather than face death, dismemberment, or banishment to the

Wilds or the mines.

Some Seelie, like my uncle, had bent the knee long before, betraying their own realm and family for an ounce of extra power and privilege. I hated him.

He never spoke of my parents. My childhood nursemaid always told me I was to honor and respect him. He took me in, despite being the daughter of traitors to the crown. He had never loved me, at least I didn't think he had. My mother was his wife's sister, and he must have loved her once to agree to take me in.

She died when I was still a babe, at the hands of the male who sat across from me.

I finished my tea and rose from the breakfast table, preparing to leave to further nurse my headache.

"And where are you off to?" Asked my uncle without looking up from his papers. I froze. My uncle never asked about where I went or what I did each day. His only interest in me was how well I would marry to secure him powerful allies at court, and bragging about his charitable nature in taking in his poor orphaned niece. It was difficult to actively deceive my extremely shrewd uncle, so I generally relied on his disinterest to do whatever I pleased and go about my work.

"I'm going into the woods," I said, mostly truthfully. "To pick the foxgloves with Aurelia. They bloom this time of year."

My uncle looked up and gave me a hard look. For a moment I thought he might forbid me from going, but he simply said "be back to dress for dinner," and went back to thumbing through reports.

"Oh no, who's coming for dinner?" said a voice from behind me. I whirled to face the voice and instantly regretted it. My headache was still murder, and I silently cursed my life choices. The male turned to me and smiled. "You look terrible, cousin."

"Thank you, Aspen. Now go away," I said with a grimace.

"Oh, don't be a poor sport," said Aspen playfully, tugging on my braid. I winced as pain shot through my temples and Aspen raised his hands in apology.

"Sorry, too much Faerie wine?" He asked, grinning at me.

"Why ask if you already know the answer," I said curtly, turning to leave.

As much as I hated my uncle, I loved my cousin like a brother. He was tall and slim and elegant, but kind and warm in a way my uncle was not. As children we had played together until he had been sent away to receive a "proper education" by my uncle. Now that he had returned to take on "the duties of the heir of a high lord of the realm," in my uncle's words, we were close once more.

"Important people are coming to dinner," said my uncle looking up from his papers. He pinned Aspen with a hard look. "As future lord of this estate you will be here. Now take your bickering outside so I can have peace."

Aspen grinned, swiping a blueberry tart from the breakfast table and joining me as I headed out of the house and toward the woods.

"I hate when important people come to dinner," Aspen signed dramatically, taking a large bite of the tart. "If meansh I hash to behaze," he said through a mouthful of breakfast. I rolled my eyes.

"At least he's not trying to marry you off to all of them," I said darkly, kicking a little spot of mushrooms that had grown up from the morning dew. "He always invites Thorn, as if we are already intended for each other."

Aspen shuddered in mock horror and I pushed him. He laughed and tugged on my braid again, eliciting another sharp pang in my head.

"Maybe you'll be mates one day," he teased. I glared at him and he put up his hands in mock surrender. "I take it back! Peace, cousin!"

Aurelia was waiting in our usual spot by a cathedral grove of elm on the border of the woods and my uncle's estate. When she saw Aspen, she blushed the most adorable shade of crimson and began to stammer as she handed me the extra basket she always brought for collecting plants and flowers.

"Oh Lord Aspen, what a surprise," she stuttered, lowering into a little curtsy and blushing furiously at Aspen. I groaned. Aspen grinned.

"Lady Aurelia, always a pleasure," he said, taking Aurelia's hand and planting a smooth kiss on her knuckles. Aurelia blushed even more crimson, which I didn't think was possible, biting her lower lip in adorable infatuation.

"Ladies, I bid you farewell. See you at dinner, Ember." With a wave, Aspen turned and walked away, long strides eating up the distance toward the stables.

"Really?" I asked, looking exasperatedly at my best friend.

"You look terrible, Em," Aurelia replied, eyes twinkling blue now without her glamour in the morning sun. Her blush began to fade. "Too much Faerie wine?"

"Ugh, you and Aspen will make perfect married

mates one day," I groaned, hooking elbows with my almost-sister and smiling fondly, despite the headache. "I don't understand why you're so helplessly in love with him, but you could do worse. Help me look for fairy caps on the way, will you? I'm almost out and we will need them soon enough for the winter colds."

We picked our way through the woods, filling my basket with foxglove and fairy caps, and a few stems of woodsorrel we happened upon as we trekked the well-known path we walked almost every day. The woods always seemed to provide exactly what I needed for my healing tinctures, and I wasn't surprised to find plenty of fairy caps as we made our way to our destination. Maybe some magic still existed in these lands.

We chatted merrily, mostly about Aurelia's undying love for my cousin, but also about some of the intriguing gossip we gathered the night before. Sprites flitted in and out of the trees, gossamer wings shining in the Autumn light as they chittered happily.

"I wish I had wings," sighed Aurelia wistfully for the eight hundredth time in our lives as she admired the sprites darting to and fro.

"If you had wings you'd catch them on tree branches and trip on them while dancing," I laughed, remembering very clearly a moment in our childhood when she had nearly broken her neck by jumping off a tree to see if wings grew.

Sprites, who weren't beholden to either court, were some of the few Fae creatures who could fly. The only other Fae who was known to have wings was the rightful Seelie Queen. No one could ever explain why to me. My childhood nursemaid said she had been goddess-blessed, which wasn't really an answer.

But the stories claimed that whenever a Seelie Queen died without an heir, a new queen would be born and recognized by her wings. When the last queen had been killed without an heir, it seemed that the line of Seelie queens was irrevocably broken. No Fae had been born with wings in over twenty years.

"Wouldn't you like to have wings?" Aurelia asked, linking her arm with mine as we neared our destination.

"No," I replied firmly. "I'd happily trade you wings to have some of your practical magic." Aurelia gave my arm a sympathetic squeeze.

"Growing plants is practical," she protested. Dear Aurelia, always positive if there was positivity to be had.

"Not when you can only grow them two inches," I laughed.

As we wandered deeper into the woods, I glanced over my shoulder, growing increasingly paranoid that someone might be following us. As far as I knew I had never been followed this far in, but being paranoid sort of came with the territory of rebellion.

We reached the caves without anyone trailing us, of course. If you didn't know it was there, it would be very easy to miss the cave entrance that was half hidden by trees and bushes, carefully tended and grown to conceal the secret that I would die to keep.

Aurelia looked over and nodded, and pushing branches aside, I led the way into the cave.

An hour later, I found myself in the infirmary, wrists deep in the bloody mess of my friend's back.

"It doesn't need stitching," Pip whined as I examined the gash that ran from his shoulder and almost halfway down his back. I had seen worse injuries, but never one on Pip, who was famously timid of any actual violence.

"How did you get this exactly?" I asked as I gathered spider silk, an ointment made of mugwort and primrose, scissors, and a very sharp needle. Pip blanched at the sight of it and closed his eyes, breathing deeply.

"I fell," he hedged, cracking one eye open and closing it again quickly when I brandished the needle at him. It would heal slowly on its own, as all Fae healed quickly, but it was deep, and a few stitches would speed the process and minimize scarring.

"That is the most obvious lie you have ever told," I said, filling a basin with warm water to clean the wound. "And that includes the time you told me that you kissed the Unseelie Prince at midnight on a full moon."

"Well that's all I can say," said Pip, brown curls bobbing as he attempted to hide his panic about the approaching needle.

Pip was a Seelie Fae of common birth, and I liked him immensely. He was kind and gentle and intelligent, and if he didn't prefer males I would almost certainly have fallen for him by now. I sighed, appraising the injury again.

"Fine, don't tell me," I said. "But this better be the only time you are injured like this," I added sternly.

"Be brave Pip," said Aurelia, who was busily grinding more mugwort in the corner of the infirmary. "Ladies love scars. If you don't let Ember stitch you, they'll all be running after you intent on bedding you."

Pip blanched. "Really?" He said, looking terrified. "Well then I suppose a few stitches will be fine."

I smiled as Aurelia laughed, and began to cleanse the wound. Aurelia finished with the mugwort and moved on to grinding some eucalyptus to use for breathing treatments. While not officially a healer, Aurelia joined me in here most days, and she was almost as proficient in stitching wounds and making tinctures as I was.

I dabbed ointment over the wound, making Pip hiss something furious. He would have to put up with the sting, as the needle would hurt him much more without the numbing ointment. I moved quickly, knowing the Commander wanted to debrief us about the previous night. Pip's injury had taken priority when I saw the extent of the wound, but her patience was not endless.

"Pip!" A voice shouted from the hallway outside my infirmary. "PIP!" A panting Fae male came charging into the infirmary, face pale and breathing ragged as he finally saw Pip sitting quite safely on my workbench.

"Oh, you're alright, thank the goddess," said Lark, looking relieved and blushing furiously as Pip took him in with wide eyes. I gave a little cough and both males jumped slightly. I smiled.

"Maybe you could hold Pip's hand while I stich him up," I said to Lark, motioning him over to where I was preparing to operate. "He needs you." Pip gave me a wide-eyed, panicked look. "To help with the pain, of course," I added somberly.

I winked at Pip, whose face was a bright pink. I knew perfectly well that Pip would feel nothing, but I couldn't resist playing matchmaker just a little.

"Of course," cried Lark, giving Pip his hand and squeezing tightly. Pip blushed more, and gruffly said,

"I'm fine, really." Despite his protests, he gripped Lark's hand back.

Stitching Pip's shoulder was a quicker job than I anticipated. Dressing the wound with spider silk bandages, I reminded him to keep it clean.

"It should be good as new in a few days," I added, thanking the stars for our swift Fae healing that made my job easier.

"Thanks, Em," Pip smiled and dropped a kiss on my head. Lark frowned slightly, then perked up when Pip grabbed his hand and led him out of the infirmary.

"Maybe you should have lectured them on other safe practices," said Aurelia slyly, grinning into her mortar. "Those two will be admitting their feelings and acting on them any moment now, with that kind of encouragement."

"Oh hush," I said, cleaning up my supplies. "Come on, we need to see the Commander."

Aurelia tidied her grinding into a corner as I swept up the snipping of spider silk. I left instructions with Nella, one of my apprentices from amongst the common Seelie Fae I had been teaching, to fetch me for anything more dire than a headache, and we left through the cave network in search of the Commander.

The caves below the woods were an extensive hidden network, and it had taken me the better part of a year to learn my way around them. As we walked through passages lit by fireflies and glow worms, we passed all manner of Fae, mostly Seelie commoners, but also a few noble of both Seelie and Unseelie courts. The Unseelie always made me feel nervous with their dark magic and wicked looks, but if they were on our side then I was grateful for their help in our cause.

After the War, not all rebel Seelie had been banished to the Wilds. Some stayed in caves like this, hidden underground and spreading the word about a growing resistance. Over twenty years the network and caves had grown, connecting Fae who opposed the wicked king from the Wilds and the courts, both Seelie and Unseelie. While most rebels were Seelie commoners and nobles who had refused to bend the knee, including myself and Aurelia, there were also several Unseelie nobles who had made enemies of the king had joined our cause, hoping to dethrone him and unite our people.

Most Seelie and Unseelie would prefer to remain separate, of course, but joining forces to oppose our common enemy was better than trying to fight several separate rebellions. The Commander had made it happen, convincing Fae from both sides to join the cause and fight for a future free of the Unseelie King and a return to our two separate realms.

We found the Commander in the kitchens, drinking tea and reading reports as if she was simply a noble lady in charge of a grand estate, instead of the most important leader of our resistance.

"Commander," I said, smiling as I sat across from her. Aurelia sat next to me and we waited for the Commander to look up from her reports and acknowledge us.

Instead of looking up, she continued to flip through papers and said, "report."

I glanced at Aurelia, who looked as wary as I felt.

"Nothing of importance from the ball," I said, "but my uncle received a letter this morning from Lord Thorn. I haven't had time to read it yet, but I will tonight."

"There are lots of nobles talking about shipments to the North," Aurelia added, glancing my way, "but no clear indication of what might be in the shipments, other than wine."

The Commander put down her tea cup and looked up. Her face was beautiful and serious, a wicked scar marring her left side from above her eyebrow to her nose, received in the Great Fae War from the king himself. Her left eye was clouded and unseeing from the injury, but she refused to wear a patch, baring her scar proudly as a token of her hatred for the king and a testament to her strength and survival.

She narrowed her good eye at us.

"Anything else?" she asked, in a way that made it clear that she felt we were omitting something vital.

"The Prince was there," Aurelia piped up. She greatly admired the Commander, and viewed her as something of a second mother. Having never known my own mother, I felt more wary around her than Aurelia did, but it was hard for me to fully trust anyone, except my best friend.

"And?" The Commander was waiting for something more, but I honestly wasn't sure what she wanted to hear.

"He refused to dance with me," I shrugged. The sting of rejection was still there, not because I was snubbed, but because it had prevented me from coaxing any important information from the Prince. "Lord Thorn introduced us. That was all," I added.

The Commander steepled her fingers and looked over them at me. Her gaze was piercing, and it was hard to hold her eyes for too long.

"There's another ball in two nights," she said, sliding invitations from her stack of reports and placing them in front of myself and Aurelia.

"You two will be attending," she added, her gaze appraising. "I need you to get close to the Prince. Ask about the rebellion, in the vaguest terms possible. See what he's heard. Aurelia, you know the drill."

I blinked, first at the Commander, then at the invitation.

"Yes sir," said Aurelia, at the same time I said, "What?"

The Commander gave me a hard look. "We need information. I can't send in a lord - the Prince would have no reason to share secrets with him. But a beautiful noble lady..." she trailed off and I realized in horror that she meant for Aurelia to actually seduce him.

"Was this your idea?" I said, turning to Aurelia. She blushed guiltily.

"It's a solid plan," she defended.

"It's a mad plan!" I replied, frustration growing at my friend's reckless need to prove herself. "If he discovers who we are, he will kill us," I protested. "This is too dangerous." Aurelia bristled at my overprotectiveness.

"I'm a trained assassin," she said coolly. "It won't be the first time I've played the seductress for information."

"Pip and Lark will be there as wait staff," the Commander interrupted, standing and beginning to walk back up the corridor, forcing us to follow. "And I'll position some of our noble men in the room too with instructions to look out for you."

"Oh well, we're definitely safe then," I said

sarcastically, earning a glare from the Commander. "That won't help her if she's trapped alone with that monster."

To my surprise, the Commander laughed.

"My dear child," she said, still laughing, "I don't need her to bed him. I just need him to *want* to bed *her*. Unless you'd like to volunteer for the job?"

I bristled.

"What about Aspen?" I said, turning to Aurelia. She blushed and lowered her eyes.

"It's a job, Ember," she replied, glancing at the Commander. "It won't mean anything."

The Commander rose from her table.

"Aurelia, will you give us a moment?" she asked, pinning me in place with her good eye.

Aurelia nodded and, shooting me a sheepish glance, disappeared back to the infirmary. The Commander turned back to me, speaking quietly.

"You swore to me when you joined our cause that you would do everything in your power to fight the Seelie King. To avenge your parents' deaths. To restore our Queen and magic."

I had been pulled into this movement three years ago by Aurelia. She had introduced me to the Commander, who was friends with her family. Aurelia's parents were also part of the movement, but their commitment was constrained by their position as lesser nobility. They were watched carefully, so their contributions were largely financial.

Aurelia had kept this place a secret for the first twenty years of our friendship. She knew my past, and knew that I felt no love for my uncle. On my twenty-first birthday, the year Fae achieved their majority, she brought me here. She told me about the movement to restore the Seelie court and realm, and to place a new queen on the throne to defy the Unseelie King. The Commander had been wary of involving me because of my uncle, but I trusted Aurelia, and Aurelia was committed, so I became committed as well.

The Commander gave me a piercing look.

"I remember," I said earnestly, "and I meant it, but…"

"Then let Aurelia do her job, and you do yours," she said, finality in her tone. "I promise, no harm will come to her."

She held my gaze. I trusted very few people, but the Commander had never led me astray, and she had proven her loyalty to the Seelie people. In the few years I had been working for her, I had come to trust her almost as much as Aurelia. I nodded.

"Good," she said briskly, "then you had better get ready for tomorrow." She turned on her heel and was gone, leaving me to my own dark thoughts.

As I tidied the infirmary and sorted my medicines, thankful that there were no patients or major injuries aside from Pip today, I thought over the plan for tomorrow night.

I couldn't risk Aurelia, no matter what the Commander said, and I knew in her heart that Aurelia didn't want to betray Aspen, even if the arrangement between them wasn't really a formal one yet. She was too in awe of the Commander to refuse, and too committed to question the mission, so I accepted in my heart what would have to be done tomorrow night.

Technically, it wasn't even defying the Commander's orders, since she had suggested it herself, I mused.

Since I couldn't let Aurelia seduce the Prince, I would

have to seduce him myself.

CHAPTER 3

These infernal dinners were a cruel torture of the most exquisite kind. I sat between two ancient Unseelie Fae lords, who spoke over me as if I were nothing more than a vaguely annoying centerpiece at the table. The dark glamours of the Unseelie guests were especially unsettling tonight, making me shiver in the warm glow of the candlelight.

Aurelia, whose family my uncle had invited as our closest noble neighbor, was at the other end of the table, too far to pass anything more than furtive glances and eye rolls at each other. We would have to wait until tomorrow to plan for the ball. Aspen was near the head of the table at the right hand of his father, deep in conversation about something that I greatly yearned to hear in case it was useful to the resistance, and

Lord Thorn was seated across from me, lecherous eyes roving over me as if he wished to possess me in the most unholy of ways.

I really hated my uncle tonight.

When I had left my room to come downstairs, looking for Aspen before entering the dining room, I had overheard my uncle and Thorn speaking in my uncle's study. Creeping quietly along the carpeted floor, I had gotten as close as I could without being seen or heard, hiding behind a potted ficus outside the study door.

"It will be done in a few days' time," came the oily voice of Lord Thorn, who must be standing only a few feet from the slightly open door. "Once we have the information his majesty needs, we will be able to move against them."

"And if he fails?" My uncle asked. It sounded like he must be some distance from Thorn, maybe looking out the windows or examining his bookshelves. "If they catch wind of it, they'll move the operation."

I frowned, wishing I had grabbed paper and pen, and trying to commit every word to memory.

"He won't fail," said Thorn. I heard him move toward the door and bolted, hoping he didn't look out until I was long gone.

Now I made every effort to ignore Thorn and keep my eyes on the meal or Aurelia. I hadn't bothered to glamour myself tonight, a fact that annoyed my uncle dearly, but he was too civilized to mention in front of "important people," and I knew I appeared dull compared to the glittering Unseelie ladies around me.

That suited me fine. The glamour was difficult to sustain at the best of times, and I still had a pounding headache from last night's ball, making everything feel more difficult than it usually did. No point in taxing my limited powers further than I absolutely had to.

Instead I had brushed powder on my cheeks and donned a pretty, but modest, dark green dress that would bring out my eyes, again with a flared skirt to flatter my waist and hips. I had braided my hair in a crown atop my head and woven little white flowers throughout. I was quite pleased with my appearance, even without the glamour, but my uncle only scowled at me with displeasure whenever he looked my way.

Aspen had moved and was now speaking animatedly to a young looking Unseelie lord seated next to him who was all dark edges and midnight glances. He was dressed in a silver coat and wore the most ridiculous set of horns I had ever seen. He winked at me when he caught me staring, and I hoped the horns caused him every sort of inconvenience possible.

I toyed with my soup and focused on the table centerpieces, making the orchid petals fan gently, as if blown by a slight breeze.

"Such an adorable gift," said Lord Thorn, from across the table. His condescending, nasal voice irritated my headache, so I ignored him and returned my attention to the soup.

"Such a pity his highness didn't appreciate it," he added, loudly enough that, at the mention of the Prince, many of the guests turned toward Thorn, anticipating some titillating gossip.

"What's that Thorn?" Came my uncle's voice from the end of the table. It carried louder than was probably acceptable at a polite dinner, and more of the guests stopped to glance our way. I felt a flush creep up my neck to my cheeks, knowing I was about to be the center of attention in a crowd whose attention I definitely did not crave.

"Nothing of consequence, my lord," he sneered, clearly reveling in the attention as he straightened his cuffs and brushed a speck of imaginary dust from his lapel. "Just commiserating with Lady Ember over her unfortunate rebuffing at last night's ball." He gave me an obviously fake sympathetic look.

"My dear girl, I do not begrudge your small magic," he crooned. I tried not to gag into my soup. "Prey grant me the honor of claiming a dance with you at the next ball we both attend."

The table burst into hushed chatter and I seethed in anger and his ability to both humiliate and manipulate me in a single statement. I met his gaze, and said, politely but coldly, "Thank you, my Lord, that would be an honor."

He smiled placatingly and the table resumed their chatter, although this time I caught words like "prince," and "snubbed," and "powerless," in the snippets I could actually make out.

I sat in silence for the next five courses, entertaining myself by imagining all the ways I might strangle Lord Thorn, until finally it was acceptable for me to excuse myself. I glanced at Aurelia as I left the table, but Aspen had moved to sit next to her, and she looked so happy to be gazing into his eyes that I couldn't bring myself to separate them.

I glided out into the rose garden past the horned Unseelie lord and took in a deep breath of perfumed air. When I was as far away from the rest of the guests as I could get, I let out a loud curse.

"Tsk, tsk, what language," sneered an unpleasantly familiar voice. Lord Thorn had followed me into the rose garden, and was slinking his way toward me with a malevolent gleam in his eye. "And after I so graciously saved you from embarrassment at dinner," he added, pretending to look wounded.

"Excuse me, sir, but you caused my embarrassment," I replied icily, taking a measured step backwards as he came toward me.

He grabbed my arm and pulled me close to him, control seeming to snap. Hot breath assaulted my ear as he said, "you should remember your place in this world, girl. You are ungifted and unclaimed by a noble house without the charity of your uncle."

He loosened his grip on my arm slightly, the illusion of respectable control back in place. "Luckily, you have other charms that make you a fair prospect for a bride for some lucky lord."

The word "charms" was accompanied by a bold appraisal of my form, and I nearly gagged.

"Is there a problem, my Lord?" Came a voice from the terrace.

Thanks the stars, Aspen had appeared, arm in arm with Aurelia, and he looked positively murderous at the sight of Lord Thorn holding me so close.

"Not at all, my lord." He quickly took a step back and smiled complacently. "Lady Ember and I were just discussing the details of our upcoming dance."

He smoothed a hand through his golden curls and smiled genially at my cousin. Aspen was unmoved. He knew Thorn's type, and he knew when a poor liar plied his trade.

"A pleasure as always, my lady," Thorn said, bowing

to me and striding swiftly back up the stairs and across the terrace. I noticed the horned lord staring from the doorway and averted my gaze.

Aspen and Aurelia closed the distance between us. Aurelia looked shaken and ran her hands over me as if to check for damage.

"Are you alright, Em?" She asked, still checking me for any sign of injury. "I should have come with you into the garden, but I…"

She glanced guiltily at Aspen, who looked at her with equal remorse.

"I'm fine," I assured them, taking my cousin's free arm and guiding them back to the terrace and the party inside. Truthfully I was shaken by Lord Thorn's boldness in approaching me so openly, but they didn't need to know that. I could handle him.

"Thorn should watch himself," said my cousin darkly as he escorted us back up the stairs. "It's clear you don't desire his attention."

Aurelia nodded fervently. I smiled and said lightheartedly, "maybe I should borrow your dagger, just in case."

I had been completely joking about the dagger, but the next morning Aurelia and Aspen practically frog-marched me out to the stables to begin teaching me "some simple moves."

They were not simple. So far we had covered stances and blocking, and now that we were on to parrying I was sweaty and sore and more than a little embarrassed at my inability to master this skill. I was a healer at heart, and it turned out I was not made out for killing.

"You still look like you're scared of the blade, Em," Aurelia sighed as I attempted to stab a hay bale with

Aspen's dagger for the tenth time. Aspen snorted in amusement. I cast him a withering look.

"I need a break," I said, handing the dagger back to Aspen handle first. Aurelia would have been a more effective and competent teacher, but Aspen didn't know that she could slice a man up in her sleep, and he would ask too many questions if she taught me. I would get her to show me everything again later in the caves when Aspen wasn't around.

"Practice makes perfect," Aspen said consolingly as he sheathed the dagger at his waist. "I should get back to father anyway, lest he disinherit me. Again tomorrow?"

He looked so hopeful that, much as I dreaded the idea of more training, I nodded.

Aspen smiled, kissed Aurelia's hand while murmuring, "my lady," and waved as he walked away.

Aurelia smiled at me, a light blush from Aspen's attention still staining her cheeks. She squeezed my arm and said, "Maybe you can imagine practicing on the Prince."

We spent a few hours in the infirmary, but there was little to do. The Commander had gone to the border with a contingent of soldiers to check our communication lines, so most of the usual Fae were gone. I also lamented that I would have to delay giving her my information about the meeting between Thorn and my uncle.

"Come to dinner at my place tonight," Aurelia said, wrapping up the bandages she had been working on and putting away her tools. "You can sleep over after! It will be frightfully dull, but more fun if you are there."

"Who's expected?" I asked, putting away the herbs we had gathered on our walk to the caves. As usual, the forest had provided, and now I was struggling to find places to put everything.

"I'm not sure," she replied, coming to stand near me. "Some other noble families I think? Father didn't say, except that this is a working dinner."

That meant he was looking for information for the Commander. Aurelia's parents often hosted nobility who were loyal to the king in the hopes of both learning something useful and keeping up appearances in society. Aurelia would be expected to be working as well.

"I'll ask my uncle," I said, smiling at my friend. "Will you help me pick something to wear?"

Aurelia's taste in dresses was very different from my own. After seeing my wardrobe and declaring all were "too dull," she insisted I wear one of her dresses, which were almost all too snug in the waist and bosom. The one she settled on was a gold shimmery dream. The material had some give, so I was able to squeeze into it, but my breasts were at great risk of popping out.

"Your parents will be scandalized," I hissed as she led me downstairs by the arm. "When you wear this it looks regal. On me it looks…" I struggled to find the right word.

"Seductive?" Aurelia offered with a grin. "Alluring? Enticing?"

"Inappropriate!" I hissed back as we entered the dining room. Aurelia looked beautiful as always in white with a crown of pink primroses circling her golden head. She was a summer goddess, and I, with my auburn hair flowing around my shoulders, was a fiery autumn siren.

I didn't love the feeling, but Aurelia insisted I looked

perfect, so I went along with it. Hopefully we'd be able to spend the whole dinner gossiping and chatting by ourselves without having to be on display or socialize with pompous males.

My hopes were dashed instantly.

"My dear," said Aurelia's father as he rushed over to us, waving behind him for someone to join him. My heart plummeted when I saw who it was.

"My dear, I think you have not had the pleasure of meeting his royal highness, Prince Hadrian, yet," said her father, doing an impeccable job of looking amiable while introducing an enemy. "Your highness, this is my daughter Aurelia and her friend, Lady Ember. I believe you are acquainted with her already."

I glanced at Aurelia's father, a twinkle in his eye. Clearly Aurelia had told him about the ball. I grimaced internally.

"A pleasure," said the Prince, bowing low with impeccable manners as Aurelia and I curtsied in response. He looked up and met my eyes, that goddess damned spark flitting between us again.

Tonight he had chosen a black (what a surprise) coat with silver cuffs and formal trousers. He had left his crown off, but the shadows that trailed him the first night we met seemed to follow him everywhere, and they were floating around him like oddly shaped wings. I quickly scanned the room, but I didn't see his guards.

"You have no guards tonight? I asked. "Are you not afraid you may be attacked?"

He gave me his wicked half smile and asked, "should I be afraid of an attack in this house tonight?

"No of course," wheezed Aurelia's father, giving me a panicked look and patting the Prince's arm. "We are all friends here."

"Good," said the Prince, holding out his arms, one each to me and to Aurelia. "It would be an honor to sit with my new friends, then, at dinner."

The goddess wanted to destroy me. That must be it. With a graceful curtsy, Aurelia took the Prince's arm. I took the other with a resigned sigh.

The Prince led us over to our seats. I noticed the name cards had the Prince sitting between Aurelia and me. I glanced at him in a challenge, silently accusing him of swapping the cards. He raised his eyebrows as if to tell me he had no idea what I meant.

For the second night in a row, I endured a painful dinner of noble posturing and pomposity. The Prince effectively prevented Aurelia and I from speaking, as it would have been rude to talk around him. Instead we sat in stony silence for a large portion of the meal, the Prince's shadows flitting about eerily. At one point I was sure I felt one snake its way up my leg, but the sensation disappeared when I glanced at the Prince.

He was just as handsome, or really eerily beautiful, tonight as he had been at the ball. His nose created a sharp, but not unpleasing profile, and his gray eyes seemed to flash silver with any burst of emotion.

"Why do you study me, Lady Ember?" the Prince asked, buttering a roll as we waited for dessert to be brought out. He turned to me. "What offends you?"

"Nothing, your highness," I replied, meeting his gaze coldly. "I am simply trying to make out your character."

"You are angry with me," the Prince said, sounding unexpectedly delighted by this. I blinked. He chuckled darkly.

"Please, tell me how I have earned your ire," he

asked, eyebrows raised in anticipation of my response. I was surprised to realize that somehow, I was not afraid of him at all. He seemed both genuinely curious and amused at my reaction to him.

Maybe it was the daring dress making me reckless, but I said, "why, my lord, I only presumed Fae of my low ability were beneath your attention."

"Ah," he turned to face his roll again, grin growing even wider. "I see. You are angry about my comment at the ball."

That his insult seemed to amuse him made me grow even more angry. Apparently I was throwing caution to the wind and letting my dislike drive my words tonight. Thank the goddess for the crowded dinner table, where no one seemed to be paying attention to our argument.

"Why no, indeed," I replied, injecting ice into my voice and turning to face my dinner again. "Why should it bother me to be so wholly humiliated in front of both courts for a circumstance that was perpetrated on my people by *your* father?"

His smile dropped away entirely and his face darkened. Tendrils of night were curling around the hem of my dress, and they seemed to expand as his temper flared. The Prince lowered his voice to a near growl.

"It is rare indeed that a lady speaks to me so openly and with such contempt," he said in a low voice, his lips quirking wickedly on one side in a gruesome parody of a smile. "You would do well to remember that we are one court now. Be careful speaking so boldly."

The Prince stood, bowing to Aurelia's father and announcing to the room at large, "Thank you for an excellent meal. I fear I have rather lost my appetite."

He walked out without another word, and the room filled with hushed whispers. Aurelia shifted closer to me and said quietly, "What in the goddess' name did you do to the Prince?"

"I have no idea," I replied, watching him walk out.

CHAPTER 4

The morning of yet another ball arrived. I woke in Aurelia's room, having spent the night as she had suggested. Her bed was large with plenty of space for both of us, and I blinked at the bright sunshine filtering through her window.

Aurelia was already up and brushing her hair, pinning little flowers in place.

"Do you just wake up naturally put together and perfect each day?" I groaned, feeling the frizzy mass of my own hair around my head. "Do songbirds and tiny woodland creatures dress you and help you get ready?"

Aurelia smiled.

"What if I said they did?" She asked, turning back to the mirror.

"I'd say you should pay them more," I grumbled,

awake enough to make myself presentable for breakfast.

Since I'd spent the night, I threw on yesterday's clothes and joined Aurelia and her parents for breakfast. They were seated together, pouring over documents while holding hands. It was adorable, and I felt a pang that I would never know if my own mother and father loved each other the way Aurelia's did.

Aurelia kissed her parents cheeks and we sat. I poured tea and bit into a raspberry scone. Heaven.

"Well, my dears," said Aurelia's father looking at us over his spectacles. "I'd say you certainly made an impression on the Prince last night." I groaned, and he chuckled.

"We didn't learn anything important I'm afraid," said Aurelia, frowning over her toast.

"No, we surmised as much," said Aurelia's mother with a weak smile. "Maybe it's a good thing though. If he dislikes Ember, he might be inclined to try to sway Aurelia against her. Maybe confide in her a little." She raised her eyebrows and I groaned feelingly again.

"You too?" I asked. "I thought you'd both be against this mad plan for tonight."

"We know our little Aury can take care of herself," said Aurelia's father fondly, using his pet name for his daughter from our childhood. "You will try to help her, rather than spend all night arguing with the Prince, won't you Ember?"

After a breakfast that was filled with scolding, I left to get ready. Aurelia planned to wear a gown "fit for seduction" in her words, and I sat down at my vanity somewhat morosely.

Aurelia was prepared to seduce the Prince, which meant I had to prepare myself to outdo her. Not only had I probably ruined my chance of that happening last night at dinner, but I thought Aurelia might be right. My wardrobe was rather dull, and not really up to the task. Most of my gowns were cut far more modestly than was fashionable. I supposed it didn't matter if the Prince refused to speak with me at all.

I had one gown that might do, with a little help from my weak glamour. Tonight I would abandon my usual role of the shadow and play the seductress, and it was going to require a lot of work and some serious acting to pull it off.

Two hours later, I shivered as the breeze chilled my bare shoulders on the terrace of the ballroom. I took a fortifying sip of Faerie wine and surreptitiously checked my reflection in the glass door.

The dress *was* fit for seduction. While my shoulders were bare, the rest of me was covered modestly, sleeves reaching my fingertips in a tapered point and sweetheart neckline not revealing too much of my décolletage. But the scandal lay in the fact that the dress was absolutely skin tight. Black fabric clung to every curve and pooled at my feet like a puddle of shadow, leaving absolutely nothing to the imagination.

I had glamoured my hair to appear shiny and smooth, rather than somewhat wavy and frizzy, and my eyes blazed a brilliant emerald, but that had taken basically all of my power. Diamonds sparkled in my ears, but my throat was bare, making my skin look less tan and more creamy white than usual against the black dress. While I felt a little too curvy and on display to be absolutely comfortable, I also felt powerful and fierce. Not a shadow ready to hide in the corner, but a Queen ready to command the floor. Tonight the Prince would bow to me, and I would make him tremble.

I downed my glass and glanced across the floor at Aurelia. She had chosen a fiery crimson for her seduction, which brought out the gold tones in her blonde hair and the warm tan of her skin. She had glamoured her dress to flicker like flames, reds and oranges swirling around her legs in a heated dance, and her eyes were a warm golden russet tonight. Many males were admiring her, both up close and at a distance. I sighed.

If she was fire and warmth, I was cold steel.

From the terrace I could see most of the ballroom, and as Aurelia's eyes and ears, I was supposed to signal her when I found the Prince. I had no idea how I would somehow seduce the Prince away from her, but I had to try, even if I loathed the idea of apologizing to and flattering the male.

As of yet, the Prince had not shown up, so we waited, she conspicuously, and I in shadow, until he arrived. Lark and Pip had been fluttering about the room serving guests and casting wary looks at us every so often, and I recognized two of the Seelie lords from the caves circling on occasion. They looked comically uncomfortable. The Commander would be furious when she heard how little they had attempted to blend in.

I sighed.

"It is an absolute bore, isn't it," came a deep, smooth voice from behind me.

I stilled, placing my glass on the ledge beside me and facing forward as my neck prickled. The Prince came to stand next to me, towering over me by at least a foot, and radiating contempt. I spared a quick glance to the side. He was again in full black, dark hair brushed back from his angular face and weaponry on display, although his guards were nowhere to be seen. His eyes flashed to mine and caught them, sending that strange bolt of electricity through me again, like the first time we had met.

"Lady Ember. A pleasure to see you again," he said with a courtly bow.

"Oh I'm sure it is," I mumbled under my breath, offering a curtsy in return.

"Excuse me?" asked the Prince.

"Nothing, your highness, I was merely exclaiming at the pleasure of seeing you again too." I had meant to sound genuine, but my voice had come out sarcastic. I cursed myself.

The Prince gave me a wry look, leaning on the ledge next to me and crossing his arms.

"You really don't like me, do you?" He asked, a smile tugging at his lips.

"I apologize if you have that impression," I said as politely as possible. "In truth I was not myself last night. Pray, do forgive me for my rudeness to you. It was unpardonable."

His brows lifted, but rather than accept the apology he held out his hand.

"Dance with me." A command, not a request. Shadows snaked around his arm as he waited for me to take his hand.

I hesitated. This would be one way to enact my plan, but I had vowed never to dance with this male, and the idea of letting him hold me made me shudder.

"I fear I have no inclination to dance tonight, your highness," I said, sipping my Faerie wine for strength while trying to think of a way to do what I had planned. In his presence it was much harder to think rationally than out of it.

"Of course not," the Prince scoffed, rolling his eyes heavenward. "You know, I don't believe in untruthful flattery, my lady," he said, stepping away from the railing and closing the distance between us. His eyes pierced mine, sending little bolts of awareness through me, and his shadows curled around the hem of my dress.

Suddenly I was furious. This male had humiliated me in public, and now had the gall to address me as if his insults had been a favor to me. I tried to maintain an icy, polite demeanor, but it was no use.

"Indeed," I replied coolly, "especially if you have no patience for small magic." He blinked as if I had struck him.

Fury was growing in me like a pillar of fire, and I needed to leave before I ruined everything. Maybe I could convince Aurelia to wait on her plan for another night.

"If you'll excuse me, your highness," I said coldly, giving a little curtsy as I turned to leave. He stopped me, pulling me back to face him and placing a finger under my chin to draw my eyes to his. His touch was far too familiar, and it sent shivers through my core.

"I also don't believe in lying," he growled, sounding murderous. "If you don't like what I said when we met you are free to ignore it, but I shan't flatter you out of some ridiculous societal notion of courtesy."

My jaw dropped and my blood boiled. The spoiled, stuck up, prideful male!

"You are a monster," I gritted out through clenched

teeth. "Why would I want flattery from you?"

The Prince let out a mirthless laugh, shadows pulsing around him.

"A monster," he said, seeming to chew over the word and deciding that he liked it. From the corner of my eye I noticed that his guards, the same from the first ball, had appeared some distance down the garden path like a pair of obsidian statues, and my blood turned to ice.

"I may be a monster," he continued, "but I always speak the truth. I abhor lies." He looked at me with disgust, leaning down to speak in my ear and pitching his voice so low he was almost whispering.

"You lie with every breath you take."

I blinked. "What?" I said, dumbfounded. He stepped back, his cold smile failing to reach his eyes. The spell between us seemed to be broken.

"Take your friend in the red dress and go home," he said, stepping away. "And tell your *Commander* that I will *not* play her games. I have proven my loyalty, and if this is how she repays it then I'm done."

Without a further word of explanation, he turned on his heel and walked away into the crowded ballroom. I stood, dumbfounded for several heartbeats while I put together what he had just said.

Somehow, he knew Aurelia and I were spies. I supposed that's what he must have meant with the comment about me lying. He somehow knew about the resistance, the Commander, possibly everything.

Panic rose, swift and nauseating. How our cover had been blown, and how we were still alive despite it, I had no idea, but I wasn't willing to tempt fate. Aurelia and I had to go now and warn the Commander, and if we had time, get everyone away before the full wrath of the

Prince of Death could come down on us.

CHAPTER 5

"How did he know?" Aurelia panted as we ran through the forest. Branches snarled in our hair and caught at our arms and legs. I felt a twig snap against my cheek and blood dripping down my jaw, but I didn't stop. The scratches would heal soon enough. We had to get to the caves and warn everyone before it was too late and the Prince came to hunt us all down.

"I don't know," I huffed back, wishing I was wearing stout boots rather than the flimsy evening slippers that squelched through the mud and caught on every root. "But it doesn't matter right now."

The forest was dark, the moon's light blotted out by the canopy above us, and we crashed through the undergrowth heedless of the noise we were making. If anyone were following us, they'd know exactly where we were. I wasn't sure if the Prince had sent soldiers after us, and I had no desire to lead them straight into the underground network that housed our resistance.

By some blessing of the Goddess, we made it to the cave entrance with no one on our heels. I descended into the caves quickly, scraping my arms and legs on stone with my clumsy descent. My lungs were on fire and my cheek still ached, but I could already feel the wound closing. We ran through the caves, our slippers scuffling on the stone floor. It was the dead of night, so not totally surprising that the caves seemed deserted, but the quiet unnerved me. What if the Prince had beaten us here?

Finally we came to the small chamber that the Commander used as an office. A thick wooden door had been built in an existing inset in the cave wall to grant some privacy, and Aurelia and I banged on it loudly as we attempted to catch our breaths.

"Enter," came the voice of the Commander. She was clearly still awake, her tone as crisp and commanding as it usually was while giving orders or strategizing attacks, and we tumbled into the room, both speaking at once.

"Sorry to disturb you, Commander," said Aurelia breathlessly at the same time I shouted "he knows about us!"

The Commander stood from behind her solid oak desk and looked at us bemusedly.

"A drink, ladies?" She said, gesturing to a small couch next to her desk. She grabbed a decanter of something amber and pulled four glasses from her desk drawer. She looked up, seeing our scrapes and cuts and bruises and added, "you look like you need it."

"We don't have time for a drink," I snapped,

wondering at the four glasses but brushing my confusion aside. I rested my hands on her desk. "We have to evacuate."

The Commander sighed, pouring the amber liquid.

"Yes, I had a feeling you'd be barging in here in a panic tonight," she said, looking pointedly at the wall next to the door behind us.

"What?" Aurelia said, sounding confused. I turned and looked where the Commander was staring and stifled a scream.

"Lady Ember," said the dark, smooth voice of the Prince, pushing off from where he leaned against the wall of the office, a smile twisting his lips. "And your friend in the red dress."

He gave a small bow to Aurelia, all the while keeping his gaze on mine. "I'm pleased to see you took my advice."

The Commander forced the amber drink into my hands and pushed me toward the sofa. She did the same for Aurelia, then turned to the Prince and offered him the fourth glass. He took it with a small nod of thanks and perched against the wall closest to me. The Commander downed her drink in one gulp, clanked her glass on the desk and turning to face us. She stood stiffly with her hands behind her back.

"How is he here?" I asked, still holding the glass and staring at the Prince accusingly. We had run directly from the ball, and there was no way he could have beaten us on foot. "There was no horse outside."

He smirked and said, "magic."

"Drink," the Commander said, as I opened my mouth to ask several hundred more questions. "And I will explain."

I shut my mouth and gulped, glancing again at the Prince, who quirked an eyebrow at me and took a sip of his drink. He was dressed as he had been at the ball, but no swirls of darkness came rippling off him, and his terrifying aura seemed to have been dampened somehow. Slowly, I took a sip as well. It burned, but it helped calm some of the panic still bubbling in my chest.

"Where to begin," said the Commander. She seemed to deflate a bit and pulled the chair from behind her desk to face me and Aurelia.

My friend and I had not spoken to each other since entering the cave, but she took my hand in hers and gave it a squeeze, knowing I needed something to anchor me in this moment.

"Two years ago," started the Commander, "I apprehended a young man who was skulking around the forest outside our cave complex. He claimed to be looking for me on behalf of the Prince, and he brought me a message with the royal seal. That message was from the Prince, claiming to have no love for his father, and offering his aid to our cause."

The Commander paused, giving the Prince a hard look, then resuming. "I had no idea if the man was being honest, so I detained until I decided what to do with him."

"You threw him in your dungeon, you mean," said the Prince darkly. He didn't look exactly angry, but it was clear he was unhappy about the way his man had been treated.

"I sent him back mostly in one piece," said the Commander indifferently, looking coldly at the Prince. "Anyway," she said, turning to face us again. "Once we were able to verify that the message was genuine, we met in a neutral location. Hadrian came unarmed and alone, and offered us his help."

"Hadrian?" I said, looking shocked that the Commander had used his name. In my mind he was always just "the Prince," with a capital P.

The Commander ignored me and continued, "the Prince has certain," she paused and gave him another appraising look, "skills and connections that have helped us greatly over the last two years. Situations have arisen that complicate his involvement with us. Tonight I sent you to that ball to set the stage for your next mission, but the plan went rather awry, didn't it?"

The Commander threw an annoyed glance at the Prince with this last bit, and he shrugged noncommittally. "I told you, either of them would do. It's your fault for not telling them."

"What situations?" Aurelia asked.

"What mission?" I asked simultaneously.

The Commander sighed. "I will explain it all if you give me a moment."

"And how can you possibly trust him?" I shouted, downing out the Commander. "He could be selling all your secrets to the king as we speak!"

"Prince Hadrian has been in these caves several times now, and none of the king's soldiers have ever ventured near," the Commander answered wearily. "He has given us valuable information and now presents us with an opportunity to learn even more and finally restore the Seelie throne."

"He's been here before?" I shouted incredulously, accidentally knocking my glass to the ground, where it shattered spectacularly. The Prince waived his hand

and the glittering glass pieces reformed. That was certainly a magic I longed to have, but it just made me angry coming from the Prince. I glared at him.

"AND," said the Commander, speaking over me. "He has put himself at incredible risk to bring us vital information."

The Prince sighed dramatically and said, "Valeria, will you please get to the point."

I sat, open mouthed. I had never heard anyone call the Commander by her name. She was always the Commander. What was this friendship and familiarity between them? Did she truly trust this hateful man? Clearly not entirely, or she wouldn't have asked Aurelia to attempt to infiltrate his defenses

"Wait," Aurelia said, "I don't understand. Why do you want to help the Seelie?" She looked at the Prince and cleared her throat.

"Your highness," she added.

The Prince smiled faintly at the deference and shrugged casually. "Because I hate my father," he said coolly, no hint of emotion in the statement, just fact. "And I will do anything to see him burn."

Something flashed in his eyes. There was a wound there that I didn't want to probe.

"And how will our lives be better if you sit on the throne," I snapped, getting a look from the Commander. I rolled my eyes and added as irreverently as possible, *"your highness."*

The Prince frowned and said, "I don't know. But I think we can do better. Be better. I think there's a way to unite our people in peace."

"Peace?!" I realized I was shouting again and lowered my voice. "Your father has been murdering innocent

Seelie and stealing Seelie land and power for over twenty years. And you have never stood in his way."

The Prince looked angry now too, and he said in a quiet deadly tone, "I guarantee I have faced more of my father's cruelty than you can possibly imagine."

His eyes bored into mine, and something coalesced in his features. Hate maybe? Disgust? Clearly he saw me as the unfairly prejudiced party, so I simply laughed.

"Oh yes, how you must have suffered in your palace with your servants and your magic," I scoffed, gesturing in his general direction.

The Prince pushed off the wall, fists clenched as darkness began to seep out around him.

"Enough," shouted the Commander, coming to stand between us. "Ember, sit now or you will be dismissed. Hadrian, please."

She turned to look at him, and I don't know what was communicated, but he nodded and stepped back to the wall.

He was breathing hard and his fists remained clenched as the Commander said, "Ember, I have the most important job I will ever ask you to take on. Aurelia, as Ember's closest friend and confidante, I am allowing you to join this meeting so you can offer support. Nothing that is said here can leave this room."

Aurelia glanced at the Prince, and nodded hesitantly.

"What if I don't want the assignment," I asked warily. The Commander sighed.

"As always, you will not be forced to take it. It will not be easy, or painless, and it will be extremely dangerous, but it could save our people and our home."

Aurelia had gone extremely pale. The Prince shifted, so slightly that I might not have noticed, but the darkness around him seemed to reach out to me slightly.

"Then I'll decide when I hear the job," I said, injecting resolve into my voice. The Commander gave the Prince a nod, and he turned to look at me.

In a purring voice he said, "I need you to be my bride."

"You are mad," I said with a scoff, standing and storming toward the door. The Prince was before me instantly blocking my path, and I snarled, "get out of my way!"

"No," he said coolly. "Sit and listen to your Commander."

I glared at him as he continued to stare me down.

"Ember," said the Commander sharply. "You haven't heard the whole job. Sit."

Her tone brooked no argument and I stomped back to my seat next to Aurelia. She was still very pale and her eyes had gone very wide. We had let our glamours go when we were running through the forest, and without hers she looked somehow younger, and smaller, and fragile. She would hate to be thought of as fragile. I turned to the Commander.

"How," I said, biting out the words between my teeth, "exactly will this save our people?"

The Prince resumed his position against the wall and said, "my father wants me to marry a Seelie of noble birth to secure his control over both realms." He drew his hand up to his face and pinched the bridge of his nose as if his head pained him. "I can't continue my work here if I have to protect an innocent female, nor am I willing to subject one to the attention of my father. I need someone who knows what I do, who is part of the cause, who can lie to my father and the Unseelie court and act like my bride."

"Ha," I laughed out loud at the suggestion and the Commander scowled at me. "You need someone to warm your bed to fool your father?"

The Prince clenched his jaw. "There will be no bed warming. There will be no marriage. The betrothal will go on as long as possible until we can get the information I need to overthrow my father, and then you will be released from the engagement."

The Commander interjected sternly, "You will be surrounded by enemies with only the Prince as your ally. You will have to convince the Unseelie court and king of your relationship long enough that the Prince can seek the information we need and gain his father's trust. Failure will be deadly."

I ground my teeth trying to wrap my mind around the assignment. "How long would I have to prepare?" I asked.

"Two weeks," said the Prince, jaw still clenched. "I must convince my father to accept you at court and your uncle to bless the union within that time, then we will travel north. It will require some," the prince paused, quirking his lips at me, "convincing acting."

"Why can't we just kill the king, if that is really your true goal?" I asked the Prince exasperatedly, refusing to acknowledge the implications of what he meant by *acting*.

"Because it will be too suspicious. The court will assume it was at my hand. It's no secret that my father and I don't see eye to eye," he said. "They will brand me a traitor and some other ruthless Unseelie noble will claim the throne. And we won't get the information we need."

"We could use poison. Make it look like an illness," I said, warming to this plan as different ways of poisoning the king raced through my mind.

"Killing the king is not our primary objective yet," said the Commander in a voice that made me turn my attention toward her. She looked at me now as if she thought *I* was the mad one. This whole plan was madness, so why not lean into it.

"Why not?" I asked incredulously. "This is the perfect opportunity! The court will be distracted and the Prince will have an alibi. We can end the war with one death instead of thousands."

"That won't end the war," the Prince said so forcefully it made me start. Once again, inky blackness blurred his edges as he lost control of his temper. "It will make him a martyr in the eyes of the Fae who support him. I will kill my father when the time is right, but all his death will achieve now is more chaos and bloodshed."

The Prince pushed himself off the wall and paced the small room. "We need information before we can move against my father. He doesn't fully trust me, so I need to convince him and the rest of the court that he can. That I am his willing successor."

He turned to look at me pointedly. "That's why I need you. He doesn't think I'll take a wife on his orders to further his aims. You need to convince him otherwise."

"Why not me?" asked Aurelia. She had color back in her cheeks now, and she was looking determinedly at the Commander. "It was me you sent to seduce him. Why change the plan and send Ember?"

My stomach sank. If the Commander sent Aurelia, I

could lose her. It would defeat the point of me speaking to him at the ball at all. Moreover, this mission would offer me access to the king, and I wanted revenge. He had taken my mother and my father from me before I had the chance to meet them. He had destroyed hundreds of families and killed thousands of innocents. As unpleasant as the company of the Prince would be, I wouldn't waste the opportunity.

The Commander glanced at the Prince and said, "because tonight was supposed to be the start of this mission, and instead of being seduced by you, Aurelia, the Prince spent the evening speaking with Ember."

I gaped. That's what tonight had been about?

"If that was the plan, why not go straight to Aurelia?" I asked, turning to the Prince. He shrugged, and met my eyes with a strange intensity.

"Because you fascinate me," he said darkly. The intensity dropped away and he shrugged flippantly. "And I saw you first."

I gaped. Curse my goddess damned luck to be outside when he decided to blow the whole plan.

"The whole court is speaking of it," the Prince continued. "My guards were listening for gossip, and you're now considered the front runner in polite society for my bride."

"All we did was talk!" I shouted, incredulously. "Now I'm supposed to be madly in love with you?"

The Prince smirked. "Apparently the other guests believed it to be a," he paused to choose his next word carefully. "Passionate conversation."

I scoffed.

"Regardless," said the Commander, "the die is already cast. It has to be you, Ember, and it makes sense considering your uncle's obvious affiliation with the crown. I didn't ask you because I didn't think you could act the part, but now there is no alternative."

"This means I only have two weeks to teach you how to properly use a dagger," Aurelia said, smiling weakly at me. I grabbed her hand and squeezed it in comfort. I knew she was far more worried than she was letting on.

"I'll teach her," said the Prince. I suppressed a shudder at the idea of letting him come near me with a sharp object.

"I'd rather take poison," I said, shooting a hateful glance at the Prince. He smirked, probably picturing stabbing me during our first dagger lesson.

"I will ask your uncle for his blessing after the Autumn Equinox," the Prince said, pushing off the wall as if he was done with this meeting. "Between now and then we will need to convince him and the nobility that we are attached. Don't start packing until he has said yes."

"And what if he says no?" I asked haughtily as he turned to leave. The Prince stopped and gave me another one of his wicked half-smiles.

"He won't."

Pompous ass.

"Can you do this, Ember?" Asked the Commander seriously. "You will have to put aside your prejudice to pull this off. Hadrian will be your ally from here on out. You will be our eyes and ears in the palace, but it will also be your job to protect him from harm, as he protects you."

She gave me a piercing look and I hesitated, glancing at the Prince. He raised a brow at me.

"If not," she continued, "we will need Aurelia to step

in."

"No," the Prince and I both said at the same time. I gave him a puzzled look, but his face betrayed nothing.

"I can do it," I replied.

"Good," said the Commander. "Then prepare yourself to be a bride."

I was already home when I remembered the conversation I had overheard between my uncle and Lord Thorn. Cursing myself for forgetting, I resolved to tell the Commander tomorrow as soon as possible.

CHAPTER 6

As if my commitment to this mission were not enough of a divine test, the goddess tested me even more the next morning.

"No woods today," my uncle said, breaking the silence of the breakfast table as he looked up from a note scrawled in an elegant hand. "For we have guests tonight."

Curse my uncle. My information would have to wait yet another day now.

"Again?" Aspen groaned, slumping over his eggs. I laughed at his show of despair.

"Yes, heir to my lands and fortunes, again," said my uncle, shooting Aspen a disdainful look.

"Who is it now?" Aspen asked resignedly. He acted

for all the world like my uncle planned social events to personally inconvenience him. A sharp look from my uncle made him rephrase.

"Who, dearest father, have you so magnanimously invited to partake of our hospitality?" I laughed again, and my uncle directed his look at me.

"Believe it or not," my uncle replied, looking at us both with annoyance, "it was not I who did the inviting. Prince Hadrian has declared his intention of calling upon us."

I choked slightly on the sip of tea I had just taken, and Aspen raised a brow at me.

"What for, Uncle?" I asked, hoping I had successfully adopted a tone of polite inquiry.

He seemed satisfied and answered, "I suspect to take my measure as one of his father's allies, but based on reports I hear, he may have," he glanced at me, "ulterior motives."

Aspen, seeing the look, turned to look at me expectantly.

"I know nothing about it," I said defensively, raising my hands placatingly.

"You will both be on your best behavior tonight," my uncle warned us as Aspen stuck his tongue out at me. "By the goddess, stop that, you are both well past your second decades."

"Apologies uncle," I said demurely, shooting Aspen an obscene hand gesture beneath the table.

"So just the Prince?" Asked Aspen, resuming his breakfast, and thus declaring me the victor of our secret war under the table. I smirked.

"No," said my uncle, rifling through his other mail. "I have invited several other noble lords to join us." He looked up at me, "but no young ladies."

"Can Aurelia come?" I asked beseechingly. I knew that the performance I would have to give would be far more convincing with Aurelia as my supporting actress. My uncle frowned.

"Why would you want to invite your competition?" He asked, narrowing his eyes at me. "Lady Aurelia is far more beautiful, she will certainly draw the Prince's gaze. Or do you not want a chance to demonstrate your particular charms to the Prince?"

I blushed crimson and tried not to let my anger show. Aspen also blushed and looked away, pretending to be distracted by something outside. We both knew what *charms* the young local lords found in me, and it had little to do with magic or breeding.

"Not at all uncle," I replied, trying to adopt my most calm voice. "I just know Aurelia's interests lie elsewhere." I glanced at Aspen. He was still looking out the window, but I saw his smirk. "And you know I will feel easier around the Prince with her nearby."

My uncle waved a hand dismissively. "Fine, I'll extend the invitation to her family. At least her family is less wealthy. That will be a mark against her."

I breathed a sigh of relief and Aspen stood suddenly.

"Care to go riding, cousin?" He asked, offering his arm.

"Do not go far," reminded my uncle as I took it and we escaped to the stables.

My uncle had forbidden us from going into the woods, but not from sparring, so Aspen took me out to one of the nearby fields, tied up our horses, and attempted to teach me some more about defensive fighting. I was abysmal, and by the time the morning had faded into afternoon I was sweaty and miserable.

"It's no good," I wheezed, falling heavily to the ground in exhaustion. "I'm just not a fighter. Old dogs and new tricks and all that."

Aspen gave me a pitying look.

"Maybe swords would be more your speed," he said thoughtfully.

"You want to give me a *bigger* knife?" I said incredulously, propping myself up on my elbows to look at him. He grinned. I threw my head back down and groaned.

"Come on," he said, offering me a hand and pulling me back up. "Father will send his dogs out after us if we are not back for luncheon. He'll want us to spend all afternoon *preparing*."

I groaned again and stood.

"What do you think of the Prince?" I asked, clambering back into the saddle of my horse.

"Why do you ask?" Aspen looked at me warily.

I shrugged. "Just curious, I suppose," I said, trying to sound uninterested. "You're always allowed to hear more than us poor, innocent ladies. I assume you all hear terrible stories when you gather for cards and things."

Aspen snorted. "I'm glad your opinion of my activities is so high," he said, bemused. "Honestly, I haven't heard much, but be careful Em. The male is known as the Prince of Death for a reason, and I'm certain it is not an appropriate topic even for cards."

I sat in my chambers that afternoon uncertain what my move tonight should be. I had agreed to this mission to fake a betrothal to the Prince, but other than "doting" I hadn't been given much direction. Was I supposed to be the sultry vixen? Unlikely. The chaste maid? Chaste was a bit of a stretch. I was not very experienced, but most girls took lovers at the Spring Equinox celebration, and I was no saint.

How about demure lady? I could probably pull that off. Maybe I could act coy and shy…no. I immediately squashed that thought. Anyone who had seen us arguing would not think me shy.

Sighing, I chose something sedate, but flattering; a simple velvet gown of deep emerald that brought out my eyes. It was somewhat shapeless, with fluttering short sleeves and full skirts. I wrapped a belt of golden leaves around my waist to cinch it, and decided to wear my hair down. I pinned one side back with a golden comb decorated with tiny metal roses, brushed some color on my cheeks and lips, and inspected my appearance.

It would do.

Guests were already arriving when I headed downstairs. Aspen sighed with relief when he saw me, already bored out of his mind it seemed. He was in a warm rich gold coat, and he looked every bit a lord of Spring.

"What's your game plan?" He whispered in my ear as he escorted me into the drawing room. This was not a ball or a dinner, but a servant was circling with refreshments, and I gratefully took a glass of Faerie wine.

"Drink too much wine and forget the whole

evening?" I asked. He smirked, clinking his glass against mine.

"Agreed."

My uncle's guests started to arrive, and positioned themselves around the room engaging in various activities. As my uncle had promised, there were no other young ladies, but many lords had brought their wives. A few young males laughed over some joke in a corner and Aspen went to join them. I sat alone on a sofa, sipping my wine and wishing Aurelia was here already.

She arrived at the same time as the Prince, and he was obliged to lend her an arm as he escorted her in. My uncle gave me a blistering look as he went to greet his royal guest.

Aurelia rushed to me and kissed my cheek, looking apologetic.

"What is your game plan?" She whispered, grabbing her own glass of sparkling wine. I laughed at how similar she and Aspen were, but before I could repeat my quip about drinking too much, I felt eyes on the back of my neck.

The Prince was watching me from across the room, pointedly ignoring the conversation of the lords trying to engage him. I felt that strange spark that I always felt when our eyes met, and I heard him interrupt the lord who was speaking to excuse himself. No need to ask what role the Prince would be playing tonight then. Rude prick, it seemed, was his only act.

"Act natural," Aurelia whispered.

I gave her a withering look.

He came toward us, taking the armchair closest to my seat and crossing an ankle over a knee. His legs were very long, and he looked almost too tall to be comfortable in that position. As usual, he was dressed in his characteristic black, and his demeanor exuded boredom.

"Lady Ember," he said, dipping his head slightly, "Lady Aurelia. A pleasure as always."

"Your highness," I said, attempting demure but only succeeding in sounding bored. He smirked.

We sat in awkward silence for a few minutes. I tried to think of something to say, but my mind had gone inconveniently blank. I looked toward the door and cursed quietly.

"What is it?" Asked Aurelia, turning to look where I stared. Lord Thorn had just arrived, and he was already heading toward the sofas where we sat.

"Not a fan?" The Prince asked, sipping his wine with a grimace. Did this male just hate nice things?

"What a charming party this is," said Lord Thorn, dropping into the seat across from the Prince. Aspen had also seen the Lord's arrival and flopped down on the sofa next to Aurelia, causing her to slide into him. She smiled up at him, and he leaned his arm on the back of the sofa, almost holding her.

"It's an absolute bore," Aspen said grumpily. "No dancing, no music. What is the point of such gatherings?"

When no one answered and the awkward silence had stretched on longer than was comfortable, Aspen spoke again.

"Do you care to dance, your highness?"

The Prince blinked, as if surprised to be addressed.

"No," he said simply.

"But how could you resist such charming company?"

Lord Thorn asked, leering at Aurelia and me in a way that made my skin crawl.

"What is your definition of charming, Lord Thorn?" The Prince asked cynically. I wasn't sure if Thorn realized he was being mocked, but he replied as if not.

"Why, beauty of course," he said nodding to Aurelia, "and wit." He glanced at me. "But I find, your highness, that few ladies are truly impressive these days. Some do have more magical talents than others," he added, glancing at me again.

I felt rage burning in my gut as the Lord clearly intended to slight me again in company. I opened my mouth to say something, but the Prince beat me to it.

"And what else, my lord? Surely that is not all you claim to find charming," he sipped his wine, hiding his grimace more effectively this time. Aspen and Aurelia glanced at me as if looking for direction, but I wasn't exactly sure where this was going either.

"Lady Ember is a skilled healer," chimed in Aurelia. Goddess bless her, she was trying harder than either the Prince or I was to make this romance seem plausible. "I believe those kinds of charms should also be considered in your estimation, your highness."

The Prince smiled what I thought might actually be a genuine smile at Aurelia and said, "Of course, you are correct, Lady Aurelia. But there is still something lacking."

"Music and dancing are important," Aspen added, smiling at Aurelia. She was a fine dancer and singer and she blushed a pretty pink that matched the dress she had chosen tonight.

"Hmm," said the Prince noncommittally. "Still not enough I think."

"Please," I interjected, my tone more biting than inviting, "enlighten us as to your preferred charms, your highness."

The Prince gave me one of his wicked half smiles. "Why, a truly charming lady must be able to defend herself with violence," he said.

Lord Thorn let out a hard laugh, and complimented the Prince on his wit. Aspen raised a brow at me, doubtless thinking of our lesson this afternoon, and I looked away out the window to my right.

"Lady Ember," said the Prince, standing and offering me his arm. "There is a rather lovely garden on your estate I believe. Would you honor me with a tour?"

"As you wish, your highness," I replied, taking his arm. I caught my uncle's eye as the Prince escorted me out and he gave me an approving nod. I resisted the urge to roll my eyes.

"Is Lord Thorn always such an ass?" asked the Prince once we were safely beyond earshot on the terrace. I snorted.

"Always," I confirmed. "He makes an art of it."

The Prince chuckled, a low rumbling noise and I looked up to meet his eyes. I felt that strange tug toward him again and looked away, trying to ignore it. I couldn't decide if I should trust him with the information about the clandestine meeting between Thorn and my uncle. I decided not to risk it.

We walked in silence for a few minutes. I noticed that darkness had begun to trail him. He had kept it hidden in the drawing room, but now he let his dark power pulse around him.

"Why are you here?" I asked, heading through the rose garden toward the little fountain at the center of my uncle's grounds. It was my favorite place in the garden, and it was generally where I ended up when I walked the grounds.

"To woo you, of course," the Prince said, giving me a sardonic look.

"No," I said flustered, "I mean why here? We could have met again at any number of balls."

The Prince shrugged. "I don't like dancing."

"Really?" I asked incredulously. "You hate dancing so much you'd prefer to endure nights like this?"

"Well it doesn't seem to matter where I go," the Prince said resignedly. "The company is tediously repetitive everywhere."

I bristled but said nothing, sitting on the edge of the fountain and looking up at him.

"What now?" I asked. The Prince glanced up at the moon.

"I suppose we stay here for long enough that we are missed and then return looking misty eyed and infatuated," he said, sitting next to me and leaning his arms on his knees.

We sat in painful silence for a while, listening to the trickling of the water in the fountain. I noticed that the weeds between the stones at his feet had withered in his presence. I shuddered.

"What?" He asked, seeing my discomfort.

"Your power is unnerving," I said, gesturing to the dead plants at his feet. He looked down and nodded.

"I've been told." He lifted his head to look back at me and frowned. "But death is sorely misunderstood."

"What do you mean?" I asked, feeling like the power of death was a pretty obvious one to fear and understand. He sighed.

"Life, the magic of the Seelie Fae, cannot exist without death," he said. "Nature requires balance. Light and dark, life and death, Seelie and Unseelie. For example," he gestured to the dead weeds, "what do you feel if you stretch out your power to them?"

I laughed, "what power?"

He raised a brow. "Try," he implored. "Tell me what you feel other than death."

I rolled my eyes but did as he asked, letting my basically useless glamour fall away so I could extend my power into the earth. I barely managed to feel anything, except...

"Oh!" I said, surprised. The weeds had been sucking the life from the flowers on the edge of the path. The Prince's power had freed them from the stranglehold of the weeds.

He nodded, looking at me intently. "Life and death go hand in hand. Death is feared, but all life ends and begins with death. One cannot exist without the other to keep it in balance."

I nodded thoughtfully and we sat in silence awhile longer. It was less awkward now, more contemplative. He broke the silence first.

"Who did you lose?" He asked quietly, examining the stones at his feet.

"What?" I asked, pulled from my reverie by the question.

The Prince turned his head to look at me. "You hate my father, more than a wealthy, privileged noble lady should. Even one of Seelie birth," he added. I narrowed my eyes.

"And you loathe me, though I have done nothing more than insult you with honesty."

I scoffed, amazed by his lack of self-awareness.

"So who did he kill?" he asked again softly. There was no mockery or sarcasm in his face. No jest or deception or game I could detect. He seemed to genuinely want to know.

"My parents," I said tightly. I didn't elaborate, and he didn't ask for more details.

"I'm sorry," he said softly after another minute. I nodded, throat tight against the emotion I tried not to let show.

After a few more minutes he said, "I think that's long enough," and stood, offering me a hand. I took it, dark tendrils of power snaking over my forearm as he helped me to my feet. I expected them to feel cold, but they left a warm tingle across my arm as they moved.

The walk back was silent, but not awkwardly so. His question had forged some sort of understanding between us. I sensed that he had lost someone too. We might not be true allies, but we could find common ground in our desire for vengeance. We returned to the terrace, and he stopped me, turning to face me fully.

"For what it's worth, my lady, I understand your loss. Your desire for revenge. I feel it too."

I looked up at him, his eyes gleaming silver in the starlight. I felt that strange tug of connection again, and I stood very still, uncertain what to do, as he leaned down to whisper in my ear.

"So let's give them a performance to remember."

CHAPTER 7

I awoke the next morning in a cold sweat, the memory of my nightmare fading from my mind. This time the dream had changed, inky blackness swirling around me as the stars began to go out and a cold wind blowing from the north. I shivered as I rose to prepare for the day.

Last night had been a minor success. The Prince had spent most of the evening brooding roughly wherever I happened to be, and he made a show of kissing my hand as he left.

Finally, I had a day with no balls or dinners or social events, which meant I could focus on work I actually enjoyed. I dressed in brown cotton britches and riding boots and, hoping to avoid my uncle's interrogation and criticism for my attire, I decided to skip breakfast and headed out into the woods.

With only two weeks to prepare for my departure, I knew I wanted to stock the infirmary and write down some common treatments for Aurelia and Nella and my other apprentices to carry out in my absence. When I thought about leaving my healing for the goddess knew how long, I felt a growing gnawing pit of dread in my stomach.

As I walked I plucked a few useful herbs and mushrooms, regretting my choice of clothing. The forest as always provided exactly what I needed, and my arms were quickly full with useful herbs and fungi. Trousers may be far easier to move in, but skirts would have served as a perfect makeshift basket. I lifted my tunic over my head to use as a basket and hoped the squirrels would not be scandalized to see my flowing white undershirt without more covering. It was a warm day anyway, and sweat began trickling down my neck as I worked.

It was truly a beautiful morning, reds and golds and oranges of autumn leaves overhead and crunching underfoot. As I moved through the forest collecting medicines, I admired the warmth and beauty. I wondered how many beautiful mornings there would be when I went north.

It would be colder and harsher for sure. Maybe it was the dark, wicked Unseelie magic that did it, but I struggled to imagine the Unseelie Prince in a sunny spring garden. The stories I had heard painted the North as a cold, dead land, and while a part of me longed to see snow and hear its crunch under my boots, I knew I would miss the warmth of the autumn sunlight on my face in our southern Seelie lands.

The first thing I did when I got to the caves was to seek out the Commander. She frowned when I told her what I had overheard between Lord Thorn and my uncle and had me write it down.

"This could be about us," I said, pointing to the line I had written about "being able to move against them." She nodded.

"It could," she said tersely. "It could also be about the Fae in the Wilds. They grow bolder with their own attacks, aided by our weapons. Or even the dwarves. Maybe they are threatening the North."

"It sounded like whatever it was they were talking about was immediate and local," I argued, handing her the transcript of what I had heard.

"I'll look into it," was the only reply I received. Sighing, I went to the infirmary.

Despite feeling that the commander had not taken me seriously, I spent a glorious day cataloging plants and making bandages and writing down notes for Nella to use when I was gone. Pip, stopped by, lamenting both that I was leaving and that the Prince had not even said hello to him. While we had all been sworn to secrecy, it seemed like the whole cave complex knew about my mission.

"Believe me Pip," I said laughing, "he's not worth your pining. Better to stick it out with Lark instead."

Aurelia also came to help, and together we compiled a veritable book of common cures for illnesses and injuries, marking each page with a note about where the items for each cure were located in my storage cabinets, and creating a cross reference for each herb or plant. I reveled in every single minute of it.

By late afternoon I was stiff from sitting over a cramped writing desk, and I felt like I had done all I could with the knowledge I possessed. Stretching, I realized that Aurelia had already left, so I packed up the room to head back home.

The forest was already growing dark in the waning afternoon light. Deciding that it would be best if I did not get caught out here in the dark, I ran, enjoying the wind whipping past me as I darted between trees and bushes, trying not to break an ankle in a tree root.

I paused, out of breath, at the tree line by the cathedral grove, my uncle's estate less than a mile away. There was still plenty of sun, and I belatedly realized I had left my tunic in the infirmary. Cursing myself, because I knew it would be missed when the housekeeper collected the laundry, I turned to go back.

I didn't notice anyone near me until I heard a twig snap. I quickly darted behind a tree and squatted, listening for footsteps or voices. The forest was still. Was it possible I had imagined the noise? Maybe it was just an intrepid squirrel. I was weighing my options for what to do next when a ragged voice croaked behind me.

"That is not a very ladylike position, my lady."

I whirled and saw the Prince just as he tumbled forward, blood splattering on the leaves at my feet.

I can't remember how I got there, but suddenly the Prince's head was in my lap as I turned him to face the sky. Blood gushed freely from a wound in his side, and I pressed down with a hand to stanch the flow.

"Your highness!" I shouted, trying to rouse him from his faint. There was no way I would be able to drag him to the caves without injuring him further, and I wasn't sure if I ran for help that he would be alive when I returned. I felt panic claw its way up my throat and pressed down more on the wound, willing the blood to slow.

The wound must be very deep to bleed so much. Most Fae began to heal from injuries instantly, and even deep wounds from a normal blade would begin to knit instantly and require only a few stitches. This injury was clearly different. How had this happened in the twelve hours we had been apart?

The Prince groaned slightly, his eyelids fluttering.

"Your highness," I tried again, trying to rouse him. Much as I hated the male, I didn't want him to die under my hands. He was an ally after all. Or, at least the Commander seemed to trust him.

"Hadrian," I said more forcefully, "Your highness, I can't get you to the caves like this. I need you to help me."

The Prince grimaced and suddenly we were surrounded by swirling darkness. The breath was torn from my lungs as we moved through nothingness. It felt like my body was coming apart into nothing, and the only thing I felt was the slick blood of the Unseelie Prince seeping between my fingers.

Just as suddenly as it had started, it stopped. I opened my eyes to find us in the assembly hall in the caves. Fae gasped around us as we appeared out of nowhere, and I bent over, retching on the floor as a wave of nausea engulfed me.

"Ember!" I recognized Pip's voice distantly as my ears buzzed and black spots entered my peripheral vision. I took in deep lungfuls of stale cave air to try to stop myself from blacking out. My hands were still on the

Prince's wound, and I vaguely realized I had been sick right next to him. Lovely.

"What in the name of the goddess happened, Ember?" said Pip, crouching by me and putting a steadying hand on my back.

Lark was hovering nearby, and I spit out a mouthful of bile and forced myself to speak.

"Help me get him to the infirmary."

Pip's face paled at the sign of the bleeding Prince, but he nodded and he and Lark hoisted the Prince up between them, his arms over their shoulders. He was so tall that his feet dragged on the floor behind them. Blood was still dripping from the wound in his side, but at least the flow seemed to be slowing.

I rushed ahead of Pip and Lark as they moved sluggishly along, the deadweight of the Prince holding them back. His head had dropped between his shoulders and I thought he must have fainted again. I pushed into the infirmary and surprised Nella, who was washing the bowls we used for mixing.

"Lady Ember!" she gasped in surprise, "what's..."

"No time," I cut her off. "Fill a basin with hot water and get me a needle and spider silk thread."

I pushed my sleeves up and scrubbed my hands, trying to remove as much of the dried blood from under my nails as I could. As I finished, Pip and Lark arrived, the Prince looking a sickly green as he hung between them.

"Get him up on the table," I said to them as I dried my hands and Nella returned with my tools.

The Prince groaned as they hoisted him up, which I felt was a good sign. Clearly he had a strong will to live, and he would need that to survive.

I realized that he was wearing heavy leather armor on his chest, which had done nothing to protect him from the blade. I began unstrapping one shoulder and Pip went to the other side wordlessly to help. We peeled the armor away, and I began to cut away his shirt. It was sticky with blood, but it was impossible to tell exactly how much the Prince had bled against the black material.

As I pulled the fabric away from the wound, I let out a curse under my breath. Nella gasped when she saw the wound, and Pip, who had a weak stomach at the best of times, turned away.

The gash was ugly, four inches long and at least two deep from a quick inspection. But the worst part was not the wound itself. Black lines spread out from the wound, like inky veins forming a web of corruption. The Prince had been stabbed with iron.

I cursed again.

"Nella, I need woodsorrel and aniseed. Grind them in equal parts as fine as you can." She nodded, looking somewhat sick, and I added, "Pip, I need you to fetch Aurelia. Lark, get the Commander."

Both males nodded and left quickly. I found myself alone with the Prince and an ugly thought crossed my mind. I could let this hateful male die. He said he hated his father, but he represented everything that his father did, and one less Unseelie Fae would make it far easier to dispose of the whole court.

I hesitated. A strange pang hurt my heart at the thought of letting anyone die, with the exception of the Unseelie King, and I shook my head chastising myself. I was a healer, not a killer, and I would not blacken my soul for the sake of this male.

I pulled a tall stool over and touched a warm, wet rag to the injury. An iron injury was rare. Iron was the only substance that could mortally wound a Fae in one blow. No one knew why, or at least I couldn't find a reason in any of the medical books I had poured through, but some property of the metal prevented our healing magic and poisoned the blood.

Iron had been banned for centuries in the Fae realms. The dwarves dealt in iron and steel, but they were natural enemies to the Fae, and had refused trade for centuries. Fae weapons were made of copper or silver or wood, or sometimes obsidian, but never iron. Even an injury from steel, though less dangerous than pure iron, would take weeks to heal, and it could be deadly if the injury were deep.

I inspected the wound again and rinsed blood from my cloth. A lesser Fae would have already succumbed to the injury. Clearly the Prince had strong magic and a will of steel to survive this injury, but without my help he would surely die from the poison in his blood.

Nella returned with the woodsorrel and aniseed, which was the only combination I knew could slow iron poisoning. Nothing could reverse it, and it would take weeks for the Prince's magic to fully heal this injury, but the medicine would help it along. I mixed the herbs with water to create a paste and finished cleaning the wound, then began to spread the paste in and around it.

The Prince, who had been groaning slightly throughout sucked in his breath with a hiss and grabbed my wrist. Sweat beaded his forehead and he opened his eyes enough to meet mine. His eyes were steely gray with determination, but his grip on my wrist was weak.

"I need to treat this wound your highness," I said, not removing my wrist from his grasp. "If you don't let me, the iron will kill you. I'll be done soon."

Gently I laid my free hand atop the one he had placed on my wrist. His eyes widened and he grunted, this time in what I thought was acceptance. He removed his hand from my wrist and gripped the edge of the table instead, nodding slightly as I returned to treating his wound.

It took most of an hour to clean, treat, and stitch the stab wound. I had to sew muscle together beneath the skin before I could knit the angry, blackened edges of the wound.

While I worked, I imagined the wound like I would a plant growing from a vine. I willed the flesh to knit, much like I willed leaves to bloom. I imagined the lines of corruption sucking back into the wound, like roots growing in reverse. Warmth tingled under my hands while I stitched and cleaned, and by the time I was done I felt completely drained.

"There," I said, mostly to myself. I looked at the Prince. He was still lying with his head back on the table, sweat dampening his brow and chest. His grimace had eased somewhat, and he watched me with an unnerving level of concentration. I cleared my throat and quietly asked Nella to go make some chamomile tea with mugwort for the pain.

"The paste should stop the iron poison from spreading further," I said, wiping my bloodied hands on a clean towel and wiping sweat from my forehead with my arm. "I'm afraid it will be a few weeks until you are fully healed, but you'll live."

The Prince grimaced again, lifting the corner of his lips in what would have been his normal wicked smile had he not been in so much pain.

"I'm sure you are disappointed," he rasped, turning to look at the ceiling. "My death would have given you great comfort I think."

He sounded so hopeless in that moment, I wasn't quite sure what to do. Probably best not to tell him I had contemplated letting him die, however briefly.

"Not at all," I said brusquely, disposing of the soiled towels and cloths in a laundry bin and putting my hands on my hips in what I hoped was a businesslike manner. "It would have been exceedingly inconvenient if you had died on me."

The Prince let out a bark of laughter, then sucked in a breath as his wound pulled and hurt with the movement.

"Inconvenient indeed," he growled, wincing.

"How did you get this," I asked, sitting beside him on the tall stool again. "Few Fae have iron daggers. someone must have very much wanted you dead."

"Other than you?" he ground out. I said nothing, uncomfortable that he might have understood my earlier hesitation for what it was. He huffed a dark laugh, my silence saying more than my words ever could. "Someone did. An assassin from my father's court perhaps. I'm not sure."

"He really doesn't trust you, does he," I said as he tried to sit up, bracing his forearm on the table, face contorting in pain as he moved.

"Wait," I said, putting my hand on his bare chest to push him back down. He was all firm skin and muscle under my palm, white scars crisscrossing his chest that I hadn't noticed before because of my focus on the wound. Another of those little electric bolts traveled up my arm when I touched him. Our eyes met again and I coughed uncomfortably, removing my hand.

"Let me get some pillows," I said, moving to the linen cabinet to grab something to prop him up on, "and I'll wrap the wound so it feels more secure."

The Prince groaned slightly as I helped him sit up enough to get the pillows under him. I cut a large square of spider silk and folded it to make a pad to cover the wound, then began wrapping more silk around his middle to keep the pad in place. His skin was warm as my hands traveled around his body, and I hoped he would not develop a fever from infection this quickly. My face was pressed close to his chest as I worked. He smelled of sweat and blood and aniseed, but also mint and forest and snow-kissed pine.

I tied off the end of the silk, feeling a flush creep up my face as I moved away. The Prince caught my hands and I met his eyes.

"Thank you," he said, his voice still gruff with pain, but easier than it had been. "You have a gift for healing."

I smiled sardonically. "It's no gift. I have done a lot of reading. My magic isn't strong enough to help with this."

The Prince frowned as I began to clean up, and the Commander and Aurelia came rushing in together.

"Oh Em, you are covered in blood!" Aurelia exclaimed at the same time the Commander said resignedly to the Prince, "what have you done to yourself?"

I rolled my eyes and grumbled, "Gotten himself half killed is what." Aurelia took over the tidying for me and pushed me to sit down as the Commander leaned against the wall, arms crossed over her chest and said, "report."

"It was an assassin, possibly from my fathers court," said the prince, a sharp edge of pain lacing his words. "He used an iron dagger. Dwarvish, I think. I didn't get a good look." Tendrils of darkness leaked out of his fingers as he spoke, and I noticed him reign them in and tamp them down with a glamour. Impressive, considering the extent of his injury. And foolish.

"Save your magic for healing," I said, nodding to his hands. The prince just scowled at me and continued.

"He was waiting in the woods and ambushed me." The prince grimaced again, clearly in pain.

"Did he know who you were when he attacked?" asked the Commander. The Prince shook his head.

"I wore a hood," he rasped. "He didn't see my face until after he attacked. "It's possible he was looking for any rebel to lead him here. Once he saw my face I knew I'd have to kill him, but he caught me in the side with his goddess damned iron blade first."

"The body?" asked the Commander, glancing at me. This could easily have been what my uncle and Lord Thorn were plotting. I pursed my lips.

"Left it," grunted the Prince, "about two miles out to the west. I couldn't move it and me."

I blinked. Somehow the Prince had stumbled a mile through the forest, gravely injured and barely making a sound when he stumbled on me. I thought of how he had transported us to the caves in a swirl of darkness.

"How is it that you found me instead of going straight to the caves?" I asked, eyes narrowed. He must have known where I was to find me so exactly. "And how did you get us here? What was that darkness you took us through?"

"We shadow-walked," he said, turning his attention

from the Commander to me, voice still laced with pain. "And I don't know how I found you. I just...knew where to go. Felt you near."

The Prince dropped his head back against the pillow and I cleared my throat, adopting my strict healer voice as I stood.

"He needs rest," I said. "Anything else should wait until tomorrow." The Commander nodded, but the Prince protested.

"I need to leave," he said, groaning as he tried to stand. "My guards will be out looking for me. They won't know where I am."

The Commander pushed the Prince firmly back down on the table. "We will come up with some plan to keep your injury secret," she said, frowning a his face blanched somehow even whiter than usual. "And we will send a message to your guards saying you are," she glanced at me, "with a lady for the evening." I blushed. "Rest a few hours, then we will get you out."

The Commander left, barking orders at everyone, and Aurelia went to find some clean clothes. Our shirts were both sticky with the Prince's blood. I sat next to the table as Nella returned with the tea. She bobbed a curtsy and left to help tidy up.

"Drink this," I commanded, holding a cup to his lips. The prince obeyed without an objection, and it worried me how compliant he was. He clearly felt terrible.

"What is it?" he asked as he finished the last sip, dropping his head back on the pillow and closing his eyes. Now that we were alone he had released his shadows again. They flickered pathetically as if wounded just as badly as the Prince was.

"Tea. It will help with the pain and sleep," I said,

placing the cup down and reaching for a cool cloth to wipe the sweat and blood from his face. He opened his eyes at my ministrations and looked at me. I tried not to let it unnerve me as I worked.

"I'll check on you in a few hours," I said, standing to take my leave.

"You are covered in my blood," the Prince said weakly. I paused, temper flaring slightly. I reminded myself that he wasn't the terrifying male I had met at a ball right now. He was a patient, and he was in pain.

"Still criticizing. That's a good sign," I said, sighing. The blouse I wore may not be salvageable. I would have to do a lot of explaining about my destroyed wardrobe. "Is there anything else you need, your highness?"

"No, I mean," he gritted out, "I am sorry about the blood. I ruined your shirt."

I raised my brows at him.

"It's not worth worrying about, your highness."

"Hadrian," he said tiredly, closing his eyes as the tea took effect. I studied him for a few moments, his chest rising slowly as sleep found him, the lines of pain in his face easing.

"Hadrian," I replied softly.

CHAPTER 8

I jolted awake several hours later, woken by the nightmare that always seemed to visit whenever I had a difficult day. This time as the stars winked out, I recognized the blackness that darkened the sky for what it was.

Blood.

I rubbed my eyes and stared in confusion at my surroundings, taking several minutes to remember where I was and what had happened. I had drifted off on the couch in the tiny infirmary office. Aurelia had insisted I eat something and lie down once I had left the Prince.

"You look half dead," she had scolded, handing me a clean shirt she had pilfered from the laundry. It was a male's shirt, but it would have to do since the alternative was remaining caked in blood. Or naked.

Once she had watched me to make sure I ate the bread and soup she brought, she had made me lie down.

"I'll watch the infirmary," she said, tucking me under a blanket like I was a child. "And I'll send a message to your uncle that you are staying with me tonight."

I attempted to protest but she pushed me firmly back onto the couch and insisted I stay there.

"Promise to get me if anything serious comes in?" I asked, finally lying down to appease her.

"I swear it," she said, hand over her heart. "Now rest!"

I hadn't intended to fall asleep, only to close my eyes for a few minutes, but I must have been out for several hours based on how groggy I was. I didn't understand why I felt so drained, but I supposed it had been a taxing afternoon. As I rubbed a hand over my face, I took a minute to examine my feelings about everything that had happened.

I had saved the life of the son of my enemy, the male who had caused all the suffering in my court since before I was born. I had saved the life of a male I didn't like very much, and had promised myself I would hate forever. But I also realized I felt a grudging respect for the Prince. He had nearly died for a cause that was not his own.

Still, though he claimed to hate his father, I couldn't see how his hate could be greater than mine, or any Seelie in my realm.

I sighed. This ruse we were planning was going to be complicated, more so if the Prince returned home visibly injured. Even with a week and a half still remaining before we traveled North, he would be in no shape to ride any distance. And somehow we were supposed to convince the court that we were, well, maybe not in love, but at least romantically attached, before leaving to face his father. I had no idea how to pull that off if the Prince spent the next week and a half in bed, or how we would account for his absence in society during that time.

I stretched. I needed to get home before I was missed, and while it was unlikely my uncle would notice my missing tunic and too-big shirt if I bumped into him, I'd prefer to have time to change before I was expected at breakfast. I could probably get home and change within the hour, then sneak back here after breakfast to check the Prince's condition.

It was at that moment that I had the perfect way to explain how the Prince and I had become betrothed, as long as we could pull it off.

It didn't take long to put my plan into action. The Commander nodded with approval when I had finished explaining my idea to her.

"Yes," she said thoughtfully, "I think this will work nicely."

Soon, I had a small group gathered in the infirmary to plan out how we would hide the Prince's injury and explain our swift (pretend) love affair.

The Prince was awake. He was still pale, his face drawn in pain, but he was alert, and his bandages were clean when I checked briefly. He hadn't bled through them, which was a sign that he was beginning to heal. He was dressed in a clean white shirt, similar to the one I wore, and he looked at me warily as I explained the plan.

"You tell the truth," I said, perching on the edge of

the bed he had been moved to, explaining my plan. "Or, mostly the truth. You must glamour the wound so that your guards can't tell it has been stitched and treated, and to hide the iron corruption. Tell them you were ambushed somewhere far from the caves, and ask them to call for me to serve as a healer. Say you have heard of my skills from the local nobility and request that I come tend to you. You'll be able to rest and heal, and we will be able to explain how we came to fall in love and become engaged."

"This is a weak plan," the Prince growled, lines of pain wrinkling his forehead. The wound must hurt savagely, but I couldn't be sure since he was usually just as disagreeable.

"This is the only plan," I retorted, crossing my arms in annoyance with his stubbornness. "You can't stay here for two weeks, and we need to appear to be courting. I can offer to read to you as you recover. Clearly my ministrations will win your heart and you'll be so overcome by my tenderness and beauty that you'll ask for my hand. It explains everything."

He laughed, then winced as it caused him pain. Served him right.

"Unless you have a better plan?" I adsked smugly.

Aurelia clapped her hands. "It's an excellent plan!" She said. "Most of the local lords and ladies have received some kind of medicine or patching up from you at some point, so they'll believe that the Prince has heard of your skill at healing. Especially since there are very few Seelie with the gift left. I can attend Saturday's ball and spread rumors of your budding romance. If I tell just a few of the noble ladies, news will reach the entire court by Monday."

"Smart," I said approvingly to Aurelia, offering my dear friend a smile.

"It's settled then," said the Commander briskly. "How will we get him back to his guards?"

I paused. I hadn't really thought that far. Brow furrowed, I suggested, "a litter?"

"We could drag him," said Pip, blushing as the Prince scowled at this suggestion.

"We could borrow a wagon from the village," chimed Lark, looking far too excited about all of this.

"I'll shadow walk," said the Prince, grimacing as he spoke, "and I still hate this plan."

"How will you shadow walk?" I asked exasperatedly. "You need all of your magic to heal. You can't walk through the forest like that. It will drain you completely and ruin all of my hard work saving you."

"I'll manage," said the Prince, sounding annoyed at my fussing.

"Good," said the Commander with her normal voice of authority. "Go now. Ember, return home at once so you are ready when the Prince's messenger arrives." She stood and began waving everyone from the room.

The Prince nodded as I stood to protest, but before the words could escape my lips, he had rolled off the bed and disappeared into shadow.

Never in my life had I gotten home so quickly. I had packed as much woodsorrel and aniseed and spider silk wrappings and tea as I could into a small pouch, and I arrived back only thirty minutes after the Prince's departure. I hoped I would have no more than an hour until he called for me, so I quickly cleaned myself up, wiping away the smeared makeup and dirt and blood from my face, rebraiding my hair until it looked somewhat civilized, and donning a simple dress. By the time I was done I felt semi-confident that I did not look like I had slept the night on a lumpy couch after being bled all over by the Prince.

The message came with one of the Prince's guards. He had dark, shoulder length hair and wore armor like the Prince's. A scar sliced across his chin, which he had clearly tried to cover with a closely cropped beard. He introduced himself as Vanth, and he bowed to me as he repeated his master's summons. I put on what was hopefully a convincing show of surprise and called for a horse from the stables, my favorite dappled gray mare. Within the hour we were riding off toward the abandoned Seelie palace, where the Prince had taken up temporary residence for his stay in the Seelie Realm.

When we arrived I lamented at the state of the palace. It had been left in a state of disrepair since the Queen had been slaughtered by the Unseelie King. No more than a skeleton staff must be on hand to keep the palace in order, and most of the windows were cracked, as well as several stones in the towers.

We were met by a young Seelie stablehand who took our horses, and Vanth himself led me through the abandoned palace to the Prince's chambers.

A strange twinge of despair filled me as I passed through the torn and burned wallpaper and carpets in the carcass of the Seelie palace. Its loss felt strangely personal for me. Tapestries hung in moldy disrepair from the walls, and the ornate tile floor was chipped and cracked. The pattern, which had once been the seal and symbol of the Seelie Queen, was almost unrecognizable. I paused, tracing the toe of my boot along the edge of one of the broken wings of the great moth. The phases of the moon and stars that once shone on its marble wings were damaged beyond repair. I sighed, continuing behind Vanth as I cataloged the wreckage in my mind.

When we arrived at the Prince's door, the other member of his guard was standing at attention. She was petite, shorter than me by several inches, and a long silver braid fell down her back. With her pale, Unseelie skin, she looked like a ghost. Efficiently and quickly, she searched me for weapons and checked my bag, her small hands flying in and out of every pocket. Satisfied, she gave a grunt and escorted me into the room.

I clapped my hand to my mouth in shock as I saw the Prince. He looked so much worse than he had at the caves, his skin gray and clammy and sweat dotting his brow.

"Your highness," I breathed, setting my bag on the bed and moving to stand behind him.

"Leave us," he croaked, and I realized he was dismissing his guard, who was standing behind me with her hand on the pommel of her sword.

"Your highness, it's not safe…" she started.

"I said leave us," he commanded. "She can't hurt me more than I already am."

His guard bowed, and left the room, closing the door behind her.

The Prince looked at me. "Calm your hysteria, I'm fine."

I watched dumbstruck as a little color returned to the Prince's face, his appearance improving enough to calm the edge of panic I was feeling. Understanding hit me like a tidal wave and I ground my teeth in annoyance.

"A glamour."

"You told me to be convincing," the Prince said with a slight shrug. He winced, his wound clearly still paining him. Good. I hoped it hurt.

"If you're quite done pretending to be dying, I need to check your wound," I said, tugging the hem of his shirt up to reveal bloody bandages. The skin of his torso was warm, but not hot as I lifted the edge of a bandage. I hissed through my teeth. Several stitches had torn, and the wound looked angry.

"I knew shadow walking was a bad idea," I said, setting out my supplies and rolling up my sleeves. "This will be even less pleasant than it was at the caves," I warned him as I pulled out a needle and thread.

"That was pleasant?" He grunted, raising a brow.

"How did you even have enough magic for a glamour like that after shadow walking?" I asked, settling into the familiar motions of cleaning and dressing a wound. The black lines of corruption had begun to recede, which was something. I saw that the room had a bathing chamber, and I went to fill a bowl with warm water.

"I have a lot of magic," the Prince said, stifling a groan as he shifted so I could set to work stitching the wound. "Or rather, my father does. Sometimes too much magic," he added tightly. "It helps to work it off."

"Must be nice to have so much magic you need to burn it off," I said, sighing. I worked as quickly and gently as I could, the Prince sitting silently throughout the process. I was snipping off the last of the stitches when the Prince caught my hand.

"Thank you," he said, eyes meeting mine. The now familiar jolt of whatever it was between us zapped my core, and I nodded dumbly.

"I'll ask the guards to bring you some broth," I said, tidying my supplies away quickly and trying not to meet his stare again. "Try to ease up on the glamour a little, or your guards will truly think you're dying."

Without another word I slipped from his room and made my request to the guards. Vanth left, I presumed to the kitchens, and the female guard turned to me.

"The Prince had requested you stay to tend his wound, my lady," she said stiffly. "I am to take you to a room and make sure you are settled."

"Oh, that's not necessary," I said quickly. "I can return tomorrow to check on the Prince."

"The Prince commands it," the guard replied, clearly feeling that this settled the issue. I sighed.

"Very well. Thank you."

She nodded and led me down the corridor, only a few doors away from the Prince.

Shutting the door to my guest room, I took a deep breath and leaned against it. The room was beautiful, but sad. It had clearly been neglected for years, and while the sheets were newly cleaned, dust was present on the furnishing and the dark blue drapes and canopy, which were worn with age.

I sighed and sat on the great four-poster bed. It was too late to change course now, but I wondered if I would regret getting myself into this mess in the morning.

CHAPTER 9

"This is healing remarkably well," I said.

It was the third day since I had arrived at the palace. My uncle had sent me a message encouraging me to stay with the Prince for as long as necessary. He was very obviously hoping to win favor and maybe marry me off, which worked nicely for my plans as well, so I agreed and made every show of concern in my reply for the Prince's welfare.

Several other healers, none as skilled as I, had been called to verify my treatment plan, and all had agreed that the Prince was safe under my care. Each had given me a knowing look as they left, and I wondered how much of Aurelia's gossip had already spread through the court.

From the Prince there was a great deal of grumbling

and sarcasm. I had actually attempted to read to him, since neither of us had much to occupy our time, but he was exceedingly critical of every genre of book ever written. More often than not. I ended up reading silently to myself while he looked out the window. There was a pretty view of the woods, but even I would grow bored and frustrated after three days of idleness. I often caught him studying me, but I pretended not to notice. I'd rather not know what he found so displeasing, if I was being honest with myself.

"Good," the Prince said gruffly, standing from the bed where he had been sitting and pulling on his shirt. "I need to resume my duties, both official and secret."

"Well, you shouldn't move for two or three more days, I think," I said, averting my eyes from the muscles that rippled over his back as he dressed. Curse my stupid heart and stomach for the little flutter it did at the sight.

I was also growing bored with the seclusion. Aurelia and Aspen had both written, assuring me that all was well in my absence and asking after my well-being. My uncle had even paid a visit in person one morning, probably out of his desire to wheedle his way into more courtly influence. The visit was short, the Prince feigning exhaustion to get rid of him, and my uncle left with prodigious assurance that I was at the Prince's disposal for as long as he needed. He had tried to get me alone to talk, but the Prince had claimed he needed me to stay. As he was escorted out, my uncle gave me a hard look that promised violence if I didn't win a marriage proposal from this.

A few times a day the guards popped in to check on us, but I mostly sat vigil alone, hoping that the court believed us to be falling in love as I nursed him back to health. And so three days had sluggishly elapsed, trying both of our patiences.

"I don't have two or three days," the Prince said, "and neither do you." He gave me a pointed look. "We leave in one week. In that time we need to convince the nobility we are courting, get my father's permission to present you, convince your uncle to release you, and make sure preparations are under way for us to communicate back with the network from the North."

I huffed a laugh. "My uncle will be glad to get rid of me to an advantageous marriage, so don't worry about that point."

The Prince frowned, clearly unwilling to bend on his desire to be doing things. In truth the wound had healed much faster than I had anticipated. Each application of aniseed had pushed the corruption back, and the wound had almost completely closed. I sighed.

"Let me at least wrap it tightly so there's less of a chance it will open back up," I conceded.

The Prince nodded and I unspooled some spider silk bandage, gesturing at the Prince to lift his arms so I could wrap his midsection. It really was a miraculous healing. The Prince must not have been exaggerating about his power. An injury like this would have put most Fae out for two weeks, if they had even survived. The fact that he was up and itching to move was a testament to his magic, or maybe just his willpower.

I began wrapping the silk bandages around the Prince's waist. His skin was pale and smooth where he wasn't laced with scars. I expected him to be cold, something about his pallor made it seem likely, but he was warm. He still smelled like mint and aniseed and pine, and it wasn't a completely unpleasant scent. My hands brushed his waist and I noticed goosebumps rise along his arms.

"Sorry," I said, still wrapping layers of silk around the wound to keep everything tightly in place. "Cold hands are an occupational hazard."

"It's fine," he replied gruffly, surprising me with his tone so much that I looked up and met his eyes. He was a good head and a half taller than me, and that zing of something passed between us again. I cleared my throat and finished wrapping his waist, tucking the end of the spider silk in so it wouldn't peek out from the bottom of his shirt.

"There," I said, adopting what I hoped was a professional and impassive tone. "Good as, well, not new, but it should hold."

The Prince lowered his hands to my arms and held me there for a moment searching my face, causing my heart and stomach to thrum. I stood absolutely still, not understanding this charge between us or what he was doing or why he was holding me.

He released my arms and walked to the armoire.

"We will be expected at the Autumnal Equinox in two nights," said the Prince, back turned to me as he began pulling out his armor. He stopped and turned, leaning against the armoire with his arms crossed. Like this, without a coat and with his shirt only partially buttoned, I could almost forget he was the Prince. I nodded.

"I'll be there," I said, adding with a wry smile, "I suppose I don't need to worry about you dancing too much and reopening your wound, but you'll need to do a better job of acting like you actually like me. Such a feat may be beyond even your all-powerful magic."

For the first time since his injury, the Prince's lips quirked up in a half smile. The movement transformed his face from terrifying to breathtaking. My cursed heart gave a little leap.

"I look forward to the challenge."

Within the hour I was packed and ready to return home. My dappled mare had been fetched, fat and happy from three days of pampering in the Royal stables. As I turned to mount, I felt the Prince's hand on my waist, boosting me up into the saddle. My heart lurched. I didn't need the help, but clearly our performance had begun. I faced him, and he took my hand in his.

Pressing his lips to the back, he said, "I owe you my gratitude, my lady."

I blushed and turned the horse to leave.

"Lady Ember," he called as the horse began to plod away. I pulled her reins to slow her and turned toward him.

"Yes, your highness?" I asked, not sure what else to say to him. Three days of proximity to him had lowered my guard around him, and seeing him weak and vulnerable had softened my disdain. But we were still enemies, weren't we?

"See you at the ball," was all he said, and he turned to walk into the palace, guards following at a respectful distance.

My uncle was sorely disappointed when I returned to the house, grumbling about wasted opportunities and cloistering himself in his study to "catch up with his correspondence." I made another mental note to sneak in to read his letters when he was next out of the house.

I spent the next day going back and forth from the

house to my infirmary, restocking medicinal herbs and wrapping bandages and writing down instructions for common treatments.

Aurelia tried to teach me a few times to use her dagger, and I had some success with defensive moves. I did not hear from or see the Prince until the morning of the ball, when I woke to find a large black box waiting for me at the end of my bed with a small gold note card attached.

I sat up and scrambled to the end of the bed to examine the note. In swirling black script it read,

> For tonight's performance.
> -H

Heart thumping rather faster than usual, I gingerly opened the box and gasped. It was a dress of the darkest black I had ever seen. The material was silken beneath my fingers, and I quickly lifted it out of the box to drape it on the bed.

The dress would sit off my shoulders, with long flowing sheer cuffs that widened and pooled into the skirt. Gold leaves and moths and flowers and ravens were filigreed across a snug bodice, and the skirts draped out from the hip in a waterfall of midnight silks.

It was beautiful. Regal. Fit for a queen.

The gold note had fluttered to the floor when I draped the dress on the bed, and I reached down, realizing there was something else written on the back.

"P.S. challenge accepted.

I fiddled with the embroidery on my bodice as Aurelia, Aspen, and I arrived at the ball. The celebration for the Autumnal Equinox was always held outside under a canopy of autumn trees that painted the sky with reds and golds. Firefly lanterns floated overhead and lit the floor as the warm glow of sunset faded into night over the canopy of trees. Sprites darted among the guests, stealing sips of Faerie wine and fluttering prettily.

We had ridden in my uncle's carriage that night. For once, my uncle had decided to attend as well. He was clearly wanting to make sure the Prince noticed us in attendance and to flaunt his new status as a favored lord over their noble heads.

He had cornered me earlier, before I had a chance to get ready.

"Do not disappoint me tonight, niece," he said, backing me into a corner of the drawing room with elegant menace. "You have the Prince's eye. Do not let it wander to any other female."

I had been unable to sneak into his office yet, and I worried what he might be planning with this new powerful alliance before him

Aurelia was in a blue so pale it was almost white. Her golden hair was loose about her shoulders, a crown of baby's breath atop her head. She looked like a princess of the Spring. Aspen was clearly bewitched, and barely glanced away from her the whole ride over.

I smiled secretly to myself as he offered her his hand to disembark, placing his other hand around her waist in a steadying gesture.

I got no such treatment when he helped *me* out of the carriage.

"Careful or your eyes will fall right out of your head,"

I whispered to him as I climbed down the carriage steps. He grunted in reply, then turned his immaculate manners on my friend, offering his arm. I grimaced, realizing that he had left me to be escorted by my uncle.

"Ah, my Lord," came an oily voice from our right. I cursed as Lord Thorn appeared, bowing obsequiously and offering me his hand. "Lady Ember, you are a vision as always."

I hid my grimace tolerably well until, to my horror, he offered me his arm. My uncle nudged me forward and I had no choice but to take it.

"Lord Thorn," my uncle intoned, with a slight nod of his head. "How fortunate we are to run into you. Would you be so kind as to escort my neice into the ball? I have some business to attend to before I enter."

"It would be my pleasure," replied the lord, leering at my chest in a way that both froze and boiled my blood at the same time.

I went with him stiffly, trying to think of every excuse possible to return to Aspen and Aurelia. They were a short distance away, golden heads bowed together in discussion. Aurelia's tinkling laugh lit up the night, and I cursed my friend for her infatuation. There was no way she would rescue me from this.

"I believe you owe me a dance, my lady," said Lord Thorn, steering me toward the floor where couples swayed to the sweet melodies of Faerie fiddles.

"I owe you nothing, my lord," I replied in a stiff tone, remembering our last encounter. He clearly remembered as well, for he frowned and narrowed his eyes.

"I believe you will owe me a great deal when I ask your uncle for your hand in marriage tonight," he said, spinning me to face him and gripping my waist in a mockery of a dance. His grip was too tight and commanding and I almost missed what he had said.

"What?" I replied dumbly. All thoughts seem to have fled my brain.

"Marriage, my lady. You are speechless, of course."

I would rather plunge my head into a grove of poison ivy. I would rather drain and stitch all the festering wounds in the court.

I would rather marry the Prince.

The realization jolted me out of stupor. The Prince. I had an escape.

"You flatter me, my Lord," I said icily. I felt no need to stroke this male's vanity, and it was incredible that he didn't realize my contempt for him. "But you assume too much. You have not yet asked for my hand, and I have not yet given my answer."

We had begun to turn with the other couples on the floor. Thorn was tall, almost as tall as the Prince, but thin and gangly. He was built like a weirdly oversized insect, and I suppressed a shudder as he leered down my dress.

"Your answer is irrelevant," said Thorn, spinning me around and gripping my waist tighter, almost painfully. "Your uncle will agree."

"My uncle is not my master," I said. I had stopped moving and stood completely still with him near the edge of the dance floor. A few couples glanced our way as they edged carefully around us.

"I will not marry you," I said, allowing my contempt and disgust to power my voice and stopping dead in the middle of the dance floor. "There is no way I would accept you, under any condition."

I turned to leave and he grabbed my wrist. His grip was hard, and he pulled me back to him, wrenching my shoulder slightly as he did so. I cried out in pain, and several lords and ladies turned to us to see what caused the commotion.

"You have no real title, no claims, and no wealth," Thorn hissed. "It is likely that no male shall ever wish to take you as a bride. I do this as a courtesy to your uncle, who is a dear friend," he paused and gave me another lecherous smile that made my gut twist unpleasantly. "You should be thanking me. On your knees. Maybe you will when we are married."

I pulled away, prepared to slap him in front of all the nobility. He lost his grip on my waist, just as a large hand landed on the small of my back behind me.

Thank the goddess, Aspen has been paying attention, I thought. But the voice that came from behind me was not my cousin's.

"Lord Thorn," came the rumbling voice of the Prince. "Release the lady."

Black swirls of night were twisting through the air around me, pulling me away from Thorn. The Prince was not dampening his power with a glamour tonight. I was surprised to note the anger that rolled off him and his shadows.

Thorn stood his ground, either oblivious or uncaring about the anger directed toward him from the Prince.

"Forgive me, your highness," he said, his tone placating. "I am pleased to see you have quite recovered from your injury. I assure you, this is but a lover's quarrel. Lady Ember and I are to be married, is that not so my lady?"

The arrogance of this male! I shook my head as I

leaned back a little into the Prince's hand.

"Indeed?" Asked the Prince before I could reply, shifting his hand to curl around my waist. Despite the chill of his icy rage directed at the lord before us, his hand was warm and solid. I leaned into his touch.

"That is a grave misunderstanding indeed, then," he rumbled, still holding me firmly. "You see, Lady Ember is my betrothed."

Thorn visibly paled in the golden firefly light and the chatter around us seemed to suddenly stop at the Prince's words. I glanced between the two males, the difference in their appearance almost comical, Thorn reedy and sallow, the Prince dark and broad, muscles clearly visible beneath his formal jacket embroidered with golden flowers and moths and ravens, the match to my dress I realized. The moth and raven were symbolic, I realized, representing the union of our courts. He had planned this well. He wore the obsidian crown and an ornamental sword at his hip, also carved from sharp obsidian. Both of us were dressed to perform the first act of our deception, it seemed.

Thorn had no hope of overpowering this male. I wondered that he hadn't already fled. We stood in tense silence, an unspoken argument passing between the two males.

"I see," said Thorn, taking a step back. His eyes narrowed at us, as if looking for the lie that I knew we were perpetrating. His eventual smile was a dark, twisted thing.

"My congratulations to you both, then."

Like a bubble popping, the chatter suddenly resumed, frenzied whispers passing between the guests as they toasted our marriage and health. Thorn bowed and scuttled away. The Prince dropped his hand from my waist.

"My lady, a dance?"

He turned to me and held out his hand. It was pale as snow, but warm and strong. I took it and let him guide me away from Thorn to the center of the floor. He placed a hand gently but firmly on my waist again and lifted my right hand in his left.

"Are you alright?" He asked softly, as he began to turn us about the floor. I met his eyes and saw that streaks of silver flitted in their flinty depths. I felt the tension in his arms and hands, and the shadows that flowed from and around him whipped in more of a frenzy than usual as we danced.

"Yes, thank you," I said finally, dragging my eyes from his and glancing about at the spectators. Nobles were still whispering behind their hands and glancing our way. I felt my stomach drop with mortification and shame.

"I'm sorry," he said.

"What?" I asked in surprise. "What could you possibly be sorry for?" The Prince frowned.

"That the bastard touched you. That he frightened you." His grip tightened on my hand and waist and I winced slightly.

"Apologies," he mumbled again, loosening his grip. "Thorn is a snake and he's forced my hand. I underestimated him."

"It complicates things, I know," I replied, looking up to meet his eyes again. "You didn't have to rescue me."

"Didn't I?" He asked, brow raising as we continued to turn slowly. "Our plan would certainly be ruined if you married another male."

I laughed bitterly. "I would not have married him," I said, injecting every word with the disdain I felt for Thorn. "My uncle is hoping I'll marry you. He'd never agree to wed me to Thorn unless that possibility were off the table. Besides, you interrupted before I had the chance to devastate him publicly."

I tried to smile, to seem nonchalant about the whole thing, like Thorn was more of a nuisance than an actual threat.

"Of course," said the Prince, brows still raised and sarcasm lacing every word. "You were just about to cut him down with bladed words and he would have had no avenue of recourse. He would have simply perished of mortification, leaving you alone forever. I am terribly sorry for getting in your way."

I rolled my eyes, but felt the corner of my mouth twitch up.

"How could anyone ever want to stab you?" I asked sweetly. The Prince glared but I saw the barest hint of a smile meet mine. He pulled me a little closer as the song drew to a close.

Belatedly I realized that I was dancing with the Prince, a male I had sworn I would never dance with. I was annoyed to realize he was a rather excellent dancer.

"I vowed never to dance with you," I blurted. I had no idea why I said it. It just came out in my panic to fill the silence between us. I mentally cursed myself for risking the tenuous truce we had built.

"And I you," he replied with a smirk. "Yet here we are." We turned in silence for a moment longer.

"Are you well?" I asked. "The wound…"

"Is fine," he replied. "It's almost fully healed." That seemed improbable to me, but before I could argue, he deposited me handily right where Aspen and Aurelia were gawking with open mouthed shock at our display.

"I'll be back," he whispered, leaning down to kiss my cheek, as he strode across the floor toward my uncle, who was surrounded by a group of Unseelie nobles congratulating him on his great accomplishment of making such an advantageous alliance.

I felt my cheek burn where the Prince had kissed me.

Aurelia, who of course knew that the Prince was supposed to be my fake betrothed, gathered her wits first and threw her arms around me.

"Oh congratulations!" She squealed in a very convincing display of girlish excitement. "I just knew he had fallen for you. To think you will be a queen!"

I turned to Aspen, not sure what exactly to expect. Aspen was no fan of the Prince or the Unseelie King. He disliked his father, but wasn't ready or powerful enough to defy him or the king yet, and since he didn't know about my secret life as a rebel spy, he had to assume the engagement was genuine.

"Er...yes," he said, lifting a hand to scratch the back of his head in confusion. "Yes. Congratulations, dear cousin." He gave me a swift brotherly kiss on the cheek, then a piercing look as Aurelia began twittering about gowns and table linens and the palace and what a lovely time Spring would be for a wedding.

Goddess bless Aurelia, for without her I have no idea how I would have survived the night. As lords and ladies from both courts came to congratulate me or make my acquaintance or take my measure as a potential bride for their Prince, Aurelia flitted about making introductions and enthusiastically discussing wedding plans and directing me to have a drink of wine or eat something to save me from the more nosy and impertinent guests.

Aspen had wandered off, probably to talk to my uncle about the news, and perhaps to get the measure of my newly intended. He returned with a dark glower. Clearly, the conversation had not gone his way.

"Lady Aurelia," he said, interrupting her litany of wedding related discourse, "will you do me the honor of a dance?"

He held out his hand to her and she flushed a pretty shade of pink. His royal blue coat complemented her dress, almost like he had planned for them to be a matching set, and he looked at her expectantly, a new set to his jaw and shoulders that spoke of determination. Of intentions.

Aurelia glanced my way. "Go on," I said with a smile, and shot my cousin a wink. He rolled his eyes and led Aurelia on to the floor. She seemed to float around him, her feet barely touching the ground as they twirled. Aspen's face softened at her joy, and soon he too was laughing with her.

"They seem well matched," came a dark voice to my left. I didn't bother to turn to the Prince with my reply.

"They are. I hope they are truly happy together."

"Marriages are rarely happy," he replied. His mood was somehow even darker than it had been when he had interrupted Lord Thorn's horrific proposal.

I glanced at the Prince. He was still watching Aurelia and Aspen, his gaze hard.

"Your uncle had given his blessing," the Prince said, still watching my friend and my cousin. "And I've sent word to my father. We leave tomorrow."

"Tomorrow?" I gasped, turning to face him fully.

"I'm sorry," he said, still not looking at me. He sighed and cast his eyes skyward. "I think we've been compromised. I still haven't found out the identity of the male who attacked me, and now with this…"

He trailed off. I assumed he meant Lord Thorn's unrequited proposal. I clenched my jaw, willing the burning feeling of loss back down. I had agreed to this scheme, and I knew the risks. And the cost. Aurelia would be safe here, and she would continue my work. Aspen would be able to follow his heart's desire of finally declaring his intentions to her. I would fulfill my mission and get my revenge.

"We should dance again," I said, hardening my voice so the Prince wouldn't hear my disappointment or my fear. Whatever tremulous alliance we had made at the start of the night seemed to have become brittle, the warmth from our first dance and his rescue completely absent in the set of his shoulders and the shadows that had begun to surround us both.

I grabbed a glass of Faerie wine and finished it in one gulp. The Prince raised a dark brow at me, but held out his hand. I allowed him to sweep me onto the floor.

I felt the whispers surrounding us again and sighed as the Prince took my hand and grasped my waist. I could feel his eyes on me as we danced, but I did my best to avert my gaze. This was a job. Just another mission. I had grown accustomed to his dark, brooding presence while caring for his injury, and I had let down my guard a bit around him, but now that it was time to embark on the mission, I needed to remember the facts. This man was dangerous, and I should remember it. He may have proven his loyalty to the Commander and her generals, but he had not yet proven his loyalty to me.

"What's wrong?" he asked, his deep voice pulling me from my dark thoughts. I met his eyes, that goddess damned spark flitting between my ribs again.

"Nothing," I replied, attempting to push away my feelings. "You dance well. I'm surprised you didn't dance at all the night we first met."

The Prince looked uncomfortable at my mention of that night. "Forgive me for my rudeness to you," he said, his voice filled with an earnestness I had not heard from him before. "I didn't know who to trust. I assumed you were a pet of Lord Thorn based on how he addressed you."

That made sense, I supposed. "When did you know I wasn't?" I asked.

"When I saw you push him away at your uncle's dinner," he said.

I looked at him in surprise. "You weren't there," I said accusingly. "How could you have seen that?"

He smirked, his features warming again. His eyes had lost their violent edge and he had relaxed into the dance. Any spectator would assume we were lovers enjoying our last night in the Seelie lands.

"I was there," he said, sounding smug as an old cat. "Silver coat. Horns." He gestured to his head.

"Prince, spy, and master of disguise?" I asked, quirking a brow at him. He gave me his wicked half smile and spun me around one final time as the dance drew to a close.

"I have many talents," he replied in a near whisper. His voice promised seduction, and I shivered slightly. His aura of darkness had calmed, but I felt a tendril of night skate deliciously up my leg. What was this thing between us? Were we allies? We didn't feel like enemies anymore at least. I was in dangerous territory. Was this all a part of the ruse we were concocting for his father? I decided that two could play this game of dangerous flirtation. I raised my brows.

"You'll have to show me more some time," I replied coyly. The Prince responded with a heated stare. Realizing that he was wrapping us in a cocoon of darkness, he spooled the shadows back into himself and tamped them down with his glamour.

"The dress suits you, Lady Ember," he said loudly, leading me off the floor. Aspen and Aurelia were waiting a short distance away.

"Why thank you, your highness," I replied, realizing we had a small audience as Fae watched us from around the room. We were performing. "It is exquisite. I believe it was a gift from an admirer."

"A male of good taste then," he said, bowing and kissing my hand before looking up and meeting my eyes. There was that familiar jolt to my chest. I wondered if I would get used to it once we were together every day.

"Oh, I don't know," I replied, unable to resist delivering one last little jab to his ego. I plucked at my skirts in emphasis. "It could probably do without the ravens."

He smirked and leaned in to whisper in my ear, making a shiver run down my spine.

"I wasn't talking about the dress."

CHAPTER 10

"What are you *thinking?*" Aspen said, gripping my shoulders and giving them a little shake. "Goddess be damned, Ember, what possessed you to say yes?"

I sighed and lowered my eyes, brushing the flank of the dappled mare I had been tending to. As expected, my uncle had been thrilled about my engagement to the Prince.

"Think of the influence this will bring us at court," he had said over breakfast as Aspen had questioned his motives for agreeing.

My uncle either didn't suspect the betrothal was insincere, or he didn't care. He went on at great length over breakfast about the impressiveness of the match, the importance of bearing many sons to the Prince (eww), and the connections this would open for Aspen's prospects in a bride.

Aspen had rolled his eyes at this, but he had said very little about my impending marriage until after breakfast, when he cornered me in the stables, where I had gone to clear my head and visit the horses one last time. The Prince would be arriving around midday and we would begin the journey north. My things were already packed, and I'd decided to do a farewell tour of the estate to pass the morning.

Aspen didn't know about my treasonous second life, and I didn't want to endanger him by telling the truth. I looked up at him and said, "It's complicated."

"Complicated?!" He raged, stomping around the stable in frustration. He ran his hands through his hair and finally stopped, looking at me with such sadness in his eyes it took me aback. "Is my father making you do this? Is the Prince?"

"No," I said firmly. I realized that as much as I hated it, Aspen would have to be the first victim of my deception. I had to make him believe I was willing, if not exactly in love, or he would fight his father on it and ruin all of my plans.

"The Prince is," I hesitated, thinking of a way to phrase this that would seem believable. I settled on, "misunderstood. He can be difficult and disagreeable," here Aspen let out a laugh of derision, "but I have seen him be kind and gentle as well." I blushed slightly thinking of the dance last night and hoping Aspen thought I was thinking of the Prince's convalescence. "I think I could come to love him as well as any Unseelie lord, and my uncle is determined to marry me off to one of them eventually."

I shrugged, trying to seem nonchalant about the

whole thing as I continued brushing the horse. "If I become a queen, maybe I can do some good and bring some peace between our realms. I could help our people, Aspen. And maybe my marrying so high will mean *you* don't have to."

He blinked. Aspen knew I meant Aurelia. He loved my friend passionately, but he couldn't act on his feelings without his father's approval, and she wasn't a high born Unseelie lady. While she was part of the nobility on her mother's side, her father was common, and though they were well off, a marriage to her would not further my uncle's position in the world. Before my betrothal, he would certainly have refused the match if Aspen had asked. If I became a queen, I would have secured the greatest alliance possible for my uncle. Aspen would be free to follow his heart.

He sat down heavily on a hay bale and put his head in his hands. In a muffled voice, he said, "you don't have to do this, Ember."

"I do," I said resolutely, replacing the brush and sitting next to him. "I want to. You have to trust that I know what I'm doing. I want to go with the Prince."

He turned his head sideways slightly and looked at me through his fingers.

"Plus," I added, nudging his shoulder playfully. "Think of the fine gowns and jewelry I'll get to wear as Unseelie Queen." I waggled my eyebrows and he huffed a laugh.

"You'll take care of Aurelia for me?" I asked. I knew the two would be happy if they were married, and maybe even mated, and if happiness could come from this ruse in any small measure, I'd latch on to it with both hands.

Aspen nodded and sighed, "Always." I gave his shoulders a squeeze, feeling the need to reassure him one last time.

"I know you don't like him," I said, "but the Prince is powerful. I'll be safe with him."

I left my cousin still brooding in the stables and found myself wandering aimlessly, realizing that I actually believed what I had said to Aspen. I was safe with the Prince, and though there was a part of me that still wished to hate him for what he represented, and for who his father was, he had given me no reason to think he was anything but a good male, at least in comparison.

There was no way for me to say goodbye to the Commander before we left. Aurelia had promised to assure her that I would pass along whatever information I could as soon as possible.

After the ball, I had told Aurelia about the change in plans. We had said our tearful goodbyes already, hugging tightly and promising each other to stay safe.

She had pushed her dagger into my hands, insisting I keep it with me at all times.

"I can't use it," I protested, trying to give it back to her. "I'm more likely to hurt myself."

Aurelia smiled her radiant smile.

"The sharp end goes in your enemies," she said, patting my hand and pushing the dagger back at me. "The Prince can teach you the rest. Don't forget to guard your left."

I had laughed at her last attempt to train me to use a weapon, and assured her I would. I gave the dagger on my hip a little pat as I headed back toward the house. With a jolt, I realized the Prince and his guards were already there.

As I approached I had a better idea of what I would be dealing with. Four black horses stood in silver livery, tails swatting at the flies that buzzed around them. It was an unseasonably warm morning, and the poor things must be miserable. They were probably used to the much colder climate of the North.

Two Fae warriors stood near the horses speaking quietly. I recognized Vanth and the female guard from the palace, although they were dressed so plainly it would have been hard to be sure had I not spent three days with them. They had forsaken their spiked armor and glittering weapons for leather pants and linen shirts, roughspun cloaks covering their hair and simple daggers in their belts.

"My lady," said Vanth as I approached. He crossed his right hand over his chest and bowed slightly. I was uncomfortable with such a show of deference.

"His highness is inside with your uncle," the female guard said in a velvety voice. Now that she was out of her armor she looked younger. She was tiny next to Vanth, and I vaguely wondered how long they had served the Prince. I also realized with chagrin that I didn't actually know how old the Prince was. He was alive during the war, but beyond that I wasn't sure. What if he was centuries older than me?

"Thank you," I said, nodding slightly and continuing in. I didn't have to go far, as I heard male voices coming from the formal drawing room off the main foyer.

"Ah, there you are, my dear niece," came the voice of my uncle as I entered the room, rushing toward me and embracing me. My uncle had never embraced me, even when I was a small child or injured or sick. I couldn't even remember seeing him embrace his own son. Rather than his grief over seeing me shipped off to be married, this embrace was malicious. "The Prince has been waiting," he whispered angrily. "Don't ruin this!"

He stepped back and smiled a false fatherly sort of smile, holding me by the arms. I stepped a short distance away and he lowered his arms awkwardly.

The Prince had been sitting with his back to me and promptly stood to face me, watching this exchange with a bemused sort of grimace. He was so much taller than I remembered, and like his guards he had forsaken armor for plain traveling clothes. Several daggers were sheathed at his waist, but the normal silver sword and obsidian crown were absent. He had dampened his power with a glamour, and though he still looked powerful, he had lost some of his terrifying fierceness like this.

"My lady," he said, making the same gesture as his guards and bowing with an arm crossed over his chest. I curtsied as best as I could in riding boots and leather leggings. Skirts were inconvenient for riding or moving freely, but they were excellent for hiding ungraceful curtsies.

"Your highness," I said, uncertain if I should speak with cool politeness or the warmth one would to a beloved. I settled for something in the middle. "My apologies for keeping you waiting."

I self consciously smoothed my tunic down in a vain attempt to look respectable, and felt Aurelia's dagger sheathed on my hip as I did so. It gave me comfort feeling like she was here with me

"Not at all," said the Prince in his usual deep voice. If he had tried to sound relaxed he had failed miserably.

He was clearly coiled tighter than a spring, and his tone made it clear he was annoyed that he'd been forced to socialize while he waited for me. His gaze swept over me appraisingly, not in the same way Lord Thorn might leer, but as a general might assess a soldier's readiness for battle. He nodded slightly, so I assumed I passed inspection.

"It's time to go," he said, turning to nod to my uncle.

"My lord, I shall protect her with my life."

"Of course your highness, please take care of my dearest girl," my uncle said, coming close to cup my face in his hands. I grimaced slightly at his closeness, and he kissed me on each cheek as he said, "you will be missed, my dear."

The look he gave me as he stepped back held none of the sentimentality he expressed aloud. It was a look that promised retribution if I embarrassed him or failed to secure this marriage. I gazed back at him without emotion and nodded once, turning to follow the Prince toward the horses.

Vanth and the female guard had already mounted. The two remaining horses were a gigantic black stallion, and a smaller sleeker mare. I admired her, patting her nose and stroking her shiny black head.

"This is Nisha," said the Prince, coming to stand next to me and patting the mare's neck. "She's yours, a gift for our betrothal."

"Oh," I said, unsure what else to say about the gesture, which was clearly part of our performance. I realized I would have to be ready to perform at all times now. I patted her neck as Nisha nosed my tunic looking for treats. "She is beautiful. Thank you, your highness."

"Hadrian," he reminded me quietly as he lifted me

onto Nisha's saddle. I swayed a little as I found my balance and grinned down at him. He quirked his half smile at me and patted Nisha once more, turning to vault smoothly onto the back of the massive stallion.

"Are you sure you should be doing that?" I called, certain that he should be saving the acrobatics for after the iron wound healed.

"I'm fine," he replied, both guards answering in unison with him. He shot them an annoyed look but I laughed out loud. Clearly I was not the only concerned party, and clearly Hadrian didn't care.

"The Prince is as stubborn as his horse, my lady," said Vanth, smiling at me kindly, the scar on his chin disappearing under his beard. "You know what they say about leading horses to water."

"As if you could lead him anywhere," the female guard added sarcastically. I smiled at the friendly banter between them all.

"Thank you for your continued confidence in me," Hadrian said flatly. "Is everything prepared?"

"Yes, your highness," Vanth replied. "Seline and I will ride ahead to make sure the way is clear. We have arranged to have Lady Ember's things picked up and transported later in a trade wagon that is heading North."

"Very well," Hadrian replied. "We'll see you at the first marker." With a nod, Vanth and the female guard, Seline, sped off before us, horses galloping away like racing storm clouds. Once again I was alone with the Unseelie Prince, and not exactly sure how I should feel about it.

Oblivious to my discomfort, Hadrian turned to me and asked, "How fast can you ride?"

"Well enough," I replied, checking my seat. "Why aren't you wearing armor?" I asked, concerned. If we were attacked I wasn't sure that daggers would be enough of a defense.

"If we traveled looking like the Prince and his guards and his future bride, we'd be a target," Hadrian replied, donning a cloak to cover his head, and tossing me one too. "Put that on," he commanded.

Once I had clasped the cloak he continued, "like this we are a simple traveling party, rather than a possible target for assassins, sent by my father or otherwise. Much of the resistance is unaware of my role, and I wouldn't put it past them to try to earn some glory with your Commander by killing me."

I nodded, understanding the logic, and gently touched Aurelia's dagger at my hip again. If we were recognized, I hoped that Hadrian and his guards were proficient enough with daggers to defend us.

"Do you think that's what happened in the woods?" I asked, nodding to the site of his injury. He shook his head.

"None of your people could identify him." Without another word, he turned his horse and started off at a gallop.

I caught up with him, flying over wheat colored fields as autumn laced trees sped past us.

"We ride till sunset," he shouted over the sound of the horses. I nodded and steeled my back and shoulders for what would certainly be a long and uncomfortable ride North.

CHAPTER 11

Hadrian's determination that we ride until sunset was short lived. If the horses hadn't needed water and rest, then my stomach growling loudly as lunch time came and went would have stopped him. We steered the horses to a little stream off the path to drink, and Hadrian jumped off his horse like a male who hadn't recently been stabbed by an iron blade. He started rummaging through a saddle bag looking for something to eat.

"I should look at your wound," I said, climbing down much more carefully than Hadrian had. "You could have pulled a stitch with all that vaulting on and off your horse."

I gave Nisha a pat as she drank and went to stand next to him, crossing my arms expectantly. He ignored me and pulled an apple, half a loaf of bread, and a block of cheese out of his bag. Tossing me the apple, he tore the bread in two and handed me half of that as well. He then set to work cutting slices of cheese with one of his daggers.

"Please tell me that's a clean dagger," I asked as he ate the first piece of cheese and handed me the second. I looked at it suspiciously.

"Of course," he said, cutting and eating another slice. "I haven't used it to gut a male in days."

I choked slightly on my mouthful and he gave a short bark of laughter. I scowled at him, realizing he was teasing me.

We passed the rest of the impromptu meal in silence. I gave half of the apple to Nisha, who gobbled it up as if she hadn't eaten in days. Hadrian was talking quietly to his horse and patting down his neck.

"What's his name?" I asked, nodding to the stallion.

"Erebus," he replied, patting the stallion's neck as he neighed restlessly. "He's Nisha's mate."

"Oh," I said, surprised first that horses had mates and second that our horses were a mated pair. "How do you know?" Hadrian looked at me with a raised brow, as if questioning whether or not I was serious.

"Because," he said slowly, "I've seen them do things that only mated pairs do." I blushed.

"That is not what I meant," I said sharply. Hadrian replied with his wicked half smile. "I mean how do you know they're mated only to each other?"

He shrugged, packing his saddle bag back up and patting Erebus on the rear. "I've never seen them take an interest in any other horses," he said, turning to boost me back into Nisha's saddle. "And sometimes," he added, tightening the stirrup and putting a large hand on my calf, "you can just tell."

His eyes met mine, and I felt that flash of something again. I swallowed as he held my stare for a moment longer than necessary. He released my calf and turned to climb back into his own saddle.

Part of me wondered if I should ask if he felt the zap of whatever it was as often as I did. I willed my heartbeat to calm and reminded myself that this was the Unseelie Prince I was dealing with. He was dangerous, deadly, and definitely not a male I should get entangled with. This was a job, nothing more.

Although, I realized that he was a job I was quickly becoming friendly with. Maybe it was something about seeing him vulnerable when he had been stabbed, or maybe just our prolonged proximity for this mission, but my feelings for the Prince were much more complicated than they had been when we first met. I hated him then. Now, I wasn't sure what I felt, but it didn't feel like hate.

We rode for several more hours without rest, slowing only when the sun had begun to set and a tavern had come into view. Although we were still solidly in Seelie lands, the temperature had begun to drop, and I shivered with only the roughspun cloak to keep me warm.

"We're staying here?" I asked. "Isn't it dangerous if you're recognized?"

"I'd rather not sleep outside tonight," Hadrian replied, dropping down from his horse and offering me a hand I gladly accepted. This was more riding than I had ever done in a single day, and every one of my muscles ached. I would give an awful lot for a hot bath to sink into right now, but I felt sure that would not be in the cards for me tonight.

"We will be safe enough as a group," he said, helping me down and steadying me as I swayed. My legs felt like rubber, and my abdomen ached with every breath. I had no idea how Hadrian could be managing with his wound.

"You should let me check that wound when we get inside," I said, shivering again as a cold breeze blew past.

"I'm fine," he said again. I rolled my eyes.

We walked the horses to the stable next to the boarding house, and I saw that Vanth and Seline's horses were already there. Hadrian flipped the stable hand, a very young Seelie boy, a silver and headed toward the entrance.

The tavern was noisy. The main room was a dining room filled with Fae from both courts. A party of Seelie males laughed raucously in a corner, and a table of Unseelie males sat in tense silence over a card game, each looking like they planned to murder the other.

Hadrian steered me past the dining room and up a set of stairs, his hand on my lower back guiding me.

"You've stayed here before?" I asked. The hallway was poorly lit, and I put my hand on the wall to steady myself.

"Many times," he replied, stepping around me and walking purposefully to the room at the end of the hall. He knocked three times and waited until two knocks answered. Then he pushed open the door.

Vanth and Seline were already lounging comfortably in the armchairs by the hearth. A fire was blazing merrily as Seline sharpened a set of wickedly curved daggers in the glow of the firelight. Vanth rose and clasped Hadrian's arm.

"Any problems?" He asked gruffly as Hadrian removed his belt of daggers and dropped them with a heavy thunk on the table. I was still wearing Aurelia's dagger, and I didn't plan to take it off any time soon.

"None," Hadrian replied. "Food?"

"On its way up," Vanth replied. Clearly this was a well known and choreographed dance between Hadrian and his guards. I felt a little out of place with them, and decided to poke around the room.

It was less of a room and more of a small suite I realized. The chamber we had entered was a tiny common room. Two doors led to separate sleeping chambers, also small, the bed taking up most of the space in each room, and a third to a bathing chamber. I wandered into the bathing chamber and filled the sink with warm water, splashing my face to refresh myself some from the ride. A bath was out of the question, as the only way to bathe looked to be an ancient shower, so I re-braided my hair, which had snarled and tangled on the long ride, and passed a damp cloth over my arms and neck. Satisfied that I had done all I could, I returned to the main room.

Hadrian and Vanth had started a game of cards I wasn't familiar with while Seline continued to sharpen her knives. I wished I had brought a book with me, but I settled for sitting in front of the fire with Seline and listening to the rhythmic sound of her daggers.

I must have dozed off, because I felt myself being jostled gently on the shoulder and startled awake.

"There's food," said Seline, who had returned her daggers to her belt. She offered me a bowl of something that looked like stew and a heel of crusty bread. "You look like you could use a meal."

"Thank you," I said, accepting the food and taking an experimental sip of the stew with a wooden spoon. It was plain, but warm and hearty, so I ate without complaint.

Seline sat and studied me, frowning a bit as she ate her own stew.

"Why are you doing this?" She finally asked. I dropped my spoon in surprise and splashed the stew on my shirt. Lovely.

"Doing what?" I asked, trying to sound innocent. "Marrying the Prince?"

She scoffed. Hadrian and Vanth had gone silent, their game abandoned. They exchanged a wary glance and Hadrian sighed.

"You might as well tell her," he said, moving to lean on the mantle next to me. I stared at him with wide eyes, trying desperately to figure out if this was part of the performance we were supposed to perpetrate.

"They already know," replied Hadrian, nodding to each of the guards in turn. "They know about me and the rebellion. Vanth and Seline are my most loyal guards, and friends. You can speak plainly."

I relaxed a little, realizing that of course they would have to know. There was no way Hadrian could have slipped away from them on the day he was attacked if they didn't know what he was actually doing.

"Why?" I asked, unsure how else to ask how they had found themselves entangled in this mess.

"My mother," said Vanth. Everyone stilled as we looked his way. His head was bowed over his stew as he spoke. "The king desired her, so he took her against her will," he added, voice dark with hatred as he spoke. He looked up and I saw the pain in his eyes. "He killed her, after she refused to bed him one night."

There was a heavy beat of quiet, and then Seline spoke.

"My mate," she said quietly, her velvet voice like a somber requiem. I felt a pang of pain at her loss. Mating was the deepest bond two Fae could experience. It was a choice to spend eternity together, to feel what the other felt, and to suffer what the other suffered. Not many Fae today completed a mating, even if they were happily married. If one lost a mate, it was supposed to be like losing a part of oneself.

"He…" she broke off shaking her head, unable to continue. Vanth put a firm hand on her shoulder.

"I am so sorry," I said to both of them, understanding their hurt. I knew those words were not enough to convey my sorrow and understanding, so I offered my own truth. "My parents were killed when I was just a baby. I never knew them."

Vanth and Seline nodded darkly.

"Among us you can speak freely. This will not be the case when we arrive at my father's court," Hadrian added, his eyes seeming to gaze far beyond our small party. He drew back into himself with a shake and added, "so make sure you are not overheard." I nodded.

"What about you?" I asked, not sure I wanted to know Hadrian's tale of loss yet. "Why do you wish your father dead?" Vanth and Seline exchanged a wary glance at this, and Hadrian shook his head.

"That is a story for another time," he said, standing and placing his now empty bowl on the table. "We should get some rest. Tomorrow is another hard day of travel."

I nodded, standing as the others also rose.

"I'll take the first watch," said Hadrian, gesturing to the rooms behind us. "Vanth, relieve me in three hours." The male nodded, and followed Seline into one of the rooms, closing the door.

"Oh," I started, blushing furiously as I realized that the room only had one bed. "They're sharing a bed?"

Hadrian shrugged, looking wistfully after them. I wondered if he felt something for Seline and wished she was sharing his bed. Or if he had someone back home he longed for. I felt a pang of discomfort thinking that this ruse might keep him from someone he loved.

"Go rest," he said again, looking at me. "Tomorrow will be another hard ride." I nodded and left him, closing the door on me as he watched. There was only one bed in this room as well, and I settled into it, wrapping myself up in the covers against the cold. The room was plain, but comfortable, a single small window shuttered against the cold and night. I blew out the candle, and let myself drift away.

My last thought as sleep claimed me was to wonder where Hadrian would sleep tonight.

The dream found me again. I sat on the same cold rock under a sky full of stars. The magic that hummed in my veins felt stronger than usual, like a pulsing flame through my blood. The sense of loss was greater too, like my heart had been ripped out of my chest and would never be replaced.

The stars began to wink out one by one, as blood filled the sky, and the dread overtook me as darkness fell.

But this time, there was something new. A sound, like crying or wailing filled my ears. I tried to cover them but found I couldn't move. The sound intensified to a scream, and I awoke once again with a start and sat up, my head splitting and my ears still ringing with the sound.

The room was dark, with only a pale sliver of light filtering under the window. It must be very early in the morning. I pressed a hand to my temples and rubbed, willing the headache away. To my surprise, it worked. It felt like a warm washcloth rinsing away the pain and replacing it with cool calm. I held out my palms in front of me and inspected my hands. They looked the same as ever. Had I healed myself? That didn't seem likely when I had never done it before and I chalked it up to exhaustion and an active imagination.

I looked around the dark room, eyes adjusting to the dim light. I had my answer for where Hadrian was planning to sleep. He was on the floor lying in the small space between the bed and the door, a fur blanket wrapped around him, head resting on his arm and shadows curled around him. I supposed the shadows had to sleep too. He must be uncomfortable, but he looked peaceful enough.

It was strange seeing him like this, without the armor and weapons and the air of violence surrounding him. I had never actually seen him enact violence, but that was his reputation. I wondered if it was more his father's doing than his own.

The likelihood of my getting back to sleep seemed slim, but I laid back down anyway and started to turn what I knew about the Unseelie royals over in my head. The Prince and the king were well known, but no others. If there was a queen, rumors about her had not traveled South. Maybe she had died, or maybe the king took mistresses instead. Again I wondered how old Hadrian was, if he had siblings, and how much of the rumors of his viciousness were true.

"You're thinking so loudly I can hear you from over here," came a tired voice from the door. I turned and saw the shape of Hadrian moving in the dimness as he turned and sat up.

"Sorry," I whispered, still lying on the bed wrapped in the warm furs. "Do you want the bed? I can go to the common room so you can sleep longer," I offered as I heard joints cracking and popping as he stretched. The floor inside can hardly have been more comfortable than the floor outside.

"You can stay," he said quietly as he stood and walked over to the other side of the bed. It was not that large, and I realized what he intended to do only seconds before he did it. With a groan he fell into the bed next to me, sighing at the soft, if somewhat lumpy, mattress.

"I can go," I said again, sitting up and shivering in the cold morning air. I had slept in all of my clothes last night, and layers of furs were between us, but somehow this felt dangerous. Like a line was about to be crossed.

Hadrian put his hand on my arm to stop me. He was also fully clothed, still wearing his gear from yesterday. He had slung his belt of daggers over the end of the bed in the night, and I was surprised it hadn't woken me.

"I didn't mean to make you uncomfortable," he said, sitting back up. "I promised no bed warming. You stay. I'm used to hard riding."

He moved to stand back up, but I covered his hand

with my free one.

"You're injured," I hissed, both annoyed and oddly grateful that he was treating me like a delicate flower. I wasn't sure what to do with his kindness. His anger and sarcasm, sure, but kindness was more tricky.

"It's fine," I added, shifting to lie back down. "We are both clothed. I doubt your guards will expect anything untoward occurred."

Hadrian raised an eyebrow, or at least I think he did in the dim light.

"Untoward?" he teased, grinning. I poked his arm and he huffed a laugh.

"Are you sure?" He asked.

Nodding, I lay back down and faced away from him, feeling the mattress sink beneath him as he got comfortable. Within minutes his breathing had become deep and even, and I could tell he had fallen asleep again.

When he woke in a few hours I would insist on checking his wound. I should have done so before. And then we'd be back on the road and I wouldn't have to think about his warm, solid presence next to me in the dark.

CHAPTER 12

"How is this possible?" I breathed, examining Hadrian's wound from every angle I could and finding the same thing. I had insisted on inspecting his wound when he woke, and he grumbled like an angry old goat at my "hysterics" over his injury. Now I could see why he hadn't felt like he needed my care.

"You tell me," he said, brows raised at me in challenge and countenance cool.

The fierce iron wound was healed. Nothing but a faint pink scar remained where he had been stabbed so viciously. The lines of corruption had faded to nothing, and as much as I poked and prodded, there was no pain or separation of flesh or even bruising. It was nothing short of miraculous.

"Did you take something?" I asked, brows furrowed

as I felt around the pink scar for any damaged tissue beneath the surface. Nothing.

"Only what *you* gave me," he said, emphasizing the "you" as if it were an accusation.

"I don't understand," I said quietly, almost to myself, shaking my head and the impossibility of his healing. He must have incredibly powerful magic to heal so quickly and so thoroughly from an iron dagger that had cut as deep as this had. He should be dead, not standing here almost perfectly healed. At the very least he should still be moving slowly and carefully and nursing stitches, not vaulting onto horses and galloping around the countryside.

"If you're quite satisfied," he said coolly, pulling his shirt down to hide the scar and stepping back, "we do have places to be."

Vanth and Seline were awake and eating breakfast when we emerged from our shared room. Vanth had raised an eyebrow and grinned at Hadrian, who immediately said, "don't even start," as he sat and began to attack a bowl of porridge.

It was cold and lumpy, but it was sustenance, and I knew I would need the energy for the day ahead.

"The horses are ready," Seline said, her voice low and commanding for such a small female. "It will be two more days before we are close enough for you to shadow walk us in. We will meet you again tonight at the second marker as long as no trouble befalls us."

Hadrian nodded and clasped arms with Seline, then Vanth.

"Goddess watch over you," he said, as they made their way out. Hadrian pulled on his cloak and tossed me mine.

"The road today will be more dangerous," he said. "We will be crossing the barrier between the realms, so you might also feel a little disoriented. Bandits use the disorientation of travelers to their advantage." He glanced at Aurelia's dagger sheathed at my hip. "Do you know how to use that?"

While the Seelie and Unseelie realms were connected, the power of our magic waned at the border between realms. It occurred to me that Hadrian's magic had been weaker in my realm than it would be in his own. I shuddered at the dark power he must be able to control within his own lands.

"Some," I replied, trying to sound more confident than I actually felt about defending myself. "The sharp end goes in your enemies," I added, repeating Aurelia's final advice.

Hadrian rolled his eyes so far back I thought they might fall into his skull.

"I suspected as much," he said, tone serious. "If we are attacked, you are to ride South, do you understand? Ride fast and hard until you make it back here. Any survivors will meet as soon as they can."

He gave me a piercing look and I nodded, feeling a trickle of fear mixing with the cold porridge in my stomach.

Seemingly satisfied, Hadrian swept out of the room and I followed. The tavern was already lively with breakfast as we passed through, and Hadrian kept his cloak up over his head until we were seated on the horses.

We started at a gallop, and within two hours I was already aching. Even though Nisha was steady and sure, she was so fast that staying atop her was taking all of my strength.

"Don't princes usually ride in fancy carriages?" I gasped out as we slowed our pace to a trot to give the horses a rest. I was breathing heavily and my legs shook from the effort of staying atop the horse. "Where is your fancy carriage?"

Hadrian laughed. "Fancy carriages are a target, my lady."

"Ember," I replied. "Or, what should you call me in front of your court?"

"Not my court," Hadrian corrected, patting Erebus' neck as he gave an annoyed whinny. "My father's court. And what would you like to be called?"

"I suppose my lady or Lady Ember is most appropriate," I replied, trying to think about what would be most strategic. 'My love' felt far too familiar, and I wasn't ready to have the discussion about our pretend romance yet, "but you can call me Ember when it's just us."

"Hmm," said Hadrian, a sly grin creeping across his face. "Maybe we should discuss pet names for each other. How about 'my burning flame' or 'my dearest darling'?"

"How about 'your evilness'," I replied sarcastically. My thighs, which were not small, had begun to chafe as I clung to the saddle, and I wanted to roundly curse everything about this mission, especially the need to ride so far.

"Why did we not just shadow walk to your realm?" I asked, discomfort rapidly turning into grumpiness. "Why ride if you have so much magic you can heal an iron wound?"

"First of all," replied the Prince, looking amused at

my ill humor, "I didn't heal that wound. You did. And second of all," he said, cutting me off as I attempted to interrupt his mistaken assessment of my healing abilities, "the jump is too far for me to manage with so many. I can make it by myself, which is how I've been assisting your resistance for two years, but it would drain me completely to take just one Fae along with me, never mind three passengers and four horses."

"Wait," I said, confused by this, "the others can't shadow walk?"

Hadrian shook his head. "It is a rare gift in the Unseelie court. Usually only members of the royal line are blessed with the gift. My father can do it, as can I. Seline has a minor gift for it, but only for very short jumps, and only taking herself."

I frowned. "Is Seline a member of your family?" I asked. Hadrian nodded.

"She is my sister." I must have gasped out loud, for he added, "half-sister, actually. And my father doesn't recognize her claim to the royal name."

I thought back in our conversation the other night about how the king had wronged this group.

"Stars above," I said in quiet horror. "He's her father?"

Hadrian nodded, expression dark and unreadable.

"And her mother? Your mother?" I asked. I met his eyes and saw pain there. It was almost like I felt the pain there, piercing through my heart as if I had been the one to lose her myself.

"Both dead," said Hadrian, turning to face the road again. "My father never kept a mistress for long. I was the only son born to any of them, so I am his heir by law, but he had no real love for my mother, and I doubt he feels anything for me."

My heart ached at the words. I knew well the pain and loss there. I too had lost my mother, at the hands of the same monster that he was obliged to call father.

"I'm sorry," I said quietly.

For a while, the only sound between us was the plodding of hooves on the dirt road and the chirping of birds in the woods beyond the path. The birds had become quieter as we moved North and the air became colder, as if the forest ahead were asleep, hibernating until the spring.

I shivered again.

"Is that why you hate him?" I finally asked. I had misjudged this male, and I felt a strange drive to puzzle him out.

"One of many reasons," he replied cagily. "What's important for you to know is this," he continued, turning in the saddle to look at me again, his brows drawn and face solemn. With anger? No, concern, I realized as he continued. "When you arrive, my father will test you. You will be manipulated and insulted and propositioned and attacked as he tries to decide if you are an ally or an enemy."

My stomach hollowed out as anxiety tore at me. I had no idea how I would fool the king into thinking me a pretty, harmless toy for his son, and I honestly hadn't given it any thought. I was so busy hating Hadrian and sparring with him in words that I had forgotten he was not the main target of this mission.

"Under no circumstances," Hadrian said, "must you bend to him. If you give in, he will know you can be broken. He respects only strength, and if he finds any weakness in you, he will exploit it." Hadrian paused, looking fierce and agonized as he added, "and I won't be able to stop him."

I nodded, understanding what my role would be. I would have to show strength at every test and assessment of my character. I must not bend or bow or break before him.

And above all else, I must kill him before he killed me.

We rode the next several hours in silence, me because of my swirling thoughts and battle plans, and Hadrian clearly reliving some darkness from his past. By the fourth hour of riding a light drizzle had begun to fall, and by the time the sun began to set I was frozen to the bone and so stiff I wasn't sure I would be able to dismount. The rain had grown heavier as we'd traveled farther North, and I decided that I already hated this near frozen wasteland.

We arrived at an inn that sat on the outskirts of a tiny, derelict looking town. It was much smaller than the tavern we had stayed at the night before and looked ramshackle in comparison, thatched roof burned in places and weeds overgrowing the cobblestones. At least it would be dry inside, I reminded myself.

Hadrian smirked as he watched me attempt to dismount without success. I was so stiff and cold that moving seemed impossible. Huffing a laugh, he took pity on me and reached up to swing me down. I was not ready for the move, and I stumbled forward. He caught me steadily and held me, arms clasped around my back and hip while I found my footing.

"Careful, my lady," he growled down at me, breath warming my frozen ear and the side of my cheek.

I met his eyes, assuming I'd see anger or annoyance there, but the look he gave me was something else entirely. It was molten in a way I had never seen before, and it chased away the frozen feeling, a line of heat racing all the way down to my core.

His grip on my hip tightened a moment before he seemed to remember himself and stepped back, planting me firmly on the ground and turning away to untack his horse. Erebus snorted irritably, as if reminding Hadrian that yes, he was here, and he wanted attention. I gave Nisha's soft nose a pat and began to untack her too.

Hadrian finished with Erebus and took Nisha's saddle from me. He didn't look at me as he said "let's go," and headed into the inn.

It was just as shabby on the inside as it was on the outside, and a small part of me wished for the luxuries of my uncle's manor. Traveling with a prince was nowhere near as lavish as I had assumed it would be, and it was clear that this group rode hard and fast without any thought for luxury.

Vanth and Seline were waiting for us, the room tiny in comparison to the last. A small fire was lit in the hearth, and there was no common room. Two beds took up most of the small room, neither seeming large enough to fit more than one person. I wondered how we were going to manage the sleeping arrangements tonight.

"You're more than welcome to sleep on the floor," Hadrian joked, watching me as I studied the room.

I scowled and he gave me a wicked grin as he passed, hanging his wet cloak up to dry and shucking off his boots with a horrible squelch. I realized that he must be just as uncomfortable as I, and resolved to tough it out. I hung up my cloak and left my wet boots by the fire to dry and Vanth and Seline made their report.

"No trouble," said Vanth in his deep, soothing voice. "We didn't meet any other travelers."

Hadrian frowned. "That's odd," he said, propping his feet up on the ledge before the fire as he sat on the end of one bed. His legs were so long they stretched the distance, and I noticed that he was leaving a wet patch on the blankets. That would be his side, then.

I missed the rest of the discussion. There was a very small bathing room attached, which was more of a bathing room in name than in actuality. There was a small brass mirror on the wall and a bucket of tepid water in lieu of a sink. I squeezed the moisture out of my hair on the floor of the tiny room as best as I could, hoping I wouldn't have to go to sleep soaking wet.

When I emerged, Seline was there, a roughspun linen towel in her hands.

"It's not much," she said in her velvety voice, "but it's dry."

"Thank you," I said, accepting the towel and looking up at her. While her silver hair and heart shaped face were completely different from Hadrian's dark, chiseled looks, I realized she had the same gray eyes. They added to her ghostly appearance in an eerily beautiful way.

I sat on the edge of the bed and unbraided my hair, toweling it dry as Hadrian and Vanth spoke in soft voices.

"He told me that you know I'm his sister," Seline said, sitting next to me on the bed.

I nodded, not sure what to say. There was not much that could be said. I had thought about her mate a great deal on the ride. Her loss was so terrible and tragic that no words would be enough.

"I'm sorry about your mate," I said quietly, feeling that it was better than saying nothing at all. She nodded. "He was a good male. I don't know that there is another like him. Or that I can feel what I felt for him again." She glanced up at Vanth and Hadrian, then quickly looked back at me.

"I am also sorry for your loss," she said sadly. "You never knew her at all?"

I shook my head. "I was a baby when she was killed," I said, repeating my story from the night before. "I don't know anything about her or my father."

Seline frowned and looked down, her hands twining together. "They must have been powerful Fae," she said at last, still not looking at me.

"What do you mean?" I asked, confused why she would think I came from any power at all. I had barely any power, and I had been far too exhausted to use any of my meager reserves the last two days anyway.

Seline tilted her head and looked at me, frowning slightly. "You don't know," she said, more to herself than to me.

"Know what?" I asked, growing more confused by the moment.

"Seline," said Hadrian sharply.

Seline started and turned to her brother. He gave an almost imperceptible shake of his head and they seemed to have some kind of furious disagreement without words.

"Will someone please tell me what's going on?" I said, exasperation growing with every second.

"Good luck with that," said Vanth sarcastically in the opposite corner, arms crossed in amusement as he watched the siblings bicker silently.

Whatever the argument was, Seline seemed to win it. Hadrian roared, "fine!" and stomped out of the room. Triumphant, Seline turned back to me and gave me a sympathetic look.

"My mother was a spellbreaker," she said, crossing her legs to face me on the bed. "It's a rare gift in the Unseelie court, and one of the reasons the king bedded her. He hoped for a son with the gift."

I noticed she did not claim the king as her father. I couldn't blame her. She took one of my hands and turned it over to examine the palm. I looked at her warily, uncertain where this was going.

"One of the gifts of spellbreakers is to sense powerful magic and," Seline paused, seeming to search for the right word, "and reveal it. Curses, enchantments, glamours, anything that can be concealed with a spell can be revealed by a spellbreaker."

"That is a powerful gift," I said. Seline nodded and let go of my hand, finally meeting my eyes.

"I don't have her gift of breaking spells," she said, "but I can sense powerful magic when it is near. This is something that the king does not know I inherited, or I'm sure he would find a way to use the ability."

I nodded, starting to get a sense of where this might be leading and already coming up with a million reasons why Seline was mistaken.

Seline sighed. "I don't know how to put this gently, so I'll be blunt. There is a powerful magic surrounding you. I'm not sure what it is - a glamour or enchantment of some kind - but if you don't know what it is, then it must have been placed on you when you were very young. Something is restricting your magic."

"Restricting?" I said, dumbfounded that this was at

all a possibility. "But I have no magic. I can barely hold a glamour for an evening, and even then it's a terrible glamour. I can make plants grow very tiny amounts, and then I'm drained for days."

Seline nodded, acting like a healer listening to me describing all the symptoms that confirmed her original diagnosis.

"You have no power because all of it, almost every drop, is tied up in this," she gestured to me frustratedly, "enchantment. Curse. Thing."

She looked helplessly at Vanth for words and he rolled his eyes at her failure to find the right ones.

"Hadrian thought you knew," she said, tilting her head and looking sympathetic. "He thought you were hiding your gifts. It's why he didn't trust you at first. But I was almost sure you didn't know. Most Fae fight against enchantments and spells when they are put on them. You seemed content to leave it alone."

I stood up in frustration and began pacing the tiny room.

"How do I break it?" I asked. Seline shrugged apologetically.

"I'm sorry," she said, and she truly did sound sorry, "I'm not sure. I tried to chip away at it a bit when you stayed at the palace, and some more last night at the tavern, but it's a stubborn thing. It doesn't want to budge for me, and I don't have the gift or skill to do more than poke at it."

She talked about this enchantment (curse. Thing. Whatever it was) like a living being. I could almost feel it now, wrapped around my magic like a great fist in my chest, sleeping soundly and refusing to wake.

Seline went on, "I think you may be the only one who

can break it. Usually childhood spells like this break on their own after reaching maturity, but yours is," she paused again, looking thoughtful, "different."

Hadrian chose that moment to come bursting back in, soaking wet, but carrying two warm loaves of bread.

"The kitchens were closed," he grunted, dropping the loaves on the table and dropping water behind him as he went to stand by the fire. "I had to walk to the bakery and wake the baker."

"You weren't going to tell me?" I shouted, striding over to him and attempting to look menacing as I stared up at him. My still damp hair had begun to dry around me in a frizzy cloud, and I angrily pushed strands of it out of my face. Hadrian winced. He at least had the decency to try to look apologetic.

"It's complicated," he sighed. Vanth's eyes widened in panic as he saw the look I gave Hadrian in response.

"Come on Seline, let's see if we can get another room for tonight," he said, walking over to her and attempting to usher her out the door.

"No," said Hadrian, turning to Vanth, "we stay together tonight. We have strength in numbers."

"I'm pretty sure you're the one who's at risk of attack, not us," said Vanth quietly. Seline winced as Hadrian responded with a growl.

"How dare you!" I shouted, fuming with anger. My heart was pounding in my chest as I realized that he knew, had known about this thing for weeks now, and wasn't going to tell me. Was going to let my magic stay locked away to wither and die.

"Ember," he said, holding up both hands in a placating gesture, "it's not that simple."

"Simple?" I said, incredulously. "Simple!? It's not

simple enough to say, 'oh by the way, we just met but I'm pretty sure you're under some kind of spell. You should look into that.'" I know sarcasm dripped from every word, but I didn't care. I was so angry I felt unbridled fury, like my rage was a physical object trying to push its way out of my chest.

A light flashed between us so suddenly it half blinded me. I fell back to sit on the hard, cold floor, stars bursting in front of me. While moments ago I had been incandescent with rage, now it disappeared like mist in the sunshine. I blinked, looking up.

Hadrian smirked his half smile.

"See," he said, turning to Seline with a look that screamed "I told you so." Her mouth had formed a perfect "O" in surprise at my sudden outburst. Hadrian turned back to me, still smirking.

"Strong emotion brings it out. I sensed it in the gardens at the ball when you were angry at me, and I felt it when I was injured. You were panicking and I was sure I felt you work magic on me, but you adamantly insisted you had no power. I assumed you were lying, but obviously you believed it."

He held out a hand, both a peace offering and a gesture of faith, to help me up. I accepted, allowing him to pull me to my feet.

"My guess is that's how you break it," he continued, crossing his arms and leaning against the mantelpiece.

"With anger?" I asked, suddenly feeling drained and hollow now that my anger had dissipated.

"No, my lady," he said, using the title to nettle me. He smirked that wicked smile. "With passion."

CHAPTER 13

Vanth grumbled and complained and whined, but I bullied him into sharing the bed with Hadrian that night. I shared with Seline, but I might as well have taken the first watch for the good it did me. I tossed and turned, unable to get comfortable and still my restless mind.

Hadrian had the first watch again. He sat on the floor, leaning on the wall by the foot of his bed, arms crossed and head resting on the bedpost. He was still as a statue, chest rising and falling rhythmically as if he was asleep. I grumbled as I tried again to get comfortable. Seline slept like the dead, and Vanth was snoring in the other bed. Maybe I should wake him up, since I was up anyway.

"I'm not asleep."

Hadrian was looking at me, head tilted almost upside down like a bat as he leaned on the footboard of the bed.

"Shhh," I chastised, closing my eyes and pretending to sleep. I was still vaguely angry about his deception and I didn't really feel like talking.

"I can hear you thinking," he replied quietly. "It's loud."

I wasn't sure what to say to that, but I opened my eyes to see that he had scooted round the end of the bed to face me. He was seated in the gap between the beds, space only wide enough for him to sit with his knees raised. He rested his arms and chin on them.

"Still angry?" He whispered with a roguish grin. It irritated me that he was able to look roguish at all in the middle of the night. My eyes were almost certainly bagged and bloodshot from exhaustion, and my braid was frizzy after the rain. His hair was still sleek and soft looking, waving gently back from his forehead, and his eyes had that steely glint of alert amusement in them.

I was annoyed at how handsome he looked with absolutely no effort.

"No," I whispered in clipped tones, which came out sounding positively furious. His smile widened at my obvious annoyance. I rolled my eyes.

"Yes," I corrected. The humor drained from his face and he frowned.

"I'm sorry," he whispered, lowering his head. That strange connection I felt every time our eyes met seemed to be growing. Even though he had looked away, I could almost imagine a golden thread connecting us now. I felt, more than saw, his remorse, and my anger waned a little more.

"I wasn't sure how to tell you. When I realized that Seline was right and you didn't know, I," he paused, searching for words. His throat bobbed as he swallowed down whatever he was about to say and looked back up at me. "I should have told you."

"You should," I whispered back fiercely, although my anger had mostly fizzled away with his apology. "Are there any more secrets you're not telling me?"

"Yes," he replied instantly. I narrowed my eyes, anger flaring again, but he continued, "some for your safety. Some because they're not my secrets to tell. Some because I am bound by my father to keep them."

I frowned and he went on, "but none about you."

I nodded, mollified by his explanation. We sat for a while in silence, the crackle of the fire and sounds of the wind outside the only noises in the room. He shifted a few times, stretching out his legs under the bed and cracking his neck. He must be exhausted, even though he didn't look it. Gradually, I felt my body relax.

"You should sleep," he said, watching me in the light of the fire. The orange glow of the flames lit up one side of his face, leaving the other in shadow. I realized that he had relaxed his glamour a bit, letting shadows creep along the floor, tendrils of darkness exploring the walls and furniture.

"Why do you hide your shadows from them?" I asked tiredly. He knew I meant his friends - his family. He frowned.

"I don't."

"You do," I responded, yawning widely and covering my mouth with a hand. "Last night and tonight, when we were safe off the road, you kept your glamour on in front of them. Why?"

Hadrian shrugged, looking uncomfortable. He looked away into the fire, making his eyes blaze gold for a moment instead of their normal silver.

"I don't always," he confessed. He turned away from the fire and looked back down at his hands, letting inky swirls wrap around his fingers.

"But," he paused, brow furrowed, "the shadows unnerve most people. My father never hides them. He flaunts them. He likes to be terrifying."

He looked up at me again and something unreadable crossed his expression. He finished, "I usually hide them when I'm not among enemies."

For a moment, we didn't speak, the sound of the fire and the wind filling the silence between us as the shadows pooled out from his hands to wrap up his arms.

"Am I your enemy then?" I asked quietly. He raised a brow at me and I nodded at his hands. "You're not hiding them from me."

"No, I'm not," he agreed, meeting my eyes again. Something about his gaze made my heart race a little. The way he was looking at me was not the way one would look upon an enemy.

I waited for more of an explanation, but it didn't come. I let the whistle of the wind and crackle of the fire lull me to sleep before I had my answer.

I woke again with a start as Seline shook me awake. Dim light streamed in from the only window, and the males were already strapping on their gear and boots. I must have slept all night, but it truly felt like only seconds had passed since closing my eyes. I rubbed my head, a faint headache forming again at the back of my skull. How I wished for my mugwort tea and a soothing bath to calm the brewing storm of pain.

I sat up, and retched over the side of the bed. Seline cursed and Hadrian dropped his belt of daggers, coming over to put a hand to my head.

"Fever," he said, darkly as I lay back down. I felt like my skull might crack in two if I sat up any longer.

"I'm fine," I croaked, my throat unexpectedly hoarse.

"The rain, you think?" Seline asked. "She was shivering when you arrived last night."

"The rain doesn't make you sick," I croaked, a hand over my eyes to try to stop the pounding in my head.

"Still diagnosing, that's a good sign," said Hadrian, retrieving his daggers and strapping them on. His words failed to hide the worry in his voice as he turned to his friends.

"Take Erebus and Nisha," he said, voice heavy with anxiety. "I'll take her on ahead of you."

I couldn't see Seline and Vanth's reactions, but their silence spoke volumes. They didn't want to let him out of their sight.

"It will be three days before we can reach you if we go by horse without shadow walking," said Vanth, concern clear in his voice.

"I know," replied Hadrian. "But what choice do we have?" With his gear prepared, he walked over to the bed and scooped me up into his arms. I attempted to protest, but another wave of nausea caused me to still, lest I vomit all over his boots.

"We could stay an extra day," suggested Seline, chewing on her thumbnail. Hadrian immediately shook his head.

"Too risky," he said, arms squeezing me a little tighter than was necessary. "We can't stay - we'd attract attention. And I am expected tomorrow night. She can't ride like this, and I can't risk my father's wrath."

Seline nodded, admitting defeat. "If we ride hard, we can be there in three days," she said. "You'll have us at your back as soon as we can be there."

Hadrian nodded and said, "go now." Vaguely I heard Seline and Vanth head out. My head was resting on Hadrian's shoulder, and I noted how nice and wide it was, glad he had opted to leave off the spiked pauldrons.

"I'm sorry for this," Hadrian said quietly to me, giving me another gentle squeeze. "You are not going to find this pleasant."

Without another word of warning, Hadrian stepped into shadow, taking me with him. He was right, I didn't like it. It was so much worse than the first time, and the darkness seemed to last forever, wiping out everything in its path. I think I screamed, and I thought I felt lips press against my temple and arms holding me tightly, but blessed unconsciousness took me, and I knew nothing but darkness.

Waking was a miserable business. My head still pounded and my gut felt hollow, like my stomach had begun eating itself in hunger. My tongue was like sandpaper in my mouth, and my eyelids felt like they had been stitched shut. It was so hard to open them, and it hurt when I tried.

"She's waking," said a quiet voice I didn't recognize.

The room beyond my eyelids was dark, and I strained to open them. I was lying on something, a bed probably from the plushness beneath me. Definitely not the bed of a tavern inn, as those had been lumpy, hard monstrosities.

I heard faint sounds like whispered instructions rattled off by an expert, and a deeper rumbling sound like a male's voice, but soon it was quiet again. While it would be easy to drift back into the darkness, the gnawing feeling in my gut made me think waking might be the better option.

"Good morning," said the dark, rumbling voice as I finally managed to force my eyelids open.

The room I was in was indeed dark. I was in a four-poster bed, the canopies darker shadows against the dark of the room. I turned my head slightly and sucked in a breath. It hurt.

"Careful," came the voice, "let me help."

A shadowy male came into view, lifting me under my shoulders to prop another pillow behind my back and help me sit up some. The nausea had passed, but I still felt like death.

"Drink," came the voice again, as I realized it held a cup to my lips. Warm liquid soothed the fire in my throat and calmed the writhing in my gut. I recognized mugwort and ginger and elderflower, the same herbs I would use for my symptoms. This tea had been prepared by a healer.

"Thank you," I rasped, resting back against the pillows and looking at the shadow.

"No thanks needed, my lady," came Hadrian's voice again as my vision cleared and adjusted to the darkness. He was sitting on the edge of the bed, gingerly returning the tea cup to its saucer on a nightstand. "How do you feel?"

"Like death," I croaked.

"The side effects of shadow walking with a high fever," he said quietly, amusement and relief in his voice.

"The others?" I asked. He knew what I meant.

"They will be here in two days I hope," he said softly, pulling the furs up to my shoulders in a tender gesture. I was not expecting tenderness from the Unseelie Prince, but I was feeling too horrible to tease him about it.

"How long…," I began hoarsely, but he interrupted me, anticipating my question.

"Only twenty-four hours," he said tiredly. "I brought you straight here when I shadow walked us in. It's almost morning."

And I guessed from the droop of his shoulders and exhaustion in his voice that he hadn't slept in all that time. He must be completely drained from shadow walking us the distance of what would normally be a three day ride.

I nodded, which hurt my head, and hissed a little at the pain. Hadrian stood and moved to an armchair near the bed, sitting heavily and sighing deeply.

"This is not the way I wanted to present you to my father's court," he said in consternation, dropping his head against the back of the chair and gazing up at the ceiling.

I looked up too and could faintly make out tiny silver stars embroidered in the canopy above the bed. Such a pretty detail in the bedroom of a Prince of Death. At least, I assumed this was his bedroom. It was too dark to really make out any details, but the furniture had a masculine silhouette, and the room was clearly decorated with darker colors. I imagined blacks and navy blues. The furs I rested beneath were soft and warm, and with the curtains drawn I could make nothing of the outside.

I was going to reply, but sleep swept me away again before I had the chance.

When I woke next it was to a room bathed in a faint golden light. I guessed it must be early evening, though the curtains were still drawn so it was impossible to tell. The pounding in my head had finally relented, and the gnawing in my stomach had become simple hunger. I sat up.

The Prince was sitting in the armchair staring at nothing, an ankle crossed over a knee as he waited. When he saw I was awake, he sat forward.

"Welcome back," he said, in his normal voice. The tenderness of the night seemed to have been replaced by the necessity of the day. He was coiled as tightly as a spring, anxiety clearly gnawing at him, although his face betrayed none of it.

"What's wrong?" I asked, frowning. My stomach rumbled and I added, "what time is it?"

"It's early evening," Hadrian said, seeming to relax a little at seeing me better. "Can you eat, do you think?"

I nodded, and he vanished into shadow, returning a few seconds later with a plate of buttered toast."

"Neat trick," I said, taking the plate from him as he sat on the edge of the bed again. He chuckled, watching me eat like I would a patient who I was uncertain would be able to keep anything down. I supposed I was the patient in this situation. I gulped down the bite of toast.

"I suppose we are even now," I said, finishing

the toast and licking butter off a finger. He watched me intently, something flaring in his eyes then disappearing just as quickly.

"Even?" He asked, raising his brows at me. I swear, this male raised his brows more than he kept them at their normal level.

"I heal you, you heal me," I replied, letting my head fall back against the plush headboard. It was a dark blue velvet, almost black, and I mentally congratulated myself at guessing the colors he would choose for his chambers.

He smiled faintly.

"The two were not even remotely the same, but if you insist then yes, I'd say we are even."

We sat there in awkward silence for a few minutes. I fidgeted uncomfortably with my braid. I must look terrible, not having bathed or eaten properly for several days of both travel and illness. I looked down to realize that I had been changed out of my travel clothes, and I blushed.

"Who," I started, gesturing at my attire. Hadrian smirked his usual smile, and said, "I assure you, it wasn't me."

I felt both relief and a pang of something else at his words. Regret? I cursed myself as he continued.

"We have a Seelie healer in the palace. She took care of you when we first arrived. My father doesn't even know we are here yet."

This time it was my brows that went up. "A Seelie healer? Where? How? Can I meet her?"

I had never known another Seelie healer. So few Seelie had magic anymore that the healing gift had all but disappeared. I had always attributed my gifts more to hard work and study and experimentation than magic, since I believed myself to be powerless. Healing was not an Unseelie gift, and when the Seelie Queen had been killed, most Seelie assumed that the healers would die out too.

Hadrian's smile was warm this time as he nodded. "We do, she lives in the servant quarters, it's a long story, and you can," he said, answering all of my questions in the same order I had asked them. "But not right now."

"Why not?" I asked frowning. The tea this morning and the toast right now seemed to have restored me somewhat.

"Because," Hadrian replied, standing and stretching, the muscles in his back and chest stretching the seams of his shirt. "Tonight you have to meet my father."

CHAPTER 14

I stood in the empty great hall of the Unseelie palace and shivered.

After Hadrian's pronouncement, he explained that his father expected him to present his bride today, as he had written ahead to inform him of our arrival. When I had gotten sick, we had been forced to come ahead of the others so we wouldn't be late.

Apparently no excuse would have been acceptable to his father for our tardiness. Someone would have to pay for it.

Still feeling shaky, I let him show me to the bathing chamber to wash up. It was a beautiful room, well appointed with marble floors and sinks, a great onyx tub sitting in the middle of the room. As much as I wanted to spend hours just lying in it and soaking away the misery of the journey here, we didn't have time. We were expected to be ready at nightfall.

So I bathed quickly and dried my hair, letting it fall loose. It would be a frizzy disaster if I did nothing to it, but I'd have to wait to tame it until it was dry.

Since none of my things were here yet, Hadrian had left to find me something to wear. When I asked where he would find a gown fit to meet a king, he smirked and vanished into shadow.

That trick was getting very annoying.

I dried my hair as best as I could and ran a comb through it to subdue some of the wildness. Since I had none of my normal tools available, I hunted through some of the drawers to find something I could use for my hair.

There were a lot of shirts and trousers, all black. Hadrian's I guessed. I finally found some handkerchiefs and, knotting two together, tied them around my head. I began wrapping strands of hair around the makeshift headband in hopes it would curl. When my whole head was wrapped, I sat with my back to the fire, still in the nightgown I had been dressed in by Hadrian's mysterious healer.

The sun was almost set when he returned and I was getting anxious. He stepped out of the shadows so suddenly in front of me that I almost fell back into the fire.

"Stop doing that!" I exclaimed as he caught my arm to prevent my imminent immolation, annoyance flailing as he smirked at me.

"What in the name of the goddess have you done to your head?" He asked, looking bemused as he let me go. He had black fabric draped over his arm, and I stood to take it from him.

"Curling my hair," I replied haughtily. "Not all of us can be effortlessly handsome like you."

"You think I'm handsome?" He said, grinning wickedly. I rolled my eyes and turned away from him, shaking out the dress. When I laid it out fully in the bed, I gasped.

It was one of the most beautiful gowns I had ever seen. Black and sparkling all over, it looked like it would sit off the shoulders, hugging the torso and fanning into flowing, glittering skirts below. Hadrian came up behind me and held out a hand. A silver necklace sparkled there, inset with hundreds of diamonds that reflected the firelight with tiny rainbows.

"They were my mother's," he said, by way of explanation. "It took me a while to find them. My father had everything boxed up after she died."

"I can't wear these," I said, shaking my head and pushing his hand back with the necklace still gripped in his palm.

"You don't have a choice," Hadrian said, bristling and sounding aggravated. "You have no other clothes. These are the best I could find."

"No, you don't understand," I said, shaking my head again and trying to explain. "I didn't mean I don't like them, I do. They're the most lovely things I've ever seen." Hadrian relaxed slighty and I continued, "I mean I couldn't. They're your mother's. They're special to you."

"She'd want you to wear them," he replied, dropping the necklace on top of the dress on the bed and stalking off toward the bathing chamber without another word.

I frowned, admiring the glitter of the gems and the

silky feel of the skirts. I was rather certain that this dress might not fit me. I was larger than I appeared to most people, and I worried my hips might not be able to squeeze into the dress. I clenched my teeth and, checking that Hadrian was still in another room, put it on.

It was a tight fit. The dress had hooks up the back to close, and I was only able to do half of them myself before I knew I would need to ask for help. It was indeed a beautiful gown. I admired how the skirts swished in the large mirror of the armoire, my hair still piled ridiculously on top of my head.

I saw that he had also brought a pair of simple flat, black shoes for me. They pinched a bit, but better than being too big and falling off me with every step. Noticing a small, satin bag on the dresser that hadn't been there before, I opened it to find some cosmetics, clearly old but still usable. Maybe also his mother's. I applied some color to my cheeks and eyes, sweeping black across my lashes, and painting my lips a much more daring shade of red than I normally would.

I remembered what the Commander had said when she assigned me this mission. "We don't need an assassin for this job. We need a shadow."

I definitely didn't look like a shadow. If anything I looked ready to seduce.

Feeling that my hair was finally dry, I unwound it from its nest and began combing it out. It was still fluffier than I would like, floating around me a bit like an auburn cloud, but I smoothed it as best as I could, using a little of my glamour to make it sit.

I hadn't tested the magic that was bottled up in me since Seline had revealed it. I had been too furious, then too sick to even remember that I had some enchantment on me. I pushed the magic a little to see what would happen.

Nothing.

Cursing, I turned to see Hadrian leaning on the frame of the door to the bathing room. His hair was damp and waved back from his face. In lieu of his terrifying armor, he had chosen an elegant coat and trousers, all black of course. Silver filigree of serpents and ravens adorned the cuffs and lapels of the coat, and he wore newly polished black boots. The spiky black crown had been replaced by one that looked to be made of black metal roses, and his glamour was dampened as he let his inky power waft through the room. He looked smug, like he knew what a fearsome and attractive figure he cast.

"The dress suits you, Lady Ember," he purred, echoing his words on the night of the ball when he had announced our betrothal. I realized that this was the second time he had dressed me, and both times he had chosen excellently.

"Why thank you, your highness," I replied, remembering what I had said to him that night. "I believe it was a gift from an admirer."

He laughed, going to pick up the necklace from the bed and bringing it over to me. It might have been his first truly unrestrained laugh I'd heard since meeting him, and it was lovely.

"A male of good taste then," he repeated, bowing and kissing my hand, just as he had done on the night of the Autumnal Equinox. He stood to clasp the necklace around my throat. The diamonds sparkled like starlight around my neck, and my eyes met his in the reflection of the mirror. There was the familiar jolt to my chest again. Something heated flashed in his vision and my heart gave a little leap as a wayward tendril of darkness curled around my ear. He batted it away.

"Are you ready?" He asked, moving away from me to open a cabinet I had not yet explored. Daggers and swords lined every inch of it, and he chose several silver and obsidian blades and began strapping them on.

Belatedly, I remembered Aurelia's dagger.

"My dagger," I started, and he nodded toward the table next to the bed.

"In there," he said as I went over to put it on, "but you won't be able to wear it around your waist tonight. The guards don't let guests bring weapons into the throne room."

I frowned and shrugged, remembering Aurelia's warning to always guard my left. I missed my friend dearly, and I felt a pant of guilt that I hadn't thought of her more on the journey north. Tomorrow I would ask Hadrian about writing to her.

"I'll strap it to my thigh then," I said, walking over to him with the belt in hand. "Can you shorten the belt for me?"

Raising a brow, his dark power pulsing slightly, Hadrian pulled a sliver blade, and knelt before me. He lifted my right leg and propped it on his knee and began lifting my skirt.

"What are you doing?" I snapped, pulling my foot back in horror. He smirked, still holding my ankle firmly.

"I have to measure," he said, indicating the length of the belt that I'd just asked him to fit around my thigh.

"And you need to lift my skirts for that?" I

asked, crossing my arms and trying to look fierce. He shrugged.

"Or you could lift them for me," he said, smirk widening into a wicked grin. I felt that twinge of heat claw its way down my spine and settle in my belly as strands of his dark power caressed my calf.

"Fine," I said, with more bravado than I felt. I put my foot back on his knee and lifted my skirts on one side to my thigh, revealing an expanse of golden leg. Hadrian went utterly still, breathing quickening ever so slightly. I triumphed internally.

"Something wrong?" I asked sweetly, reveling in the feeling of having bested him. I'm not sure what exactly I had won, but it felt like a victory of sorts. Maybe it was just unbalancing him a little.

"No," he growled darkly, lifting the belt and beginning to buckle it around my thigh.

I shivered slightly at his touch, and he paused in his work, glancing up to smirk at me as he asked, "something wrong?"

"No," I replied curtly. He smirked, fitting the belt around my thigh and buckling it to fit. His hands were almost white against my skin, but they were warm as he gripped the back of my thigh to test the belt's tightness. I felt goose bumps rise on my leg as more tendrils of his power wrapped themselves around my calf and thigh. He cursed softly, batting them away.

"They like you,"

"They?" I asked in surprise. I had always assumed the power was an extension of himself, not a sentient entity. He didn't answer, sheathing Aurelia's dagger and threading it through the belt, tightening it once more.

"There," he said, a little more gruffly than I think he

intended, giving my thigh a final squeeze. He cut the extra length of the belt and stood quickly, holding it out to me. I dropped my leg and my skirts and took it wordlessly. For a moment we just stood there, looking at each other. This thing between us was pulsing again, and I found it very hard to look away. Then I remembered the hooks on the dress.

I cleared my throat. "I uh, also need your help with these," I said, turning my back to him and sweeping my long hair out of the way so he could see the unfastened hooks at my back.

Still not speaking, I felt him tug at the back of the dress to close the hooks that I hadn't been able to reach. He made it three quarters of the way up before he said, also clearing his throat, "I don't think these ones will close."

"That's fine," I said, turning and acting like I hadn't been put off kilter by our exchange. "I think the dress will stay up without them. If not, your whole court is in for quite a show."

He didn't laugh or even smile at my joke, just looked at me with that same spark of heat. He frowned.

"Ember," he started, looking out the window. He cursed. "We're going to be late."

He grabbed my hand and spun us into shadow. We emerged in the great hall and I took a deep breath of freezing air.

Shadow walking short distances was not as unpleasant as the long distances, but I still felt like I had been torn apart and put back together. I shivered again.

I hadn't been awake most of the day to see what it looked like outside, but based on the temperature here, it must be frozen.

My breath formed little white puffs in the air before me. Glancing up at Hadrian, I saw that his was doing the same. Frost had formed on the roses of his crown, and the diamonds around my neck felt like tiny points of ice against my skin. They contrasted sharply, beautifully even, with the darkness rolling off him.

"Whatever happens, you do not bow," Hadrian growled darkly, as if preparing me for battle. He looked down at me and squeezed my hand. "You do not flatter or beg. No matter what is said or done, you do not yield to him."

I nodded and he turned to face the great obsidian doors that separated us from the throne room. "You are the future Unseelie Queen, and you bow to no one."

"Not even to you?" I asked, hoping to inject some warmth into his frosty demeanor and see the male who had joked with me about lifting my skirts.

He didn't look at me, only squeezed my hand tighter as he replied, "Not even to me."

CHAPTER 15

The king sat upon a throne of what looked to be black, pointed ice. It shone darkly in the light of the dozen fireplaces in the throne room, flickering their eerie light off the black, stone walls. Not ice, I thought as we drew closer, making our way slowly down the central aisle in the crowded room. Obsidian, so sharp it could cleave a Fae's skull.

The room was silent as we entered, broken only by the occasional sip of wine or clink of a glass as the Unseelie court watched our progression.

Everything in this realm was dark and colorless. Most of the Fae had skin as pale as Hadrian's, though some were a pale shade of blue like frost, and others had skin as dark as the obsidian throne. Black seemed to be the only fashionable color. Even the ladies who dared to wear gowns of red or green or blue wore a shade so dark it was almost black. Sneers and jeers met us as we walked, directed at me or at our joined hands, I realized, and I straightened my shoulders, staring past them all.

Each fireplace was surrounded by a dark stone mantle, carved with the two headed raven that was the symbol of the Unseelie court. I had been taught as a girl that one of the heads represented death and the other decay, the hallmarks of Unseelie magic. Guards were stationed at the side of each fireplace and around the back of the chamber. If things went badly, there would be no escape for me. I repressed a shudder as we came to stand before the man who had murdered my parents and Hadrian's mother.

He was old, I realized with a shock. I had never seen a Fae of his age before. Most Fae lived for so long, hundreds of years, that they had to be very old indeed to show any signs of age. I made a mental note to ask Hadrian how old his father was. Maybe death by poison could be mistaken for a natural death after all.

Like Hadrian, the king had dark power rolling off him, but it was different somehow. More evil. Hadrian's power was night and velvet darkness. His father's was oily and slick and somehow putrid.

"Well boy," he boomed as we approached, looking surprised and a little annoyed, "you have returned with a Seelie bride as promised."

Hadrian said nothing as he stopped at the foot of the dais on which the obsidian throne sat. The king's face was so wrinkled it was almost impossible to tell if his eyes were open. Two beady black points were all I could see of his eyes. A mass of brittle white hair clung to his head, and on his shoulder sat a very much alive two headed raven. It regarded me with red eyes, squawked, and flapped down to land on Hadrian's shoulder. I felt him tense as the bird regarded him, one eye glowing as it peered into his.

"Ah, yes I see," mumbled the king. Was the bird seeing Hadrian's thoughts somehow? How could he hide his hatred for the king like that? Hadrian didn't move, only let the bird intrude upon his mind. Seeming satisfied, the king turned to me.

"Come here pet, you look familiar to me," he said, almost kindly as he beckoned me forward. His sickly handles curled around my arms and legs, tugging me forward. "Let me inspect my son's chosen bride." I almost took a step, but Hadrian's hand gripped mine tighter, his own shadows chasing his father's away.

"No," he said, voice lacking any warmth. His darkness pulsed menacingly. This was the cold hard prince I had met at the ball, disdain for everyone around him. Except me.

"No?" Repeated the king, looking at me, rather than Hadrian.

"As my betrothed wishes," I said, injecting ice into my words and trying to sound as indifferent and cold as Hadrian.

The king laughed. "I see you've prepared her. Very well boy, I will take the measure of her later. What news? What was this assassination attempt I see in your mind?"

Hadrian began speaking about troop movements and rebel forces, most of which I knew had to be lies. He did it so smoothly, I would never have known. I wondered momentarily if he had lied like this to me before shaking away the intrusive thought.

He went on to talk about the assassin and my healing, inventing a convincing tale of whirlwind romance borne of gratitude and proximity. While he spoke, he kept a firm grip on my hand, his other resting on the pommel of a sword at his hip.

"I don't need you to like her, boy, just to bed her," the king growled, frowning at his hand on my waist. Hadrian dropped it as he continued explaining my connections.

I stood throughout, enduring the stares and whispering of the court. This was not the first time we had been the subject of gossip. Let them look their fill and say their worst, I thought to myself, willing my heart to slow my mind to empty.

After a while, the Raven flapped up and over Hadrian's head, coming to sit on my shoulder. It turned its beady eye to me, and I felt a cold slick of darkness enter my mind. The king was using the raven to read my thoughts. I willed my mind to stay blank, but it wasn't necessary. The oily darkness pushed and hit an invisible wall. The king let out a hiss of pain.

I blinked as the raven left my mind. It squawked unhappily and fluttered back to the king.

"What magic is this?" The king hissed, pointing a gnarled finger at me. "Your mind is shielded. How?"

I tried to keep my demeanor indifferent and free of surprise as I said, "Seelie magic is not all gone, your majesty."

I felt Hadrian squeeze my hand again in what I hoped was approval. His dark power licked up my arm where our hands were joined, tickling slightly as it caressed my skin.

"If that is all, my king," he started, pulling my arm

through his, "it has been a long journey. With your permission I will escort my bride to her chambers."

"Nonsense," grunted the king, clapping his hands and calling for music. "You will stay and dance. Show off your bride." He sneered and added, "You can have her all to yourself later. Plus, we don't want to risk your royal neck with an assassin roaming about. You stay."

I tried to hide my grimace as Hadrian gave a nod and replied, "as you say," escorting me to the dance floor where other members of the court had begun to spin and twirl in a foreign dance I didn't know.

Hadrian gripped my hand and waist and led me into the dance.

"I don't know this one," I hissed, my cool facade cracking with my impending embarrassment on the dance floor.

"Let me lead," he replied coldly. I tried. It wasn't perfect. I know I stepped on his toes more than once, but he didn't rebuke me. He didn't speak to or look at me at all actually.

"Are you alright?" I asked tentatively, wondering if this cold, aloof Hadrian was the one I would always see when at court.

"Not here," he replied, and my heart sank. I was tired and still aching and hungry. I missed my best friend and my cousin, and even Vanth and Seline, little as I knew them. I did not want to spend all night dancing with a cold prince in too tight shoes, even if I did adore how the skirts of the beautiful dress swirled around me and twined with his darkness as we danced.

After suffering through three dances like this, my feet and ribs aching, Hadrian finally led me off the floor toward a table of refreshments. My relief was short-lived when I saw the food on the table. From a distance, it had looked crowded with meats and fruits and all manner of delicacies. Now up close, I saw that every item on the table was putrid with decay. Maggots crawled from a suckling pig and beetles scurried between rotting fruits. I turned my face away, worried that I might be sick in front of the whole court.

"Don't react," Hadrian said, handing me a glass of sparkling red wine, "this is safe. The rest is part of his test, of you and the rest of the court. He likes to remind them where their magic comes from."

I contemplated the Unseelie court's death magic while taking a sip of wine. It was slightly bitter with a tang of something I didn't recognize. While it wasn't like the sweet Seelie wine in the south, it was tolerable. I took another sip.

Remembering Hadrian's lecture about balance, I frowned. There was no balance here, only death. I wondered how Hadrian had turned out so different from his father. The only thing that made sense was that his mother must have shielded him from his father's worst qualities.

"You did well," Hadrian murmured quietly, leaning close under the pretense of whispering in my ear. "Just a little longer."

I shivered as he pulled away, and he twirled a wayward strand of my hair around his finger, admiring its color in the firelight. Strands of his velvet power wrapped themselves around me as well, as if building a cocoon to protect me from the rest of the court.

Pretending. Right. This was a mission. I gave him the most sultry smile I could manage under the circumstances and leaned close to whisper, "please tell me there will be real food later?"

He choked on his wine, stifling a laugh. There was my Hadrian, I thought, smiling faintly. I mean, the one I knew. Not mine really. But the one I liked better than the cold unfeeling Prince.

He snaked his hand around my waist and pulled me close again. Even though I knew this was an act, my heart beat a little faster as he replied, "anything you wish is yours, my lady."

As I was trying to think of something to say in response to that, the heavy wooden doors of the throne room burst open. The court stilled.

Guards dragged a beaten and bloodied Unseelie male behind them, blue skin stained red and black in the places he had been injured. The healer in me instinctually moved to help him, but Hadrian's hand tightened on my waist.

"No," he whispered, holding me in place and looking impassively at the prisoner.

"At last, the entertainment has arrived," the king boomed, motioning the guards forward with their quarry.

"Charges?" He asked, sounding gleeful rather than solemn at the prospect of sentencing a prisoner.

"Trespassing, my liege," replied one of the guards in a monotone that betrayed no hint of emotion. I wondered if that was the only way to survive here - forcing yourself to feel nothing.

"Excellent," said the king, "boy!"

With a start I realized he meant Hadrian. He shot me a warning look and stepped forward, striding up the room to stand before his father and the prisoner the guards had dumped at his feet.

"Entertain me," said the king darkly to Hadrian.

Hadrian didn't move, fighting some internal battle with himself.

"Mercy," croaked the male at his feet, blood dribbling down his chin as he attempted to speak. "Mercy please."

Hadrian looked up at his father, then down at the male. I felt frozen in place. I knew what he was about to do, but I wasn't ready for it when he drew his silver sword from its scabbard and plunged it into the male's heart.

With an awful final gasp, the male's eyes went dim, blood spilling to puddle on the floor. Hadrian's darkness pulsed outward as if angered.

"I said entertain," snapped the king, glaring at his son before him, his own darkness pulsing furiously. Hadrian wiped the blood off his sword with the dead male's clothing and shrugged.

"He was almost dead already," he said coldly. "There was no sport in it."

Here was the Prince of Death, the unfeeling wicked male who made Seelie children tremble and maidens weep with terror. I wanted to run, to scream, to flee from this monster, who moments before had been whispering into my ear. Nausea swirled in my gut, and it took everything in me not to move.

Without another word, Hadrian turned and met my eyes.

"What do you think of your betrothed now, pet," shouted the king, who was also looking at me in challenge. All eyes of the court turned to me as Hadrian strode to my side. He didn't touch me, and I could practically feel the anger and revulsion pouring off him in great waves.

"I think," I said, voice stronger than I had expected it to be with the writhing nausea in my gut, "that violence is a weapon of the weak."

The king boomed a laugh and the rest of the court joined in. Hadrian stood immobile, still ice cold and unfeeling as we faced the court. I felt sick and exhausted, and I wanted nothing more than to go back to before this horrific night had started, before I knew what awaited me here.

"Very well, take your bride and do what you will with her," the king said, waving us away. "I expect you back here tomorrow night."

The court was still laughing when Hadrian grabbed my hand and spun us into shadow.

CHAPTER 16

We stepped out into the woods, the Unseelie palace some distance away. Hadrian turned and fell to his knee, vomiting into the snow.

I crouched down next to him, willing warmth into my body and shaking from more than just the cold. I reached out anyway and put a hand on his shoulder.

"Don't," he said harshly, spitting on the ground. He turned to look at me. "Now will you call me a monster, my lady?"

He spoke with such self-loathing, I didn't know what to say. Truthfully, I was terrified. This male had just killed another male in cold blood after he begged for mercy. I knew his reputation, but seeing it carried out was far more chilling.

But I remembered warm hands squeezing my leg, tea

being held to my parched lips, his pale face so close to death after being stabbed, how gently he lifted me to shadow walk me when I was sick. This was the same male, and I had to reconcile both parts of him somehow.

Not knowing what else to do, I wrapped my arms around him and held him tightly.

He stilled, unmoving as I held him. Slowly, he returned the embrace, wrapping his large arms around me. We sat there in the snow for several long minutes, wet and cold and in shock, waiting for the terror of the night to pass and saying nothing.

Eventually he spoke, barely a whisper against the crown of my head.

"It never gets easier."

I didn't know what to do or where to go from here, but I could offer him this, whatever it was. Comfort, acceptance, understanding maybe. How many times had he been forced to kill for his father and act like he didn't care?

"What would have happened if you had said no?" I asked in a small voice, still not looking at him. Darkness pulsed around him again and began to wrap around us. It was warm, a welcome relief from the cold of the night.

"He would have tortured me until I did it," he replied, hatred in every syllable. "Or tortured the Fae male and made me watch."

He pulled away a little and I looked up at him. He was bitter and angry and full of despair. "Or tortured you."

The darkness pulsed angrily again, wrapping around me a little more closely. I pulled away to lift my hands and cup his face.

"You made it quick," I said, understanding what the

blue Fae had meant by requesting mercy.

"I can't always," said Hadrian, looking down so as not to meet my eyes.

I nodded, still holding his face as we sat in the snow. My dress was soaking and his face was cold. Something wet hit my fingers and froze. A tear.

"I'm cold," I said quietly. He looked at me then, face strained under the weight of his sorrow. He nodded, and wrapped us in shadows. We emerged in his bedroom, the fire still blazing in the hearth. He stepped away from me and the cold seemed somehow deeper than when we had been sitting in the snow.

"I'll be back," he said without looking at me. He disappeared again into the shadows and I sighed. We would have to talk about this disappearing-without-communication thing.

My dress had partially frozen as I had been sitting in the snow. I managed to ease it off in front of the fire and put on the dry nightgown. I would really need to find some more clothes tomorrow. Wrapping myself in furs from the bed, I put the frozen gown in the tub, hoping it wouldn't be ruined. Then I sat in front of the fire as close as I could get, still shivering from the cold and terror.

Hadrian reappeared and strode wordlessly into the bathing chamber. I watched his retreating form, trying to catch a glimpse of his face. I had no idea how we would move past tonight. Clearly I had seen a side of him he hated. He could barely look at me knowing that I knew the worst of him.

Or maybe there was still worse to know.

He returned a few minutes later in dry clothes, a white shirt partially unbuttoned and left untucked from plain black trousers. He grabbed another fur from the bed and came to sit beside me. His feet were bare, and he sat with one knee up, an arm resting on it as he gazed into the fire. We leaned against a low table that had been placed in front of a plush couch, and while I was sure it would be more comfortable to sit there, I preferred being close to the fire.

For a minute he didn't say anything. I turned to look at the fire again and he finally spoke.

"Food is being sent up."

"Thank you," I said, turning to look at him again. He still wouldn't look at me, gaze far away looking into the fire.

I huffed a frustrated sigh and turned to face him, sitting cross legged in front of him with the fur around my shoulder for warmth.

"Tell me the worst of it." I said, injecting as much command as I could muster into my voice.

His brows furrowed but he still didn't turn to look at me. "What do you mean?" He asked.

Growing more frustrated I scooted closer and cupped his face again, forcing him to look at me.

"I've seen the monster now," I said, regretting ever using that word in front of him. "Tell me how much worse it gets, and then there won't be any surprises that can be used against me."

He took my hands in his and removed them from his face, holding them in front of us and looking down at them. He was still letting his dark power roam freely, and it curled up my arms, warming them. He didn't let them go when he said, "He made me kill my mother."

I sat unmoving, still holding his hands and turning his words over in my mind. He had said his mother was dead, I remembered that, but he hadn't specifically said that his father had killed her.

"It was to protect Seline," he continued, still looking down at our joined hands. "My father wanted her dead, and he offered me a choice." He looked up, searching my face for my reaction. "My mother made the choice for me."

He shook his head and leaned back on his heels, dropping my hands.

"I'm sorry, Ember," he said, putting a few inches of distance between us. "I shouldn't have pulled you into this. I didn't mean to frighten you. I hate that this is who I am, that you had to see it."

I looked again into his eyes and saw honesty and heartache. He had told me that he did not lie, and he was right. He omitted truths certainly, but he hadn't hidden who he was from me. He showed me everything.

I leaned forward, shifting on to my knees. Tentatively, I reached out and rested my palm on his cheek, giving him time to stop me if he didn't want to be touched. When he didn't stop me, I spoke.

"You don't frighten me," I said, "and you are not a monster."

He turned his head into my touch and brought his own hand up to meet mine, placing a tender kiss in the center of my palm. I felt the kiss all the way to my toes. He met my eyes again.

"I am," he said resignedly, "but I will gladly be the monster to protect what I love."

We sat there for a long moment just looking at each other, his darkness still swirling around me somewhat chaotically like it couldn't settle.

A knock on the door drew his attention and he gave me a look that said, "don't move," as he reached for one of his abandoned daggers and went to the door. I heard mumbling and his thanks, and he returned with a tray full of steaming food. My stomach gave a deafening rumble. He smiled faintly.

"You should eat something."

"Will you stay with me?" I asked as he put the tray on the low table in front of the fire. He hesitated, clearly battling with himself over some task he was steeling himself to carry out.

"I have something I need to do," he said carefully, looking at me earnestly as if willing me to trust him. "But I'll be back soon."

"Alright," I said, standing and suddenly feeling bone weary. It must be very late, or very early, and the emotions of the evening were catching up to me.

He hesitated again, then closed the distance between us and cupped my face in his hands. They were still cold from the snow, but warm tendrils of dark power raced along his fingers to warm my face.

"Eat, and sleep," he said, frowning at me and seeing my exhaustion. "I'll put wards on the door until I return. If you want I can have another room made up for you, but I'd feel safer if we stay together in my father's court, at least until Vanth and Seline return."

I nodded, and gave him a weak smile, and he turned and vanished again into shadow. I swayed a little on my feet, moving to sit on the plush couch before the small feast that had been brought up for me, feeling colder in his absence.

I ate, tasting only ash, and thinking. I had told Hadrian he didn't frighten me, and I realized it was true. Now that I knew his history, the choices and actions he'd been forced to take to survive, I felt pity. And rage.

More than ever, I had a reason to destroy the Unseelie King.

I must have dozed off at some point, because I woke up with Hadrian crouching in front of me, the fire burning low. I was lying on the sofa, and the food on the table had grown cold.

"Take the bed," Hadrian said, nodding toward the giant four-poster. "I'll sleep here."

"It's fine," I said, closing my eyes and trying to roll over and go back to sleep. The sofa wasn't really big enough for sleeping. Hadrian sighed and stood. In one move he had scooped me up and shadow walked me over to the bed. He dropped me onto it unceremoniously.

"That's cheating," I groaned, trying to scowl at him in the semi-darkness.

"You'll thank me in the morning," he replied, pulling furs up over me as I settled in, silently thanking the goddess that he had insisted I sleep here. It was so much more comfortable than the sofa.

He turned back to the couch, and before I could overthink it I said, "wait."

"My lady?" He turned, brows raised sardonically, half amused and half irritated that I was ordering him around in the middle of the night. Clearly whatever he had done had lifted some of the burden from him. Thank the goddess for that too.

"We can share," I said, voice smaller than I'd intended. I cleared my throat. "It's a big bed and there's plenty of room. You can take the other half."

He didn't move, only raising one brow a little higher. "Are you sure?"

I nodded, not really feeling that this was my greatest

plan ever, but also realizing that I didn't want him to be so far away. I felt very alone in this place, and even though Hadrian and I had started as reluctant allies, if not outright enemies, I realized that I would need him here more than I originally thought.

Warily, as if waiting for me to change my mind, he prowled around the bed to the other side. He was still barefoot, still in his casual and now a bit rumpled clothes from earlier. I couldn't see his darkness well in the dim light of the fire, but I felt it humming around him still. He sat and I turned to face him as he waited to see if I'd snap at him and send him away.

"Lie down," I said, irritation flaring. He smirked.

"As you say, my lady."

I threw a pillow at him and he laughed, catching it.

"This is mine now," he said, turning over to face away from me and pulling some furs up over himself, all while hugging the pillow tightly to his chest.

I smiled a little, glad I was able to coax him out of the darkness a bit. I sighed, lying back down and turning my back to him as well. I would ask him about his mother in the morning. And everything else I wanted to know. And then we would plan for battle.

CHAPTER 17

I woke to pale sunlight streaming through the curtains, which had been left open the night before. From my comfortable nest I could see snow glistening on branches outside and icicles dripping onto the window ledge below. I shifted slightly, feeling something heavy lying on me.

Hadrian had moved closer in the night. His arm was draped over me protectively, but there were several inches of distance and layers of furs between us. I stilled, not wanting to wake him, but I was too late.

"Good morning," he mumbled groggily from behind me. Groaning, he stretched, removing his arm. His dark power had also wrapped us in something of a cocoon in the night. It dissipated as he stretched, and I felt colder without both his arm and his power around me.

I turned to face him, resting on my hand as I watched him stretch. He was rather like a forest cat I had seen once as a child, long and sinewy, but powerful as it stretched its claws and yawned in a warm patch of sun.

He finally stopped and turned to face me, mirroring my position with his face resting on his hand. In the pale morning light, his cheekbones cast shadows in the hollows of his face. He looked tired.

"Breakfast?" I asked hopefully. He turned on his back and laughed, swinging his legs over the bed and standing.

He pulled each arm across his chest one arm at a time in another stretch and asked, "are you always hungry?"

"When I haven't eaten properly in three days, yes," I replied defensively. He chuckled and bowed, vanishing into shadow, and reappearing a few seconds later in the same spot.

"Have you heard of knocking?" I asked, raising myself on one arm and giving him a scathing look.

"It's my room," he protested, a faint smile warming his face. There was still a hollowness to his eyes, but he seemed better than he had been last night.

"Plus," he added, crossing his arms at me and leaning on a bedpost. "It was to summon food for *you*."

"Oh very well," I said begrudgingly. Sitting up, I remembered clearly why I needed more than just a nightgown to wear. I crossed my arms over my breasts to cover my nipples, which had peaked against the thin fabric in the cold. Hadrian either didn't notice or was too polite to mention it.

"Where can I get some clothes?" I asked self-consciously. Hadrian smirked. He had definitely noticed.

"Your things will be here in a few days," he replied and I gawked at him. "A few days" could mean a week. He laughed at my expression. "But I'll call for a seamstress to come today. They can maybe get you something that's ready made, and fit you for more appropriate gowns as the future Unseelie Queen."

I frowned. "Hadrian," I started, not entirely sure how to ask this question. "How long will we have to pretend like this?"

He had sat on the edge of the bed to pull on socks and boots, but he stopped and turned to me, giving me a thoughtful look.

"It's likely that my father will want the wedding to occur on Winter Solstice," he said, returning his attention to the boots. "It's the time of greatest power for Unseelie Fae, and a symbolic day for our realm."

I swallowed, realizing that the solstice was two and a half months away. That meant both two and a half months of surviving this court and pretending to be Hadrian's intended, and only two and a half months to figure out how to kill the king without it looking like he had been murdered and without Hadrian knowing I'd done it.

Hadrian narrowed his eyes. "What are you plotting?" he asked warily.

"Nothing," I lied, wrapping one of the big fur covers around me modestly so I could get out of bed without scandalizing him or myself. A knock on the door drew his attention away from me, praise the goddess, and he gave me his "don't move" look again as he went to answer it, spooling his shadows back into himself and tamping them down with his glamour.

A small female barreled into him, hugging him

around the neck. Seline and Vanth had arrived. I felt some of the tension go out of me as I realized we would have reinforcements.

"We brought food from the kitchens," said Vanth, carrying another steaming tray of food that he placed on the low table. He turned to me and bowed respectfully. "Glad to see you're well, my lady."

I threw my arms around him in a hug that surprised both of us and he chuckled, blushing a bit as he pulled away. Hadrian shot a murderous look at him that cleared when he realized I was watching him.

I laughed. "I am so happy to see you both," I said, taking a respectful step away from Vanth. Seline came to clasp my arm, then pulled Vanth down onto the small sofa to eat. Hadrian locked the door and came over to us, hesitating a moment before sitting down next to me on the floor.

"What did we miss?" asked Vanth through a mouthful of pastry. Hadrian recounted the details of my recovery and the assembly last night while I ate, spearing sausages with a dainty silver fork and popping them gratefully into my mouth. When he got to the part about the Fae he had been forced to kill, he paused.

"We know," Seline chimed in, putting a hand on his arm. "We found the widow like you asked. She'll want for nothing."

Hadrian nodded gratefully and I stared, a sausage paused halfway between the plate and my mouth.

"That's where you went last night," I said, putting two and two together. Hadrian nodded and took a sip of something steaming hot from a mug. It wasn't tea, definitely something more bitter. I missed Seelie drinks so much more than I thought I would.

"It's something we always do after," he hesitated, glancing at Seline. "If I can find the next of kin, I make sure that they know what happened and leave them with as much silver as I can spare."

"Don't they hate you?" I asked, wincing when I realized how callous the question sounded. "I'm sorry, I didn't mean…"

"It's fine," Hadrian said curtly. He sighed and scrubbed his face. "Yes, they hate me. But it's the least I can do."

"It was fast," Seline said, looking at Hadrian with grim understanding. "That's the best any of us can hope for in this court." Vanth nodded his head in solemn agreement.

I nodded too, studying his profile. "Do they know that you don't want to do this?"

Hadrian shook his head. "I don't know how they would. Some of the families may understand, but most probably think I'm sent by the king to buy their complacency."

He gave me a cynical look and added, "I don't exactly ask them when I make the deliveries."

"I know that," I said exasperated, "I'm just trying to think. If you lead a rebellion against your father, who will stand with you?"

"It doesn't matter, as I'm not leading a rebellion yet," Hadrian said sharply. "We can't move against him until we know who he's been allying with, and I haven't been trusted with that information yet."

By this time he was fully facing me, knee still raised in the too small space between the hearth and the table.

"That's why you were dragged into this," he went on, gesturing to the room in general, clearly growing increasingly annoyed that he had to spell it out for me. "To prove my loyalty, to agree to do his bidding, so that he will give me the information we need to destroy him. Killing him does nothing if we don't know who his allies are, their numbers and strength, what he has promised them, and where they are stationed."

"He doesn't trust you," I said. It wasn't a question.

"No," he said bitterly. "That damn raven can see my hatred. I can hide my actions, mask my other feelings, weave a false history, but I have never been able to disguise my hatred."

Vanth cut in, turning to me and asking, "did he have that demon bird search your mind too?"

"Yes," I said, frowning over the sausage that had never made it to my mouth. I put my fork down. "But something blocked it. I think the curse enchantment thing stopped it from seeing into my mind."

Seline raised a brow at me. "Then the spell on you is a blessing. I'd be wary of trying to break it while you are in this court. You haven't learned to shield your mind the way we have, and it takes more time to learn than we have."

I nodded, frowning.

"Enough of this," said Hadrian sharply. "We need a plan going forward here. I've convinced my father that I'll do his bidding, despite my hatred. I doubt that will be enough to earn his trust, but it's a start."

I rose and went to the dark wooden desk in the corner of the room, digging through the drawers furiously.

"What are you doing?" Hadrian asked, bemused by my frantic search.

Triumphant, I held up paper and pen. "Making a list!"

I exclaimed with probably too much excitement. "It helps me think."

"We'll have to burn the paper after," Seline protested, clearly thinking this was a waste of time.

"Fine," I said, resuming my seat on the floor and shifting my plate so I had room to write. "But I'm still making a list."

Hadrian still looked bemused, but a smile tugged on the corner of his mouth. "Very well, my lady, what is first on this list?"

"First," I said, ignoring his teasing tone, "I need to write to Aurelia. She needs to know I arrived and we need to establish an open line of communication."

"Your mail will certainly be read," Vanth said. I looked up and saw he was toying with Seline's braid over her shoulder. I smiled sadly, realizing that Vanth was deeply in love with her. I could tell Seline trusted him and liked him, but it was clear she either didn't or couldn't return his affections. Maybe because she had already lost a mate.

"Probably," I agreed, "so I'll have to write in code. I'll use references only she will understand. Second," I continued, stopping Hadrian from butting in with his sarcasm, "I need to meet your healer."

He barked a laugh. "Why in the name of all that is unholy would you need to do that before anything else?"

"Because," I replied haughtily, "I need to thank her." Hadrian's humor dissipated slightly as he met my eyes. I quickly looked away.

"I also want to learn what she knows of healing, and having a Seelie ally in your court might be an advantage for me."

Hadrian nodded. "Fine. Third, you need to see the seamstress."

I paused, pen poised to write when I turned back to him with my eyebrow raised. He smirked.

"Fine," I agreed coolly. "Third, I see the seamstress. Fourth, you attempt to join your father's strategic meetings."

"Oh, so simple," Hadrian mocked. "Why didn't I think of that?"

"Can't you slip into the shadows to spy on his meetings?" I asked, genuinely curious about how the shadow walking worked. He shook his head.

"He shares the same power. Truthfully, the power is his. Until he dies, I am merely able to tap into it." His expression was dark, recounting his father's control over him. "He'd sense me if I tried."

I sighed. "Then convincing him is the only way. How do we do that?"

No one answered. Clearly, this was a problem that was not new. I chewed on the end of the pen, an idea coming to me.

"Your father favors viciousness, yes?" I asked. Hadrian nodded, eyes dark.

"And he believes you are not vicious enough?" I pressed.

Hadrian met my eyes, narrowing his suspiciously. "Yes. Why?"

"We will have to show him that he's wrong," I shrugged, the plan coalescing now in more detail in my mind.

"How?" Seline asked warily.

"Using me," I said firmly, deciding that this was the only way. "Your father saw you protecting me last night.

It weakened your position. Tonight, you must show him you own me."

Hadrian bristled. "I am not leaving you alone with him."

"I'm not suggesting you do," I replied, meeting his gaze evenly. My stomach twisted a bit at the prospect of what I was about to suggest, but I couldn't think of a way around it. If this mission was going to be successful, Hadrian needed his father's trust.

"I already don't like this plan," he growled.

"Agreed," said Vanth. "Whatever you are about to propose, my lady, there must be an alternative that keeps you out of harm's way."

I turned to Vanth and gave him a warm smile. "Call me Ember. And I promise, I won't be in any real danger."

I turned back to Hadrian, and said, "I'm changing the order of the list. I'll need to see your healer first to prepare the next part of our act."

CHAPTER 18

The kitchens felt oddly out of place with the rest of the Unseelie palace. While the rooms I had seen, except for Hadrian's, were dark and cold and uninviting, the kitchens were the opposite. A fire burned merrily in a stone hearth, not the black obsidian of the throne room, but a warm brown soapstone that was rounded and polished with age and wear. A large wooden table took up most of the floor in the center of the room, and racks of drying herbs and flowers hung above a sink. Evergreen boughs had been placed over the mantle, as if welcoming the Winter Solstice early, and something that smelled like cedar and honey bubbled in a pot over the flames in the hearth.

Honestly, the room felt more like my infirmary than a kitchen, and I felt bizarrely at peace in this tiny slice of warmth.

An elderly female sat by the fire, loudly clacking away with knitting needles. She was bundled in scarves and shawls, even though she sat in front of a roaring fire.

"Ah, you finally came," she intoned in an impatient voice, not rising from her knitting. "About time too."

I blinked at her lack of deference to the Prince, but he smiled fondly at her.

"Mother Vervain," said Hadrian, pulling me forward by the hand, "allow me to properly introduce you to Lady Ember."

"Just Ember is fine," I corrected, as the female rose, placing her knitting carefully on a tiny rickety table and standing to greet me. "Are you too cold?" I added, concerned that she had to be so bundled up. I was beginning to sweat in the warm kitchen.

Mother Vervain gave me an ancient smile.

"This dreadful cold is too much for an old Seelie like me, my dear," she said, taking my hands in hers and studying me. Her face was aged, not as old as the king's, but enough that she must be several hundred years old. Her eyes were a bright green, similar in shade to mine, and she smiled, her eyes crinkling as she took me in.

"Well you do look quite a bit better," she said, patting my cheek and quite suddenly bustling off with good-natured efficiency.

"Sit here please," she added, pushing me into a chair and adjusting her shawls to sit more securely on her shoulders. "We must have tea."

Despite her age, Mother Vervain was spry, and she flitted around the kitchen, making tea and ordering everyone here or there, and putting Vanth and Seline to work fetching cakes and trays of food.

She was undoubtedly Seelie. While her hair had lost its color, her skin was a warm tan, closer to mine than Hadrian's pale complexion. She wore a stained gown of bright green on her ancient frame, and her apron was embroidered with pinks and greens and purples - wildflowers, I realized. How she had come to serve the Unseelie King was a story I was anxious to hear.

I glanced at Hadrian, who shrugged slightly and took the chair next to me.

Soon we were settled in front of the fire with cakes and tea, and it felt so much like being back in the Seelie court, I almost forgot where I was.

Seline and Vanth had insisted upon standing guard at the door, but Mother Vervain had forced a flowery teacup into each of their hands. I didn't have the heart to tell Vanth how ridiculous he looked, his broad frame dwarfing the tiny cup.

"Now," said Mother Vervain, setting Hadrian with a hard look, "what is this I hear about dancing? She was to be resting."

Hadrian held up his hands in defense. "I would have kept her away from court forever if I could," he said. His voice betrayed none of its usual gruffness or cynicism, and he smiled fondly at her as she tsked.

"And you, my dear," she said, turning to me and pointing at me somewhat fiercely with her flowery teacup, "what do you have to say for yourself, letting the fever get on you while traveling. Did you not bring your tea as you crossed realms?"

"I'm sorry, what?" I asked, confused.

"You told me she was a healer," she said sharply, turning her teacup on the Prince sitting next to me.

Again, he lifted his hands, grinning a bit at her attack.

"Do they teach you young persons nothing these days?" She asked exasperatedly. "Seelie must always drink a tea of elderflower and yarrow root while crossing into Unseelie lands, else the fever lays them out."

I gawked. "I've never heard that before."

She tsked again. "Shows you what happens when they let the old magics die. And you," she added, pointing to Seline and Vanth at the door, then back to Hadrian, "you clearly took your tea when entering her realm?"

"Of course," Hadrian said, holding her hands and smiling.

"Hmm," she said, withdrawing her hand to sip her tea again. "Well now you know. Never travel the realms without your tea."

This last was proclaimed, as if it were knowledge we must engrave on our hearts and embroider on our cushions. I smiled, liking Mother Vervain very much. I imagine if I had a grandmother, she might be something like her.

"Well then," she said, fixing her attention on me again. "Tell me about this iron wound you healed on the reckless prince."

I raised my brows at Hadrian, but he just smirked at the title like it was a compliment. So I told Mother Vervain of my finding the Prince, of the herbs and tincture I had used to treat him, and of how quickly it had seemed to heal.

"And what of your magic?" She asked when I had finished.

"Oh, I didn't use magic to heal him," I replied,

not certain if she already knew about my spell-enchantment-thing, or if I was supposed to tell her.

"So you say," she said. She put down her teacup and, rubbing her hands together to warm them, asked, "May I?"

She gestured to my face and I nodded, not knowing exactly what she wanted, but not being brave enough to tell her no. She placed her gnarled hands on either side of my face and closed her eyes, breathing deeply. It was almost like when Seline had told me about the spell on me, but I didn't sense Mother Vervain prodding at me. It was more like she was trying to *see* the spell.

"Yes, it's holding fast," she said, still holding my face with her eyes closed. They darted around under her eyelids as if she were hunting inside me for something. She smiled suddenly and released my face.

"Well, I expect you know you're spelled," she said, gesturing toward Seline with her chin. "That one's probably already told you."

"Can you break it?" I asked, suddenly hopeful that this female could release my magic. She shook her head, shrugging her shawls up a little higher over her shoulders.

"No," she said, although she didn't seem too sorry about it. "It's been rooted too long. Only you can break it now, I'm afraid. And best not to try while you are in this castle."

I nodded, disappointed. Hadrian cleared his throat.

"Ember, what did you need from Mother Vervain?" He asked, redirecting the conversation which would clearly twist all over if someone didn't take charge of it.

I nodded again and said, "I have many questions for you, Mother Vervain, but they can wait. Would it be alright if I visited you down here again?"

Mother Vervain nodded absently and said, "and?"

I grimaced slightly. She would know exactly what I had planned for tonight if I told her what I needed. I hoped she could be trusted. I rattled off the list of herbs and plants I would need and a sly smile spread across her wrinkled face.

"You're in for quite a night, my dear. Are you sure?" She asked, standing from her chair and moving to the sink where she started pulling all manner of plants out from little boxes and dishes and vials. I nodded.

"Well then," she said, "I have everything you need."

The rest of the day paled in comparison to meeting Mother Vervain. I scrawled off a quick letter to Aurelia, explaining that I had arrived safely and gushing about the beauty and grandeur of the Unseelie Court. I was hoping she would read the unwritten truth between my overenthusiastic lies.

As promised, Hadrian had called for a seamstress, and I spent an interminable afternoon being poked and pinched and measured and moved and generally henpecked by the irritable Unseelie female until she was satisfied and finally packed her things. She left me with some ready made shirts and trousers that were still a bit too big in some places and too small in others, but they would do if I wasn't needing to look presentable. She also left two plain, ill-fitting gowns, which were all she had available. She promised to have more clothes sent by the end of the week, and even more at the end of the month, so I thanked her as politely as I could before flopping onto the sofa in front of the fire.

Hadrian had excused himself to run drills with the king's guards, and Vanth had gone with him, leaving Seline the sole witness to my misery.

"Cheer up," she said, from her perch near the fire. She was sharpening her daggers again, and I really thought they were probably sharp enough by now.

"Your things should be here in a few days," she continued. "Then you never have to be measured again if you wish it. Except for your wedding gown," she added with a wry glance at me.

I groaned. "There will be no wedding gown. At least, I hope there will be no wedding gown," I added darkly. Seline put her daggers down and looked at me.

"Do you?" She asked. Her tone was serious and I gaped at her.

"How can you possibly ask?" I said, laughing at her serious expression. "This is not a real engagement. As soon as we have the information Hadrian needs, I get to return home, and I will not miss the Unseelie Court. And I doubt your prince will be sad to see me go either."

She was still looking at me, her expression skeptical. "I think he will."

I scoffed, but she didn't smile.

"Seline," I said, sitting up and adopting a serious expression, "we don't like each other. We barely get along."

She raised a brow at me and turned back to her daggers. "If you insist."

"I do!" I said, more forcefully than was necessary. "How can you think otherwise?"

"I've seen the way he looks at you," she said, still sharpening her daggers, "and you at him."

She looked up and met my eyes. "It may have once been hate and distrust, but I don't think it is anymore. Not for a while now actually."

I fidgeted, feeling uncomfortable. If I was honest with myself, I didn't hate or distrust Hadrian anymore. In fact, I think I trusted him more than I should. And there had been moments between us that felt like he didn't hate or distrust me either. My stomach flipped at the way he had curled my hair around his finger, how he had knelt before me to buckle the dagger to my thigh. How he had returned my embrace in his moment of despair and shame.

But he was the Unseelie Prince. Nothing would come of anything between us, not even friendship. His place was here and mine was at home, teasing Aspen and treating patients and…

And what? What was waiting for me at home? I sighed. Seline came to sit next to me.

"Hadrian is one of the best males I know," she said. "I know he has a terrifying reputation. He encourages it to convince his father that they share the same goals. And he has done some terrible things." She paused and then added, "we all have. We need to, to survive."

I nodded, still feeling confused and uncertain.

"But you don't have to decide how you feel right now," she continued. "Just know that what he feels for you is certainly not hate."

She cocked her head and gave me a mischievous look.

"Now, let's practice using these daggers," she said, standing and sliding a sheathed blade to me. "You can pretend I'm the seamstress."

CHAPTER 19

If my plan was to work, it needed to be utterly convincing. Hadrian scowled, stomping angrily around the room getting ready, throwing me annoyed glances as I took pains to make sure my appearance was perfect.

"This is a mistake," he growled, strapping what seemed like far too many daggers to himself.

I ignored him and continued my work, turning back to the mirror in front of which I sat. Mother Vervain had indeed had everything I needed to pull this off. Stinging nettle, touched in just the right spot, had caused an itchy, painful swelling to emerge under my right eye. Dried and ground up indigo and black walnuts, mixed with some water and dabbed around the eye, had turned the skin black and blue in a fair imitation of a painful, fresh bruise.

I dabbed some of the blue and black pigment on my upper arms, making it look like I had been grabbed violently, and I had chosen a dress with short sleeves to make sure they were visible. I had to be careful not to smudge any on the dress. They would stain terribly.

I put a few, fresh chokeberries in a little pouch hidden in the bodice of my dress, hoping that they wouldn't smash before I needed them at the finale.

"Everyone important knows it's not real," I said, finishing with some more of the bruise coloring to my neck. I needed it to look like I had been handled roughly, and I inspected my reflection, frowning.

"Come here please," I asked, turning in my chair to find Hadrian glaring angrily at my reflection. I turned back to the mirror and had to admit it was almost perfect. My eye stung something fierce, but it gave the appearance of having been hit quite hard by something.

Hadrian came over looking like he wanted to do anything else. "I have never beaten a female," he said, scowling at the false bruises.

"And you won't have to," I said, irritably. "Give me your hand."

He obliged and I curled his hand around my throat to try to estimate the correct placement of bruises where fingers would have been. Horrified when he realized what I was doing, he snatched his hand back.

"No one will believe this," he growled. "They saw us last night. They saw how…" he stopped, breathing deeply. He seemed to change his mind about what he was going to say and finished, "they saw that I was gentle with you."

I finished pinning my braid atop my head, making sure the bruises were visible. I had decided to craft a crown of baby's breath, woven through my braid, and I thought it came out rather well.

I turned to face Hadrian, giving him a severe look. "Then you will have to convince them that you were not gentle after we left."

He scowled more deeply at the insinuation in my tone and growled, clenching his fists on the back of the chair.

"What kind of male…"

"A vicious one," I said, standing and putting my hands on his clenched fists. "A ruthless, cruel one. A monster." He glared down at me, eyes flashing silver in his fury, but I put my hand to his face and added, "not you, Hadrian. The one you must pretend to be."

He stilled at my touch, taking in my bruised appearance and wincing. Gently, he cupped my chin in his fingers and tilted my head to examine my eye.

"Does it pain you?" He asked gently, almost tenderly. I smiled faintly.

"A little," I confessed. His grasp on my chin tightened slightly, and I added, "but it will heal in a few hours."

He nodded, still taking in my appearance angrily. The dress I had chosen tonight was one of two Hadrian had brought me as options, both having come this time from Mother Vervain.

That surprised me, but he said she had insisted. Apparently she had been keeping them for some occasion that never presented itself, wrapped carefully in tissue in a chest in her rooms. Both were stunning, but I had chosen one of pure white, capped sleeves adorned with tiny crystals that looked like frost had gathered around my shoulders. The neckline was high, but the back dropped into an almost scandalously low vee down my back, closed with tiny buttons that trailed all the way down the silken skirts. It fit my curves so snuggly I was a little self conscious of my shape, but it was almost like it was made for my measurements. I couldn't imagine Mother Vervain, always bundled up in her many colorful shawls, ever wearing anything like it, but I would gladly make use of it.

Tonight, Hadrian would play the dark Prince, and I his icy, defenseless bride.

I gently removed his hand from my chin and went to the armoire, raising the spiked silver crown I had chosen for him from its resting place. It was not as intimidating as the obsidian one he wore in the south, but more elegant and terrifying.

Returning to him, I reached up, having to stand on my tiptoes to place the crown on his head. I brushed his hair artfully aside with my fingers and stepped back to admire the whole picture. He was staring at me blankly, jaw rather slack.

"What?" I asked, glancing down at the dress and turning to try to see the back of it. "What's wrong?"

He shook his head slightly. "Nothing," he said, stepping toward me and gently clasping my shoulders to stop my futile spinning. "Nothing. You look..." he paused again, frowning.

"Is it that bad?" I asked, half laughing and half anxious that I had forgotten to fasten my dress.

"No," he said quickly. "You look like a Queen."

"Oh," I said, feeling relieved. "It will do?"

He coughed, and said rather roughly, "yes, it will do very well."

I felt a flush creep up my face under his regard.

"Turn," he commanded.

I did so slowly, not even thinking to protest his command. I felt his eyes on me the whole way around, and when I finally turned back to meet them, that molten, heated look was there again, the connection thrumming happily between us. He took a step toward me and stopped.

"Beautiful," he said.

He wasn't smiling, his expression too intense and weighted for a smirk or a grin. My stomach gave another little lurch as he closed the distance between us, a curl of his shadows cupping my face.

"What are you doing?" I whispered as he tilted my chin up again. He was looking at me like I was something rare and precious. Like I was something he desired. Silver flashed in his eyes, and I saw a need there. I wasn't quite sure I understood it, but I seemed to feel it deep in my core.

"I honestly don't know," he replied quietly, slowly closing the distance between us. I parted my lips as his neared mine.

A knock on the door broke the spell. Hadrian cursed and stepped away from me so fast he tripped and fell, almost hitting the floor before he vanished into shadow and reappeared at the door. He glanced my way, and I had to bite my lip to hold in my laugh.

Scowling, he opened the door to find Vanth and Seline waiting outside, full black spiked regalia on display.

"Are we interrupting?" asked Seline, throwing a knowing glance my way.

"No," Hadrian barked, scowling at Seline, then turning back to me. "Ready?"

And we were back to one word sentences.

I smiled, lifting my head high and adopting an indifferent tone. "As you say, your highness."

Vanth and Seline stomped behind us as we glided down to the throne room for the second night in a row. Hadrian had warned me that we would be summoned most nights, until his father decided he was bored of testing me.

As we approached the doors to the throne room, Hadrian paused, turning to me.

"Are you sure about this?" He asked in a low voice. "I don't want to hurt you."

I gave his hand a squeeze and smiled reassuringly. "You won't. Are you ready for our performance?"

He sighed, but squeezed back and turned to face the doors, and lowering his mask of cool indifference. He let his shadows loose, directing them to curl around me more than they had yesterday. I was ready. Putting my arm through his, he nodded to the guards at the door, and we entered the throne room together.

The court went still as we entered, making the long trek down to the dais where the ancient king sat, malice and cruelty pouring off him in thick, oily waves.

As we passed, the whispers began. I straightened my back and kept my expression blank, following Hadrian's lead.

"What have you done to your pet, boy?" The king asked as we stopped in front of the dais.

"She displeased me," Hadrian said, eliciting more whispers from the Unseelie courtiers surrounding us.

Tendrils of the king's dark power snaked around me, prodding and poking at my bruises. I pretended to wince, not having to do much acting when he prodded my cheek. I shuddered at the oily touch. Whereas

Hadrian's power felt like warm, soothing night most of the time, the king's was viscous and putrid. He spooled it back and smiled widely, showing all of his rotting teeth.

"Tell me, pet," said the king, looking me up and down in a way that chilled me to my marrow. "How did you displease my son?"

"That is my business," Hadrian said sharply before I could reply. This was going as planned so far, I just needed to make sure Hadrian could keep up his act long enough to be convincing.

"Yes, well don't damage her too much," said the king with a dismissive wave toward the assembled court. "At least not until you've wed her."

Hadrian nodded, teeth clenched in fury, and led me away from his father to mingle with the court. I gave his arm a subtle squeeze of reassurance, Vanth and Seline following at a discrete distance to watch our backs.

The next hour passed as tediously as the balls in the Seelie Court. Hadrian spoke to several generals and advisors, asking questions that gave me a general feel for how the king's forces were organized. All the while I remained a statue, silent and cold attached to his side, searching for my mark. I finally found him and gave Hadrian another squeeze, letting go of his arm and gliding toward a table of the bitter red wine.

A lone Unseelie lord had been watching us from a distance, and I glided over to him, offering him a smile as I took a glass of wine and managed to sip it without grimacing. The goal was to make this all look worse than it was, and I felt a little bad about what was about to happen, but Hadrian had assured me that most of the males in the court probably deserved it.

"My lord," I said, curtsying slightly and I approached him. The Unseelie lord smiled lasciviously, clearly interested in what I might be coming to offer him. I made a point of sipping my wine slowly, catching a wayward drop on my finger and sucking it into my mouth. The lord grinned and moved a little closer.

"My lady," he said in a smooth, refined voice. "It is an honor to meet the bride of the Unseelie Prince. I hope he has not damaged you too gravely?"

"Oh no," I assured him, moving a little closer and lowering my voice to a sultry purr, attempting to channel Aurelia as I added, "I like it rough."

Desire flashed in the male's eyes, and I knew I had him.

"And you, my lord?" I asked, moving closer until we were almost touching. "Are all Unseelie males so…" I paused, biting my lip as I looked him up and down. He was fine looking, but nothing compared to his Prince. Finally, I added, "vigorous?"

His smile widened, and he lifted his hand to trail a finger down my spine.

Night crashed into him, throwing him against a nearby wall, then lifting him up, dark power circling his throat. Hadrian burned with an unholy fury, eyes silver as he pinned the male to the wall and stalked toward him. He spoke in a voice that was both quiet and somehow loud enough for the whole room to hear. It was a voice of rage and possession and murder.

"Do not touch what is *mine*," he growled, squeezing the male's throat until his face turned red as he fought for breath. The whole court was silent and still, watching the display with fascination, and some with excitement. I held my ground, willing Hadrian to stop before he went too far and regretted it.

He released the male, who slumped to the ground, gasping in great gulps of air. He seemed otherwise unharmed, and a large part of me sagged with relief.

Hadrian turned then and stalked over to me, eyes blazing with fury and…jealousy? I did not think that was part of his act. I stood my ground, which was difficult considering the terrifying force of nature that was the Prince.

Dark tendrils wrapped around my arms and waist. To the court, I hoped it looked like I was trapped and terrified, bound by this male who proclaimed to possess me. But Hadrian's power was a soothing embrace, reminding me that he was not the monster, that he was my friend, and that he did not want to do what I had asked him to do next. The shadows allowed me enough of a distraction to retrieve the chokeberries and pop them in my mouth.

He growled when he reached me. "You dare let another male touch you?" He roared, slapping me hard across the face. It stung, but he had pulled back to make the slap look far harder than it was. I bit down on the chokeberries as he made impact, and a line of red dribbled down my lip and chin as he breathed hard, glaring at me.

For a moment, his mask almost slipped. I saw the anguish on his face as the juice of the berries, a deep blood red, dribbled down, marring the beautiful white dress with a red stain. I had chosen the dress for the impact this would have, but it killed me a little to ruin something so lovely. Maybe Mother Vervain would know how to save it.

Grabbing my arm where I had painted on the bruises,

Hadrian whisked us into shadow back to his room.

We had barely stepped back through the shadows when he dropped the act completely, cupping my face in his hands.

"Did I hurt you?" He asked, his voice filled with anguish as he scanned my face for lasting damage. His shadows curled around me still, as if embracing me in regret and comfort.

"No," I said, lifting my hands to where he held my face. "I'm fine. You were perfect! Very convincing."

I gave him a wide smile, but he still looked tormented, running his thumb over my cheek where he had slapped me. The sting had already faded. Before I realized what was happening he had bent his head and pressed his lips to mine.

The kiss was soft and tenuous at first, hesitant but tender and lovely. He hovered there, waiting to see if I would pull back. When I didn't, he dropped one arm from my face to wrap around my waist and pulled me closer, deepening the kiss. His other hand wound into my hair, and fire lit up my insides as desire swept through me.

I met his lips eagerly, not really thinking about what this meant or why it was happening. His tongue swept over mine, soft and exploring at first, then more insistent and urging as I opened more to him, wrapping my arm around his neck and sliding my fingers into his soft hair. He groaned and retreated slightly, planting soft kisses on my lips as if in apology, and promise. My heart beat wildly as he pulled back enough to meet my eyes.

"I have to go back down," he rumbled, face so close to mine I could see the swirls of silver in his gray eyes.

I nodded, feeling like words were beyond me at that moment. He pressed another soft kiss to my lips and rested his forehead against mine.

"Seline will guard your door," he said, still a low rumble as if he wanted to keep me his own private secret for a little longer. "I'll be back as soon as I can."

One moment he was holding me close, and the next he had swept away into shadow, leaving me cold and wanting. I pressed my fingers to my lips and wrapped my other arm around my middle, heart still beating a furious tattoo against my ribs.

The Unseelie Prince, the Prince of Death, the story of nightmares and scourge of the Seelie realm, had just kissed me. And goddess help me, I wanted him to do it again.

CHAPTER 20

Hadrian didn't return. I stayed awake, waiting for him to come back, but the night grew later and later and he didn't come. At some point I fell asleep, and I woke to gray morning light as I finally heard his booted steps moving around the room.

I sat up, and he winced.

"I'm sorry," he said quietly, "I didn't want to wake you."

He unstrapped his weapons, taking meticulous care to replace them in their correct place in his cabinet and unbuttoned his coat, throwing it across a chair before heading into the bathing chamber.

I sat there, not quite knowing what to do or say. While I obviously wanted to know where he had been and what he had been doing, the memory of our kiss hung over me. Did we need to talk about it? Did I want to? Was it a one time heat of the moment spontaneous lapse in judgment, or the beginning of something more? I had tormented myself with my own thoughts about it for hours before finally succumbing to sleep, and now they came roaring back into my brain.

He returned a few minutes later, hair and shirt sleeves damp. Before I could turn he was pulling his shirt off over his head, muscular torso fully displayed in the pale gray morning light, my stomach flipped again. He was the most attractive male I had ever seen, and it didn't help that he appeared to be chiseled from marble itself. I looked away, hoping he hadn't noticed my state as he donned a clean shirt and sat down, pulling off his boots before flopping down on the bed.

I clenched my jaw. He was going to make me bring it up. Well, I would delay that task until absolutely necessary.

"What happened?" I asked, pulling a blanket around my shoulders to cover myself. The single nightgown I had, while long, was not opaque, and it did little to hide my figure, especially in the light.

"Your plan worked, is what happened," Hadrian said tiredly, turning on his side to face me. His eyes were bloodshot and his face was haggard, but he seemed hopeful in a way he hadn't before this.

"After our little performance, my father decided it was time to take me into his confidence. I spent the last six hours attending meetings with his generals and advisors." He yawned. "They're not all convinced, but my father insists on my attendance moving forward."

"Good," I said, both excited and disappointed. If the plan worked, the mission would be over faster. I should be happy about that. But last night something had changed, and I felt a twist of misery at the thought of leaving.

"I need sleep," he said, pulling me from my spiraling thoughts. I nodded, but he sat up, rather than turning over.

"Last night," he said slowly, as if trying to think how to navigate treacherous waters with the least amount of damage. My heart cracked a little, realizing what he was about to say.

"I know," I said, "it was the heat of the moment. I understand." I hugged my knees to my chest, resting my chin on them, trying not to look crushed. My throat felt tight, and I willed back the emotion, refusing to fall apart for this male I barely knew.

He frowned. "No," he said, looking at me with his brows furrowed. Understanding lit his face. "No." He repeated, shifting to his knees and closing the distance between us. I froze a little, not sure where this was going, or where I wanted it to go.

"No," he growled fiercely, taking my face in his hands and lifting my chin. "Not a mistake," he rumbled. He leaned down, brushing the lightest kiss against my lips. I closed my eyes and sighed a little. He brushed a kiss to each closed eyelid, then each of my cheeks, my nose, and my lips once more. When I opened my eyes, his were there, swirling with silver and lit with desire. My stomach flipped as heat washed through me again.

"Not a mistake," he repeated, holding my gaze. "A beginning. If you want it to be."

It felt impossible to look away at that moment. In him I saw longing and desire. The pulse between us hummed and his shadows snaked around me, making me shiver pleasantly.

I nodded. To my embarrassment a tear trickled down my cheek. Before I could swipe it away, he had caught it, brushing it away and kissing the spot where it had fallen.

He gave me his wicked half smile and bent to whisper in my ear, making goosebumps run down my arms. "You have no idea how glad I am that you agree." He brushed his nose against my ear and I shuddered slightly, whispering his name.

I felt him smile as he moved to my other ear and whispered again, "because if you hadn't, I would have had to do something drastic." I wrapped my arms around his neck, enjoying the shivers that ran down my side as his nose brushed my ear again.

He wrapped his arms around my waist and pulled me down with him, keeping his eyes on mine as he said, "I really do need to sleep, but please know it's not because I don't want to explore where this might lead." His hands trailed down my side a little and I shivered again.

Stars, this male was making me look like a fool with the slightest touch. Goddess help me when he decided to really try.

"Then sleep," I said, holding his gaze, and pressing a light kiss of my own to his lips. His eyes grew heated. I smirked, tucking myself into his side and resting my head on his shoulder.

The knock on the door startled me awake again

when the morning had fully dawned, bright cold light streaming in from the massive window.

Hadrian still slept, one arm wrapped around me as he held me to his side. My heart fluttered as I stole a glance at his face. Some of the exhaustion had smoothed from his face in sleep, and I extricated myself from him as gently as possible before another knock could wake him.

Checking that the blanket was wrapped around me firmly, I paused at the door.

"Hello?" I said in a soft voice.

"My lady?" Replied a gruff voice, "Your things have arrived." I threw open the door and hugged Vanth tightly.

"Thank the goddess you are here!" I cried.

"Um…yes," said Vanth awkwardly, pushing me away from him with both eyebrows raised at Hadrian, who groaned as he awoke. Seline grinned behind him.

"She's just happy you brought her clothes," Seline said, patting him on the arm and pushing him ahead of her into the room.

I nodded enthusiastically and Vanth rolled his eyes.

"Females," he mumbled under his breath, earning him a jab in the ribs from Seline.

I made my escape into the bathing chamber with my favorite dress of satin gray. I smiled as I thought it was the same shade as Hadrian's eyes, except for the silver streaks. I looked in the mirror, seeing my hair frizzing all around my braid, and sighed, doing my best to comb it out with my fingers and re-braid it.

When I re-entered Hadrian's room, the three of them had moved to the fireplace, taking up seats around the low table. A platter of breads and meats had appeared, and more of the hot, bitter Unseelie drink. Hadrian was animatedly discussing the meetings he'd had with his father's generals and advisors.

"I'll have almost back to back meetings most days going forward," Hadrian said. "Vanth, you'll serve as my personal guard."

"Seline," he said, turning to his half-sister. "I need you to stay with Ember over the next few weeks and keep her safe." She nodded.

"And," he added, "I need you to teach her to defend herself."

"Gladly," she said, grinning a little wickedly, looking very much like Hadrian in that moment. She turned to me. "We can pretend to practice on the seamstress," she added, winking. I smiled as she reminded me of Aurelia, even though I knew that teaching me to fight was a losing battle.

"And I need you to work on breaking her spell," Hadrian added. We both turned to him saying "what?" at the same time.

"I know Mother Vervain warned against it," he said, meeting my gaze with a hard look. "But I'd rather you have magic to defend yourself than not."

"What if my magic isn't defensive?" I asked, an anxious knot building when I thought about being vulnerable to the king's raven. "What about the bird?" I added.

"I'll work on helping you shield your mind," he promised, leveling me with a serious look. "But I need you to try and free your magic. I can't think of how else to keep you safe here." He reached over and put his hand on mine.

Seline saw it, and shot me a smirk and a raised

eyebrow as if to say, "told you so."

"So while you're in your meetings, what should I do?" I asked, unsure what role I needed to play during the day to keep up the appearance of our engagement.

"Other than training with Seline?" Hadrian asked. "I suggest writing to Aurelia, and making sure some of the letters are totally innocuous so my father doesn't get suspicious. The more you write to her about things that bore him, the less likely he'll want to read your letters."

"Okay, and?" I asked, waiting for something more vital than writing to my friend.

"And…" Hadrian hesitated, looking to Vanth and Seline for back up. Both quickly looked elsewhere. I scowled.

"And you can do whatever you want that keeps you safe," he added lamely. "I had hoped you might help Mother Vervain and learn from her. I know she says she can't break your spell, but I have a feeling she's not telling me everything. I'd invite you to my meetings, but my father would never allow it. Seline is barely allowed in as a guard as it is."

"Because she's your sister?" I asked.

"Because I'm a female," Seline corrected with a growl.

"And because he's a paranoid maniac, which has kept him on the throne for almost a thousand years." Hadrian added darkly.

"A thousand years?" I asked, incredulous. The Fae were long lived, but that was unusually long even for us.

"Wait," I said, seizing the opportunity to ask something I had been meaning to for several days. "How old are you?"

Hadrian gave me a bemused half smile. "Worried

I'm centuries more experienced?" He teased. I blushed faintly, glancing to the others who were watching us with interest.

"No," I said sharply. "I just want to know." I shrugged, trying to act like I didn't really care.

"I am in my fourth decade," Hadrian said. Part of me felt relieved that he didn't dwarf me in years by so great a number. "I was a boy during the war, but Seline and Vanth fought in it."

"You're older than him?" I asked, turning toward Seline. She was such a small female that I had always assumed she was his age, or younger.

She smirked. "By two decades," she confirmed. "But Vanth is the truly ancient one. He just passed his first century."

Vanth growled, giving her braid a tug. "I'm experienced."

"Is that part of why the king distrusts you?" I asked, turning back to Hadrian. "Because you are young?"

"Young and untested in his mind, but to be fair, he is right to be wary of me," he said, gesturing to the room at large where we planned rebellion. "He had been trying to produce an heir for over seven hundred years. He had all but given up when I was born, and he didn't become interested in me until I reached maturity. That was when he began to test me."

Hadrian's voice had grown darker as he recounted the history. "He knows that his time is fading," he went on. "He is hoping to mold me into a copy of him before he passes into the dark. His commanders also grow concerned, and more eager than ever to recruit me to their brutality."

I nodded, feeling like I had more to think about at the

very least, even if I didn't have much to actually do.

"Okay, so," I said, ticking off items on my fingers. "You attend the meetings and report back as much as you can. I write daily to Aurelia so that when we need to, we can hopefully slip useful details into my letters. I occupy myself with Mother Vervain as best as I can between learning defense with Seline and shielding with you. And then…" I trailed off, feeling like there should be more to this plan.

Hadrian was smirking at me. "An admirable summary," he said, finishing his drink and putting the cup down on the table. "And then," he continued, taking up where I left off, "we plan a war."

Seline and Vanth excused themselves then to don their armor and gear up, promising to be back in no more than ten minutes. Hadrian strapped on his spiked armor and helm and more weapons that any one male could possibly need.

I watched him as he buckled straps and sheathed blades. He was clearly a warrior before everything else. He turned to look at me, and scowled.

"You're staring," he said, buckling a sword to his back and clanking over to where I sat on my side of the bed. Did we have sides? I supposed we did now.

I smirked up at him. "Just watching the great Prince prepare for battle," I teased.

He knelt down before me so he could meet my eyes and my heart stuttered a little as he released his glamour and let the darkness flow around him.

"Your shadows are different from your father's," I said, watching as tendrils curled playfully around my fingers. "Are you controlling that?"

He smirked. "Not right now. I told you, they like

you."

"Why do you let me see them when you hide them from the others?" I asked. I had asked him before and I hadn't been given an answer. He studied me for a long moment.

"Because I want you to see all of me. To know all of me. For good or for ill, I will never hide from you."

He planted a gentle kiss on my lips, adding, "we will talk more about this," another kiss, making heat curl low in my belly, "tonight."

CHAPTER 21

"Plants have a special kind of magic," intoned Mother Vervain as she watched me grind up some yarrow root for her. She stood over me, her many layers of colorful shawls wrapped around her like the wings of an oversized bat. "They heal, and they can harm. They shelter and nourish, not just the body, but the soul. Plants are magic directly from the goddess."

I finished grinding and smiled. The number of things Mother Vervain said that I wanted to emblazon on a cushion was growing rapidly. She took the yarrow root from me and added it slowly to the tincture she was creating for one of the Unseelie ladies who had recently given birth.

"Yarrow to purge the womb and fight infection," she mumbled to herself. "Yes, that should do it."

Mother Vervain seemed to have an endless number of tinctures and potions and teas brewing simultaneously. Cooks and kitchen maids bustled busily around the kitchen preparing food, all following commands that Mother Vervain issued from a chair near the fireplace. Occasionally she moved to attend a potion or a brew herself, but I hadn't seen her do any heavy lifting or chopping or preparing of food. In fact, the rest of the staff seemed to treat her with a reverence befitting an older, infirm relative, and I think she liked them to believe she was frail and incapable.

When I had asked her where her staff had been on the day we visited she made a vague excuse about giving them the morning off. I had a suspicion she had known we would be visiting and wanted them out of her way.

"Mother Vervain," I said, turning toward her, "how did you come to serve the Unseelie King?"

"It's a strange story," she replied cryptically, mixing her potion and pouring it into a glass vial for her patient. "And a long one. Too long for now. The short version is that I am a prisoner of war, and that's all you need to know."

"A prisoner?" I asked, rage rising on behalf of this poor female who had clearly been taken at an advanced age. "Of the Great Fae War?"

"Yes," she replied, bustling to her herb cabinet and plucking several sprigs of different plants. "And no. That war raged for over two centuries, my dear. How long do you think I have been in this castle?"

She paused her work, looking at me expectantly.

"I don't know," I replied, taking the herbs she offered me and adding them to the mortar for grinding. "A hundred years?"

She smiled sadly, her ancient face falling at the memories, and adjusted her shawls around her.

"It's a story for another time anyway," she said briskly, gesturing to the bowl of herbs. "Grind."

"What kind of tincture is this for?" I asked, grinding the herbs with the pestle, enjoying doing something that I felt competent at, unlike learning to fight with Seline, which had been a disaster as predicted. I examined the herbs in the bowl, identifying rosemary, thyme, sage, and something nutty. "I don't know this mixture."

"That, my dear, is for the roast duck," said Mother Vervain in total seriousness. "Best be off, my dear, dinner prep has started and I'll not make any more potions today. Come back tomorrow with more of your questions."

Mother Vervain took the bowl from me and waved me away. I wiped my hands on my apron and hung it on a hook by the door. Smiling and giving her a small wave as I met Seline in the hallway outside. She was slumped against the wall with her arms crossed, examining her nails. She cast me a bored look.

"Sorry you got stuck babysitting me," I said good humoredly, giving her a smile.

"Not babysitting," she assured me. "You are much older than a baby." I gave her a withering stare as she smirked.

"What now, my lady?" She asked, clunking behind me in her heavy armor.

"I suppose I should write to Aurelia," I mused, having little else to do. Hadrian had supposedly been in meetings all afternoon, and I hadn't seen or heard from him since this morning.

"You'll be expected at court again tonight," she said. I groaned feelingly. She gave me a sympathetic pat on the shoulder.

"You and his highness will have to do a better job of acting than you have been doing in front of me and Vanth," she continued. I stopped and turned. Her gray eyes twinkled with amusement.

"What do you mean?" I asked, concerned that someone at court suspected the engagement was not real. "Were we not convincing last night?"

"Oh no, you were," she said, nudging me ahead until we were out of the narrow hallway and we could walk side by side. "I just don't know that you'll be able to keep up the icily indifferent fiancée act."

"I thought we were supposed to be acting like we were in love?" I said.

"Until last night, yes. But your performance in the throne room changed that," she said, leading me up the stairs toward Hadrian's rooms. "Now you'll have to act like you don't like him. Like you fear him."

"Well that won't be hard," I laughed as we entered his chambers. He wasn't there, as expected, but at least I'd have peace to write my next letter.

"Won't it?" Seline asked, with a knowing smile. I scowled. "Happy writing," she smirked, closing the door behind me to stand guard outside.

It was snowing outside the large window in Hadrian's room, and I perched on the window ledge to write my letter to Aurelia so I could look out at the snow. So far the only time I'd been out in it was the first night in the throne room when Hadrian shadow walked us to the forest, and I didn't really feel like that counted.

I wrote to Aurelia about the castle and the nobility,

keeping my account factual and dull. What the ladies wore, what the wine was like, what the snow looked like out the window, that kind of thing.

Only at the end did I add something that she might be able to relate to the Commander.

"My future husband seems to have the king's trust. I do not see him much as he is always in meetings."

There, that seemed innocuous enough. Hopefully they'd get the message that our ruse was working.

Seline had taken a crack at my magic earlier today during our training session with no luck, so I decided with the rest of my free time I might as well see if I could at least nudge it around a bit.

I closed my eyes and felt internally for that gaping vacuum where my magic should be. It was less a hole and rather a block of nothingness where light ought to be. I gave it a mental prod. I imagined solid black walls all around it, caging my magic in. I mentally tapped around the walls to see if there was a weak spot with no luck.

I opened my eyes, frustrated and suddenly exhausted. Whatever the spell was, it was designed to drain me if I tampered with it too much. I wondered for not the first time who might have put the spell on me.

If my parents were rebels, they might have done it to protect me, if my magic was stronger than usual. The fact that they were murdered by the king didn't necessarily mean they were rebels, but it was the only idea I could come up with. Unless I had been cursed as a child? I felt like I would remember something like that, but who knows. I added it to the list of things I would have to ask Mother Vervain the next time I saw her.

Hadrian came crashing into the room, interrupting

my thoughts. I must have looked odd, sitting on the window ledge, but he didn't comment, just threw down his sword and belt of daggers angrily in a pile on the floor and started unbuckling his armor. The dark power around him flickered erratically.

"What's wrong?" I asked, hopping down from the window. He looked up, surprised to see me there, and some of the frantic lashing of his power seemed to soothe. As I got closer I realized that his face and armor was splattered with blood.

"Are you hurt?" I asked, rushing over to him to look for signs of injury. He grabbed my hands before I could frantically start hunting for a wound.

"No," he said darkly. His face was pale beneath the blood, which was normal, but the haunted look in his eyes was not. He looked away quickly, letting go of my hands and continuing to unstrap his bloody armor. Drops of blood were splashing the floor like a grotesque murder scene.

"Not in here," I said, pushing him toward the bathing chamber. I left him there and took a wet towel to wipe the blood off the floor of his bedroom. Other than a small stain on an ornate rug, it hadn't done any lasting damage. When I returned to the bathing chamber he had removed most of the armor, leaving a bloody pile in the middle of the floor.

"What happened?" I asked, leaning against the wall a short distance from him. He clearly didn't want me close to him right now, so I waited until he was ready to tell me. He didn't answer as he stripped off greaves and bracers, adding them to the bloody collection.

"Hadrian," I said softly. He stopped moving and bowed his head, still not looking at me.

"Another test," he growled, going to the tub and beginning to fill it with hot water. "He had me interrogating prisoners all day. I was not..." he stopped and swallowed. "I was not able to be gentle."

I stood silently, understanding his anger and self-loathing. Unsure what to say or if saying anything would make things worse, I waited.

Hadrian stripped off his shirt, muscles rippling as he added it to the pile of bloody armor and turned to face me. The white scars that crisscrossed his chest stood out sharply against his pallor. I took a step toward him and stopped.

"How can I help you?" I asked in a small voice. He shook his head, unable or unwilling to speak. Making up my mind, I went over to the tub and turned off the water. It was scalding hot, and I was about to add some cold when he said, "leave it."

I turned to look, then turned around equally swiftly. He was removing his trousers. I felt my face warm, and didn't turn again until I head the splash of him entering the bath and risked a look.

He sat in the near boiling water starting at the wall, eyes still haunted by what he had been forced to do today. I didn't think talking would help him, so I went and grabbed a clean cloth and a bar of soap from the counter and knelt by the tub. I pressed the cloth to his face and began gently washing away the blood.

"The first time I saw a death was in the infirmary," I started, moving the washcloth gently from his face to his neck. He closed his eyes.

"One of the fighters had been sent north to track troop movements. He'd been caught and barely made it back alive. When I got him into the infirmary and was able to see his wound, his guts were barely being held in by the shirt he had wrapped around his waist."

I rinsed the cloth, water turning slightly pink as the blood mixed with it. I lathered the soap and put the cloth to his chest, attempting to wash away the gore and sweat and horror of the day with gentle strokes.

"I stitched him up as best as I could," I continued, remembering the stench of death as it had become clear that I couldn't save the male. "No one was there to teach me, so I did what I could, but the wound was already festering. It took him three days to die, and I had to watch most of it."

I stopped as Hadrian gently grasped my wrist. His eyes were storm clouds of remorse and fury.

"You didn't torture him first," he said darkly, looking like he wanted to rage but holding it in.

"No," I agreed, "but it wasn't quick. It was long and agonizing, and I was too afraid to put him out of his misery. At the end, he begged for death, and I couldn't do it."

I cupped my free hand to his cheek and added, "did they beg?"

He nodded, swallowing.

"And did you make it quick?" He nodded again.

"Then you did as much as you could," I said, not knowing if it was right to justify his killing, but also knowing that he didn't really have a choice. He had to follow orders or risk being killed himself, and risk the whole movement with him.

"What if I can't stop?" he croaked, and I frowned, not understanding his meaning.

"What if that bastard poisons my mind, turns me into him. Makes me a monster and a killer and I can't..."

he took a breath, panic lacing his words.

"You are not a monster," I said, still holding his face. "True monsters don't fear their own monstrosity."

He turned away and I dropped my hands, sighing.

"Will you come out now?" I asked, standing to go and find some clean, dry towels. "Or do I need to come in?"

He let out a humorless laugh. I raised my eyebrow at him.

"Do you not think I'd do it?"

"No," he croaked, "no, I think you would." He tipped his head back against the edge of the tub. "I can't decide if it would be a good thing or a bad thing."

It took me a moment to decide what to do, but I chose to throw caution to the wind. Dropping the towels on the floor next to the tub, I kicked off my shoes and climbed in, still completely clothed. I was both impressed and a little horrified at my own daring. I was no saint, but I was also not usually the first to make any overtures, and this was fairly overt.

Hadrian was equally surprised and sat up, eyes wide as I sat straddling his legs, my skirts billowing around me as water sloshed over the sides of the tub.

"You are not a monster," I repeated softly, putting my hands on his bare chest. His hands went to my waist under the water, and I wished for a second that I had removed the dress before climbing in.

I met his eyes and the connection thrummed between us, making me gasp in a breath.

"You feel it too," he rumbled, sliding a hand up my back and into my wet hair.

I nodded. "What is it?" I whispered, half hoping and half afraid that he would have an answer.

"I have a theory," he said, voice low and silken,

darkness reaching around me, to cocoon us where we sat in the hot water.

He pulled my head forward and our lips met. I closed my eyes and opened for him as his tongue swept into my mouth, exploring and teasing. His free arm wrapped tighter around my waist as he pulled me closer, and I melted into him a little more with each sweep of his tongue. Heat pooled low in my core, curling deliciously between my legs.

I felt the evidence of his own feelings hard against my thigh, and it snapped me out of whatever trance I had fallen under. I pushed back, practically panting for breath as I put a few inches of distance between us. He was breathing hard, flecks of silver swirling in his eyes as he stared at me with blatant desire.

"What's wrong?" He asked, almost growling with the intensity of his desire. I shook my head, not sure I could put words to it. He didn't push, didn't pull me back down to him or insist I tell him. Just waited patiently for me to get my bearings and collect my thoughts. One of his hands was still in my hair. The other at my waist made gentle strokes at my ribs with his thumb.

"I don't understand," I said finally once I had recovered myself enough to speak. "This thing between us. I don't understand why I feel what I'm feeling." I met his eyes, and he looked at me seriously. I continued, "I hated you. Loathed you. And now I'm here, sitting in a bathtub with you, wanting…" I trailed off, unable to voice what I wanted.

"Wanting what?" He asked, voice rough with desire. The hand in my hair moved to my neck and he gently caressed the pulse point there, sending good bumps down my arms.

"Wanting more," I breathed. He nodded, as if he understood how I was feeling exactly. He sat up a little to press his forehead to mine, closing his eyes as he brushed his nose against mine.

"I don't understand it fully," he rumbled. The water had begun to cool and I shivered as he continued. "But I want to explore it. As fast or as slow as you want." He brushed a soft kiss against my lips and it felt like butterflies were erupting inside me. I had never felt this way about any male, and I couldn't reconcile the feelings with the fact that he was the Unseelie Prince.

"Let's get out before the water gets cold," he said softly, still pressing his forehead against mine. I nodded and rose, splashing water all over the floor as my sodden dress cascaded around me.

We dried off in silence, the heat between us having cooled a little with the bath water. We were expected at court again in less than an hour, and the thought further cooled some of the desire that had swept through me.

Without discussion we dressed, Hadrian in his usual black and I in one of my dresses from home. It was the midnight blue one I had worn the first time I met him. I brushed color on my cheeks and lips, then applied some of the black and blue paint to my eye and neck, hoping it looked like it was growing more faint with healing, rather than being newly brushed on.

"I remember this dress," he said, coming to stand behind me as I finished getting ready. "I remember thinking that you were the most beautiful creature I had ever seen."

I laughed, blushing slightly, remembering our first meeting very differently.

"You certainly didn't act that way," I said, shaking out my hair and deciding to wear it loose. I combed and smoothed it as much as I could before hiding the frizz behind a weak glamour.

"No, I had to pretend not to recognize you," he said, turning away to select daggers that were not covered in blood to finish his own attire.

"Recognize me?" I asked, turning to face him. "You had seen me before?"

Hadrian nodded. "At several balls and functions when I wasn't supposed to be attending as the Prince," he said, as if this were not news that should surprise me. "I danced with you at one of them actually," he added, giving me his wicked half grin before adding, "and a few times in the caves."

I frowned. "Surely I would have spotted you in the caves," I said. He gestured around himself at the pulsing darkness. "Shadows." I rolled my eyes.

"Prince, spy, and master of disguise," I said, remembering my quip from the Autumn Equinox. He grinned, bending down and planting a kiss in the hollow where my neck met my shoulder. I shivered.

"I'm sorry, for what I said to you that night," he said quietly.

I shrugged. "You were playing a part," I said, remembering the fury that had burned inside me. "The part of a pompous ass."

"I was an ass," he said, smiling against my neck. "And I misjudged you. I sensed the magic in you, and assumed you were disingenuous when Thorn claimed you had little power. I assumed you were hiding something, and I'm sorry."

"That should teach you for believing anything

Thorn says," I said, turning to meet his face with a smirk. His face was serious and I let my smile drop.

"I'm sorry for misjudging you as well," I said. Turning to face my reflection again, I added, "you told me, in the caves, that you had faced more of your father's cruelty than I could imagine. I didn't believe you either. I was so determined to be hateful toward you."

"Hmm," he said, dropping his face to kiss my shoulder, sending a shiver down my back. "What a pair we make."

He stepped back to let me finish getting ready and perched on the end of the bed, watching me.

"Seline knows?" he asked. I nodded, thinking of her meaningful glances and not needing him to elaborate.

"More like she suspects. I haven't confirmed anything," I replied, finishing pinning a comb of silver roses in my hair. I turned to face him.

"What do you want to do about it?" I asked.

"Tonight," he said, standing and offering me his hand, "we play our parts. The Prince of Death and the Ice Queen, indifferent to each other but bound by politics."

"And here I thought I'd have to pretend to like you," I said, giving him my own version of his wicked smile.

He laughed and pulled me close, practically growling as he rumbled in my ear, "My lady, when I am done with you, there will be no need to pretend."

CHAPTER 22

If I had thought the evening court gatherings could not get any worse, I had been sorely mistaken.

Rather than entering through the main door, Hadrian shadow walked us into a dark corner of the room directly. The sensation was still unpleasant, but I was becoming more accustomed to the lurching, sickening sensation, enough that small hops didn't bother me.

We were late to the party, and the evening was already in full swing. Some lords and ladies danced, Seelie and Unseelie servants delivered drinks and carried trays of food, most of it decayed. The normal whispering that followed us was absent, since we had appeared without ceremony. I saw that Seline and Vanth were posted strategically in opposite corners of the room. Vanth nodded his head a fraction, acknowledging our arrival from across the room. Seline was closer, and moved to stand next to me when we arrived.

Hadrian left me to walk the room, making appropriate and very dull small talk with the various commanders and lords with whom he was supposed to be gaining favor. Seline trailed me from a small distance as I wove between groups of guests, maintaining my icy demeanor and looking hatefully at everything while trying to glean any useful information I could.

The males gave me a wide berth, no doubt fearing what Hadrian might do if they got too close. Good. That was an unexpected perk of last night's performance.

I had already made three tedious turns of the ballroom hearing nothing useful when I heard my name, spoken in an oily wheedling voice that chilled me to my bones.

"Lady Ember, such a pleasure to see you settling in here." Lord Thorn was approaching me, striding across the room purposefully. Seline was instantly at my side, but she needn't have worried. Hadrian stepped out of the shadows next to us and intercepted him before he could reach me.

"Thorn," he said, spitting the lord's name with contempt as Thorn smiled beatifically up at him. "To what do we owe this displeasure?"

Thorn smirked, shoving his hands in his pockets and adopting a casual pose that I suspected was just as practiced as everything else about him.

"Why, I am here to pay my respects to your noble father," he said, nodding toward the ancient king, who was deep in discussion with an Unseelie Fae lord about something. He continued, "and to ask for his blessing for my upcoming marriage."

"Marriage to whom?" I asked, shocked that any female would agree to marry him. I moved to stand next to Hadrian. He clasped my forearm lightly in warning, but I didn't need to be reminded that Thorn was a snake and I should watch my tongue.

"Why, I am surprised you have not heard of it," said Thorn, looking affronted and putting a hand to his heart. "Being such a close friend, I would have assumed she would tell you the happy news herself."

My blood chilled at his words. He couldn't mean her. It couldn't be.

"Explain yourself, Thorn, or get out of my sight," Hadrian growled. Lord Thorn turned his poisonous smile to me.

"Lady Aurelia and I are to be wed next week."

It took every ounce of restraint I had to not murder Thorn where he stood.

"You lie," I snarled.

"You can ask the king if you like," replied Thorn smugly. "He has just blessed the union. My bride is already on her way north to my holdings at the border of our realms."

He paused, a snakelike grin lighting his face. "So many happy marriages on the horizon. It's quite a new dawn for our united realms, don't you think?"

With a courtly bow, Thorn waltzed away to preen at some of the other lords and ladies. I stood in shocked bewilderment, unable to move or think or breathe. Aurelia, my Aurelia, could not marry this male.

It took prodding from both Vanth and Seline to get me back up to Hadrian's room. I didn't notice that he wasn't with us until he appeared out of shadow, fuming.

"He speaks the truth," Hadrian said, grinding his teeth. "My father confirmed it."

"How can this be?" I cried, pacing and wringing my hands while Seline and Vanth looked on in bewilderment. "She loves Aspen, I know she does. Why would she do this?"

Hadrian stopped me with his hands on my arms.

"I don't know," he growled, "but I know how we can find out. Seline, Vanth," he turned to his guards. "No one enters this room until I open the door. If anyone asks for me, I am enjoying the company of my fiancée."

Vanth and Seline glanced at each other, and Vanth nodded.

"We can give you three hours," he said, and they left the room to take their positions in the doorway.

"Get changed," Hadrian said, throwing off his weapons and tearing off his dark shirt.

"Into what?" I asked, rushing to unhook my dress and remove the silver comb from my hair.

"Something unremarkable," he replied, throwing on his brown travel clothes and cloak. I did the same and went to him when I was ready.

"Brace yourself," said Hadrian, holding me around the waist.

"What are we doing?" I asked, panic momentarily outweighed by confusion.

"Going to see your Commander," he replied, and turned us into shadow.

Blackness, inky and consuming surrounded me. I felt like I was everywhere and nowhere, spinning into nothing. The black pressed in on my eyes, and I focused on the feeling of Hadrian's arms wrapped around me, of his warm breath on the top of my head.

When we emerged an eternity later, I fell to the ground, bringing up everything I had eaten that day. Hadrian wasn't sick, but he looked exhausted as he leaned against a tree for support.

"I thought you couldn't make the jump with anyone," I wheezed, spitting phlegm into the nearby grass.

"I normally can't," he replied, voice raspy with exertion.

I looked up to find he had brought us to the cave entrance. It was pitch black, and I knew the Commander might be asleep, but I pushed myself to my feet and forced myself forward.

The caves were quiet, as it was the middle of the night, but I sprinted as fast as my nauseated body could to the Commander's door. I thumped hard, uncaring if I woke the whole complex.

The Commander finally opened the door and sighed.

"I had a feeling I'd be seeing you two sooner than later. Come in."

Hadrian had followed me and entered behind me, shutting the door.

"I assume you're here about Aurelia," the Commander said, sitting behind her desk and steepling her fingers. Her injured eye looked more gruesome than usual in the dim light.

"Is this a mission?" I asked. She would never marry Thorn if not.

The Commander sighed, opening her desk drawer and pulling out a stack of papers with a wax seal. She handed me the stack, and I saw the green sigil of

Aurelia's house.

"She knew we'd likely be in communication before she was able to reach you," she said sympathetically. "Hadrian, since you're here you may as well update me."

Hadrian cast me a concerned look, then turned to the Commander, taking a seat in front of the desk. I drowned out his report as I read Aurelia's letter.

> My Dear Ember,
>
> I assume if you are reading this, then you have found out about my "marriage" to Lord Thorn. I am so sorry you couldn't hear it from me, but everything happened so quickly after you left.
>
> Thorn came to my parents the day after the Autumnal Equinox to ask for my hand. Initially, I refused, for you know how I detest that serpent. It was clear he was asking me to revenge himself on you, and you know that I love someone else.

Part of the line had been smudged by what must have been a tear. Oh Aurelia, what did you agree to?

> I told the Commander of course, and she agreed that marrying him for information was not worth the sacrifice, but within hours we heard from some of our border scouts that legions of troops had been seen entering Lord Thorn's lands. They had no good intelligence on where they were sent from, but the easy assumption is that they are Unseelie troops loyal to the king.
>
> Thorn's lands are heavily guarded, and the easiest way in was through me. So I agreed, on the condition that I could end Thorn if I felt my

life or freedom were in danger at any point.

The plan is to stay for two weeks, learn as much as I can about the situation here, then sneak out and head south. Our scouts know my position, and I am prepared to fight my way out if necessary.

Em, please tell Aspen, if you speak to him, that I will explain everything when I get back. He has a right to know, and I know he won't betray me. I know I have probably wounded him deeply, but I hope all will be repaired soon enough.

Guard your left,
Aurelia

I dropped the pages, tears lining my eyes. Hadrian and the Commander had finished their debrief, and both looked at me expectantly. I cleared my throat.

"We need to bring Aspen in," I said, realizing that the only way to salvage this was to tell him as soon as possible. "He'll support the cause, and he should know."

"No," said the Commander.

"What?" I asked, shocked that she didn't see the logic behind my request.

"I said no," she repeated coldly. "Use your head, Ember. If your cousin loves Aurelia, he will go charging after her and put this whole mission in jeopardy. Lives are at stake, including hers. It's too dangerous to compromise her."

"But," I started.

"No," she repeated. I swallowed.

"Let me write him a letter then, telling him that there's more to this."

The Commander shook her head. "You put Aurelia

in danger by making decisions based on feelings rather than logic," she said sternly. "As soon as Aurelia is safe, I will give her permission to bring him in. No earlier."

I clenched my jaw, ready to argue.

"And if you tell him against my orders, I will pull you from this mission, and the whole movement," she added, looking fierce, but softening slightly when she saw my pained expression. "I have known Aurelia since she was a child. I trust her to be safe. Have faith in her, Ember, like she has faith in you."

"Time to go," said Hadrian gently, lifting me by the arm to stand with him in front of the Commander's desk.

"Your word, Valeria, that you will pull her if she is in danger," he said, giving the Commander a dark look. She nodded and, satisfied, he swept me from the room

"We have to tell him," I said forcefully to Hadrian as he walked me back up the passage to the woods outside. He shook his head.

"You have orders, Ember." He looked down at me sadly. "Even I won't countermand them."

"Please, let me just go speak to him," I begged as he turned to face me. He still looked exhausted, but he was clearly ready to spin us away into shadow.

"Ember," he said, resting his hands on my arms. Frustrated, I lashed out.

"Don't," I cried. "Don't condescend to me or placate me or remind me of my duty. He is my family. SHE is my family, as much as Seline is yours. You can't expect me to do nothing."

Hadrian looked at me pityingly. "I'm sorry."

Before I could protest more, he had already swept me away.

CHAPTER 23

If the previous night had felt like a beginning between us, this one had felt like it might be an end. Hadrian and I didn't speak, even as I heaved my guts up after shadow walking so far. When he tried to offer me comfort, I brushed him away. He slept on the couch that night, so drained from using almost all of his power to shadow walk that he didn't even have the energy to argue.

I spent a long time lying awake. At first I cried, but eventually the tears dried and I started to plan. I did trust Aurelia, despite the Commander's assumption. It was Thorn I didn't trust. And I would make sure she had a way to protect herself.

Getting out of the bed, I lit a single candle and penned two letters. The one to Aspen was short, letting him know that I had heard about Aurelia and that he needed to wait for her for two weeks. I didn't care what the Commander said, he should know.

The second was for Aurelia, congratulating her and explaining how to use the "useful powder" I was including in her letter to please her husband. I took the letters and crept from Hadrian's room to the kitchens. Removing the little pouch where I had kept the chokeberries, I filled it with ground hemlock and folded it into the letter. I sealed both, and gave them to the night maid, a timid looking Seelie female, with strict instructions to make sure they went out in the mail the next day.

Hadrian was still asleep when I returned, and I quietly locked the door behind me and crept back into bed. Feeling like I had done something marginally useful, I finally slept.

When I woke the next morning, Hadrian was already gone. I found a note in his hand waiting for me on the desk, and I opened it cautiously.

> Back tonight.
> ~H

Sighing at the cryptic message, I dressed for the day and went to help Mother Vervain in the kitchen. Seline was waiting outside the door for me as usual, a grave expression on her face.

"What happened?" She asked. I told her about the mission and about my orders to stay out of it. She frowned.

"Did you and Hadrian fight?" I nodded.

"Less of a fight and more of a falling out. Why?" I asked.

"Because he left in an almighty temper this

morning," she said, darkly. "More than usual anyway."

I sighed, resigned that today was going to be terrible all around.

"I'm sorry," I said. "I know this thing between us complicates everything."

Seline stopped me with a hand on my arm.

"You made him come alive," she said, finality and warmth in her voice. "Don't ever be sorry for that."

Seline stayed guard outside the kitchens as usual as I went to work with Mother Vervain. The old female had no patience for my ill humor.

"If you keep grinding them like you want them to die, they'll be no use to us," she scolded as I mashed some dried elderflower viciously with the pestle. "What ails you child?"

I shook my head, not knowing what to tell Mother Vervain, or how much to trust her with.

"My friend has done something reckless," I said, turning my anger on some dried stinging nettle. "And there's nothing I can do to help."

Mother Vervain nodded thoughtfully.

"You know what always helps me when I am feeling helpless?" she asked with a kind smile.

I laughed a little. "Tea?"

"Well, I was going to say whiskey, but if you insist, dear, then a spot of tea would be lovely."

Mother Vervain bustled around making tea while I surreptitiously wiped my eyes on my sleeve. I wondered if this was what it was like to have a grandmother or an aunt. Someone to take care of you and offer wisdom, as well as ridiculous platitudes about tea.

Mother Vervain insisted that Seline join us, and the three of us sat rather awkwardly drinking our tea by the fire, Mother Vervain wrapped up against the cold in layers and layers of shawls in a hundred different fabrics. She instructed us both on the proper ways to stitch wounds, to disinfect festering wounds, and to set dislocated shoulders. By the time we left, I was buzzing with new information, and Seline looked rather green.

There was to be no throne room gathering tonight, as it was the new moon. Both courts viewed the night of the new moon each month as a time for self-reflection, and it was considered bad taste to have gatherings outside of one's family.

I was looking forward to not having to pretend in front of the court for a night, but I was anxious about seeing Hadrian. I had never quarreled with a male other than Aspen, and I felt unsure how to proceed. My feelings for Aspen were very different from my feelings for Hadrian, and I didn't want to be at odds with him, but I was still angry that he had backed the Commander over me. I tried to tell myself that she outranked us both, but it still stung.

I refused point blank to spar with Seline that afternoon, which caused her to spend a great deal of time lamenting my fate as a future stabbing victim, but she eventually agreed to help me work on unlocking my magic instead.

I tried to describe the block of nothing where I felt like my magic should be, and we spent several hours poking and prodding at it. A few times, I thought I felt something shift inside of me, a prickling at my back and core that might be magic, but it never lasted long.

By the time the sun set, we were both tired and rather grumpy, and my magic was no more unlocked than it had been before.

"Maybe we should try strong emotions," suggested Seline, who was lying with her feet on the arm of the couch, her head resting on her arm behind her. "Maybe if we try it while you're being fitted by the seamstress…"

I laughed and sent her off. She looked exhausted, and I knew I probably looked no better. Assuring her I would unlock the door for no one but Hadrian, she took her leave.

It was two hours before Hadrian returned to his rooms. I had already bathed and dressed for bed, wearing soft leggings under one of Hadrian's shirts. It smelled like him, and I had wrapped myself in it while trying to decide what I would say to him, and decided that it was now mine. When he entered I was sitting on the bed, cross-legged with my eyes closed, trying to move my magic.

He paused in the door.

"This might be my new favorite way to enter my room," he said tiredly, dropping his weapons in an untidy pile and unstrapping his armor.

No blood today, I noticed, releasing a breath I hadn't realized I was holding in.

I didn't say anything, unsure of what to say. We were still at odds, and I didn't know how to move past it. He removed his armor and changed into a clean shirt and loose pants, then came to sit next to me on the bed.

"Aurelia is safe," he said, holding out a paper written in her hand.

I snatched the paper and opened it, eager for news from my friend.

Ember,

Tell your Prince that the next time he

interrupts my work, I will personally assassinate him.

Aurelia

I winced.

"She was not happy to see me," he rumbled, looking down at the note. "But she is safe."

I looked up at him, meeting his eyes, and I felt our strange connection thrum and stutter, as if unsure where it stood between us.

"Aspen was not happy to see me either, but he didn't give me a letter," he continued. I looked at him in shock. How much power had he used today for me?

"Is he alright?" I asked, worry about my cousin's mental state moving to the forefront of my mind. Hadrian sighed.

"He is confused, I think," Hadrian said. "I told him to wait two weeks, and he wanted to know why. I couldn't tell him, but I told him the message was from you and he should trust you."

I stared at him, mouth hanging open. "You went today? To both of them?" He nodded, looking utterly drained.

"Ember, I…" he started. Before he could continue I threw my arms around his neck.

"Thank you," I whispered, holding him tightly until his arms wrapped around me in return. Loosening my grip I looked up to meet his eyes.

"I was angry and upset, and I took it out on you," I said, feeling uncertain what to do with the knowledge that this male had shadow walked all over two realms for me today, against the orders of his Commander. "I'm sorry."

Rather than replying with words, Hadrian planted his lips on mine in a searing kiss. It felt like he poured all of his remorse and relief into the kiss, drawing out my apology and gratitude in return. He broke away, leaving me breathless.

"I didn't want to wake you this morning," he said quietly, lifting his hands to cup my face and stroking my cheeks with his thumbs. "For what it's worth, I'm sorry too."

I nodded, pressing my forehead to his. "Despite that, the next time you pull rank on me, I'll have to come after you with one of Mother Vervain's deadly teacups," I joked.

He smiled wryly. "Goddess forbid."

He kissed me again, this time slow and deep and plundering, tongue sweeping over mine in gentle strokes as he explored. His arms tightened around my waist and I let out a breathy moan, much to my embarrassment. He chuckled.

"As slow, or as fast as you want," he said roughly, reminding me of his promise in the bathtub. His hand found the bare skin beneath the shirt I had stolen and stroked my ribs, causing me to shiver with pleasure.

"How about slow, then fast," I murmured, biting his lip gently in lieu of a kiss. He growled, and heat curled low in my belly as the sound seemed to travel through me.

Suddenly he was kissing me again, passionately and desperately. It felt like an exploration and a conquest as he moved his hands up my sides to brush the undersides of my breasts. I gasped.

"Too fast?" He asked, pulling away a little. I shook my head. He nipped my lip between his teeth. "I need to hear you say it," he growled.

"Not too fast," I breathed. He smiled, rewarding me with another kiss.

"If you want to stop, you tell me to stop. No questions asked." He said again, his voice rough with desire. I could see him straining to control himself, and my heart cracked a little. How had this good, kind, thoughtful, loving male been raised by such a monster?

"Don't stop," I breathed.

"Thank fuck," he groaned, pressing his lips and body to mine.

We fell back on the bed, his body covering mine as he explored me with his hands and mouth, planting soft kisses down the column of my throat, across my bare stomach, and up my chest as he unbuttoned the shirt I was wearing.

My heart thrummed in my chest and I felt heat pooling in my center, wanting more of him as he teased me too slowly. I lifted the shirt up over my head and tossed it away, his eyes flashing silver as he took me in. I honestly didn't think he saw the slightly too soft stomach, the too round hips, or any of the other imperfections I often wished away.

"You are perfect," he breathed, leaning down to suck a peaked nipple into his mouth. I gasped, tossing my head back and reveling in the sensation as he rolled my other nipple between his fingers.

"Fucking perfect," he repeated, licking a line of heat up the column of my throat. This male was going to make me combust at this rate. I reached up to pull his shirt over his head, feeling like we should at least be even on that front. He grinned as I gently stroked his bare torso, sliding my fingers down from his defined shoulders, across his pecs, and down the muscles of his abdomen. I gently caressed the iron wound scar and he shivered slightly.

"Perfect," I agreed.

His eyes met mine with blazing intensity, and I realized that we were on the threshold of something that there would be no turning back from. I burned for his touch, the feel of his mouth and fingers on me, like I had never burned for another male.

He lowered his lips back to mine, kissing me deeply as he moved a hand down my leg, over my backside, and between my thighs. I gasped at the sensation, and he ground himself against me at the sound, the evidence of his own arousal impossible to ignore.

"Stop?" He asked roughly, barely speaking above a rumbled growl.

I shook my head. "Don't stop."

He ground against me again, stroking with his fingers over my leggings. I shuddered as sensation washed over me, both too much and not enough. Darkness tumbled out of him as he released his glamour, and warm tendrils of inky black wrapped around my arms and legs and body, stroking and teasing as he touched me.

"Let me taste you," he rumbled in my ear. I nodded, too wrapped up in sensation and pleasure to deny him anything.

Gently, he removed my leggings and undergarments until I was bare before him. I shivered a little, and his darkness descended around us, warming me and wrapping us in a cocoon of dark privacy.

He kissed down my body, my stomach, my thigh, until he rested at my core. Pushing my knees up, he swept his tongue over my center. I gasped again, having never experienced a sensation like it. No male had ever tasted me before, and it felt both sinful and right as he licked and teased me, searching for the spot that would bring me the most pleasure.

My hips rocked shamelessly against his face as he moved, my hands sinking into his hair as I felt like I may come apart if I didn't have something to hold on to.

"How is this?" He asked, gently kissing my folds and running his tongue up the center of me again. I shuddered.

"Good," I replied breathlessly, barely able to form a cohesive thought. I felt him smile against my inner thigh.

"And this?" he asked, sliding a finger inside me. He groaned at the wetness he found and I clenched around him, unable to do more than make a noise of approval deep in my throat.

"And how about this?" He asked, sliding in a second finger and pumping gently. I rocked against him, moaning shamelessly and hoping to the goddess his darkness blocked out sound as well as light.

"That's it," he said, pumping gently again as he resumed licking and stroking me, his tongue teasing and sucking above where his fingers had entered me. Tension built, causing me to move my hips more frantically, needing more friction, more sensation, more everything. I shattered, his mouth still pressed against me and his fingers inside me, moaning with pleasure as he wrung my orgasm from me in great waves of pleasure.

I shuddered as he continued to stroke and tease with his mouth and fingers, little bolts of lighting coursing through me at each touch. I looked up, realizing my eyes had been closed, and met his gaze. His eyes were still hungry with need.

"What are you doing?" I gasped as he continued his attentions. He lifted his mouth long enough to say, "making you come again."

I shuddered as he pushed a third finger inside me, wringing more pleasure from me than I thought possible as he pushed me over the edge again with his wicked tongue.

After that, I was done waiting for him. I raised myself up, straddling his knees and feeling wetness drip between my thighs. He moved his hands to my back, holding me as I unbuttoned his pants.

"Are you sure?" He breathed. I met his eyes and saw longing and need there, but I knew he would wait if I wasn't certain I wanted this.

Instead of answering I kissed him fiercely, heat flooding my core again when I tasted myself on him. He helped me remove his pants until the length of him was finally freed, pressing hard against my thigh. Still, he waited for me to make the first move, to decide I was ready.

I bit his ear lightly and whispered, "please. I want you inside of me."

That was enough to snap his restraint. He hoisted me on top of him, lowering me gently onto his length. I gasped as he filled me and he stilled, letting me adjust to the fullness and sensation before gently thrusting his hips upward. I shuddered, delighting in the feel and the scent and the taste of him as I kissed his neck, his jaw, his ear, whatever I could reach.

He growled in my ear, "since the moment I saw you, I

knew it would end like this."

"Like what?" I gasped as he increased his pace, moving a little faster with each thrust.

He nipped my ear. "With me inside you. With you coming apart around me."

I shuddered, feeling the tension build again as he moved, each thrust creating a new spark of pleasure, making me feel like I might combust.

He groaned, moving faster, each thrust deeper than the last until he came, roaring as he spilled inside me. The feeling lit something in me, and light exploded around us as I joined him over that edge, twining with his shadows and scattering like stars as we rode the last waves of pleasure together.

CHAPTER 24

I lay on my stomach, completely bare, my head on Hadrian's shoulder and his arms around me as we breathed heavily.

His hand stroked gently up and down my back, and I shivered, feeling overwrought with sensation and pleasure as my heart thumped in time with his.

He kissed my sweaty temple, and I closed my eyes, sighing as for the first time in a long time I felt truly safe and whole.

The light that had exploded from me faded just as quickly, and I assumed it was my magic reacting to my strong emotion that had caused the outburst.

"You are exquisite," he said, still stroking my back and lifting his other hand to tangle in my hair. "A goddess. A queen. You literally glowed."

I smiled at his praise. Lifting my head, I rested my chin on his chest so I could meet his eyes. He was frowning at me slightly, but his expression cleared when he saw I was watching him.

"You're not so bad yourself," I teased, earning myself a gentle pinch on my bottom.

"Do I want to know how many other males have had the pleasure of experiencing you in all your glory?" He asked darkly, eyebrows raised in challenge.

"Hmm," I teased, pretending to count in my head. Another light pinch had me laughing and planting a kiss on his lips, still swollen from our lovemaking.

"I've been with a few males," I confessed, earning a scowl and a rumbling growl. "But none did what you did."

"Worshiped you?" Hadrian teased, punctuating the statement with a kiss. "Wrung such pleasure from you?" Another kiss. "Altered your existence?"

I bit his lip gently, effectively ending his list. "Made me feel alive," I said, meeting his eyes again with a more serious look. "Made me feel cherished."

He stroked a strong hand down my back again, gazing at me with contentment.

And love. The thought popped into my head unbidden, and I quashed it. He would say it if he felt it, when he felt it. I wasn't even sure I knew what it felt like to be in love. The swooping excitement and anxiety in my stomach whenever he touched me or looked at me felt like it might be.

"And you?" I asked, raising my brows at him, chin still resting on his chest. "How many females should I be jealous of?"

He smirked. "None," he replied lazily.

"Really?" I asked, sitting up suddenly so he had a view of my bare breasts. "You've never taken a female to bed before?"

He smirked again. "Oh I have. Just none you need to be jealous of." He pulled me back down toward him, kissing me soundly.

I squawked in protest. "That's not a real answer," I laughed, feigning annoyance.

"Hmmm," he said, kissing me again, this time languidly, exploring and tasting and teasing with his tongue.

"Neither is that," I admonished. He ignored me, flipping me into my back and nuzzling into my breasts.

I stroked a hand down his back and let out a contented sigh. A month ago I had loathed this male, and now I was willingly and gloriously naked in his bed. I wasn't quite sure what to think of myself.

"Hadrian," I said, dragging his attention away from my breasts and back up to my face.

"Hmmm?" He said again, kissing a line of fire up the column of my throat as he finally lifted his head to meet my eyes.

I hesitated. I didn't want to break this spell we were under, but I wasn't good at playing things by ear or going with the flow. I liked to plan and know things and see how pieces worked together, and this was no different.

"What is it?" He asked, propping himself up, suddenly serious as he sensed my hesitation.

"What are we?" I asked, feeling like it wasn't quite the right question to ask, but not sure what the right one was.

His serious expression relaxed and he stroked my

cheek, looking down at me.

"Lovers," he said, placing a soft kiss on my lips. He lifted back up and added, "partners," followed by another soft kiss on my lips. He grinned wickedly.

"Very, very good friends?" I laughed and he kissed me again. "We are whatever you want us to be."

I smiled, unable to resist him when he was being affectionate.

"And what do you want us to be?" I asked, smiling up at him. He gave me a long look, and bent to kiss me once more.

"Everything," he rumbled, kissing my neck, my jaw, my collarbone. My stomach flipped as I realized he was serious, and that I might feel the same.

Sighing I wrapped myself into his arms, legs tucked between his, and let sleep claim me.

I woke still in his arms as pale daylight escaped the curtains.

"Good morning," he rumbled, planting a kiss on the top of my head.

"Did you sleep?" I asked, frowning up at him. He had spent two days shadow walking the countryside, and I knew he must be tired.

"Some," he replied, pressing his lips to mine. I smiled up at him as he gently stroked my face.

"You can sleep more if you need it," I said. "I know you're tired." He shook his head.

"I have a long list of things I would rather do right now than sleep," he rumbled, bending to kiss my eyelids, my nose, my forehead, before slowly moving down my neck.

My stomach fluttered as he woke me in the most delicious way possible, licking and kissing and nipping until I was humming with need again.

"I think," he said between languid kisses, "that if I could spend the rest of my life like this, I would die a happy male."

I nipped his lip. "No dying," I chastised, heart thumping painfully at the thought. "Just kissing."

He smiled against my lips. "As you say."

Before we could explore more exciting avenues for the morning, a knock sounded on the door.

"I swear, I will burn this damned castle to the ground the next time someone interrupts us," Hadrian growled, standing and pulling on his pants as he tossed me my clothes from last night. I laughed, throwing on the stolen shirt and leggings before he reached the door.

"What," he growled. Seline smiled, looking around him at me. I blushed.

"About time," she purred. Vanth followed, glancing between us.

"About time for what?" He asked, looking bewildered.

"About time that they admitted their feelings for each other," Seline replied, sitting smugly on the couch. I glanced at Hadrian, who raised his brows at me. I didn't bother telling Seline we hadn't specifically admitted any feelings - just acted upon them.

Vanth still looked confused, but sat with Seline.

"What news?" Hadrian asked, leaning on his desk near the couch, arms crossed as if anticipating the worst.

"We managed to set up a chain of communication to

Lord Thorn's holdings," Vanth reported, pulling a paper from under his chest plate and handing it to Hadrian. He scanned it, nodded, then tossed it in the fire.

"Good," he replied. "What else?"

"Lady Aurelia is still half a day from his estate," Seline added. "Plenty of time for Vanth to intercept if you shadow walk him there."

"What are you talking about?" I asked, frowning at Seline, then Hadrian.

"His highness has asked me to guard your friend," Vanth said. "I vow to protect her with my life, my lady" he added, bowing slightly to me.

I looked at Hadrian, who shrugged. "Vanth will glamour himself to be part of her household guard, assigned to stay with her through the wedding," he said, still leaning idly on the desk. "That way, if anything happens, we can easily get her out."

I stood, mouth open in shock.

"You did this?" I asked Hadrian. He nodded.

Heedless of the watching eyes and the roles we were supposed to play, I strode over to him, lifting onto my toes to kiss him fiercely. His arms and darkness wrapped around me, as I whispered against his lips, "thank you."

Seline coughed politely, and I turned slightly. She was grinning, and Vanth stared at us open-mouthed. I smiled shyly.

"And thank you, Vanth," I said, arms still around Hadrian's neck.

"What, no kiss for him?" Hadrian teased, nipping my earlobe.

Seline laughed and Vanth grumbled, his cheeks going slightly pink.

"I suppose I owe you a silver," he said to Seline, irritation bleeding into his voice. She smiled at him.

"Now that everyone knows everything," Hadrian said, removing my arms from his neck and tucking me into his side, "I think it's time to plan the third act of this little venture."

"Third act?" I asked, craning my neck up to see Hadrian's face.

"Hmm," he said, dropping a kiss on my temple, "yes." He faced his friends and advisors. "It's time to get Ember out."

"What?" I shouted, pushing out of his arms toward the couch and whirling on him. "What do you mean, get me out?"

Hadrian crossed his arms in my absence. "The plan was never to keep you here long term," he said sternly, narrowing his eyes at me. "You've helped me win my father's trust. Your mission is done."

"Like hellfire it is!" I shouted. "What will happen to you when your Seelie bride suddenly disappears?"

Hadrian shrugged. "It won't matter. You'll be safe."

"I am not leaving," I said, crossing my arms to mimic his position and adopting my fiercest look.

"You are," Hadrian said, as if the matter were settled.

"Not without you," I countered. "We can all go. Once you have the information you need, we can all make a stand with the Seelie rebellion."

Hadrian shook his head. "I can't leave. My father will bring the might of his armies down on the south if I betray him. I won't risk it."

"If I may," Vanth interjected before I could respond, "I think Lady Ember is right."

We both turned to Vanth, Hadrian with a glare and I

with an encouraging smile.

"Pray go on, Vanth," I encouraged.

"Yes, pray go on," Hadrian mocked. I scowled at him.

"Hadrian, see reason. If your bride flees in the night and you don't go retrieve her, the king will assume you allowed her to leave," Vanth said, looking darkly at Hadrian as he spoke. "It won't be long until he sends his own soldiers to retrieve her, and they won't be gentle."

Hadrian growled low in his throat. Seline rolled her eyes.

"They're right," she said. "If she leaves now, the king will suspect you at best. He won't keep you alive if he thinks you have betrayed him. Either we all go together, or we all stay."

"Then with *that* settled," I said, giving Hadrian a hard look until he sighed and nodded his assent, "we need a plan for all of us to go, or to remove the king and place Hadrian on the throne. I still vote for poison."

Hadrian stiffened.

"It is not so easy to murder, my lady, even with hatred in your heart," he said darkly. "And it would be near impossible for any of us to escape if we murder the king, which someone will suspect me of doing."

"Why not do both?" Vanth asked, brows furrowed in thought. "We plan an assassination, and flee before it is carried out? Head south and hole up with the rebels while recruiting others to our cause?"

Hadrian frowned. "How will we recruit from that great a distance?"

We were silent for a time, contemplating how we might manage both tasks without being caught or accused of murder and treason.

"We'll think on it," said Seline seriously, and she and

Vanth stood. "Hadrian, you'll be expected in the king's councilroom shortly," she reminded, and he nodded as the guards filed out. "Vanth, you should leave now to intercept Lady Aurelia's party."

"I'll pack. Ready in ten?" He asked Hadrian. Hadrian nodded, and Vanth hesitated, looking at us both.

"The mission comes first," he intoned gravely. "Whatever this is," he continued, gesturing between me and Hadrian, "remember that. Goddess knows I want to see you happy, Hadrian. Just be careful." I looked at Hadrian, who was frowning at his friend.

Vanth looked at me and gave me a curt nod before striding out, Seline close behind him.

Hadrian and I stood facing each other for another moment. I wasn't sure what to say after Vanth's warning. Finally, he pulled me toward him, leveling me with a piercing look.

"Ember," he started, lifting a hand to cup my face. "If you stay with me you could be damning yourself to whatever my fate will be." I met his eyes. They shone with fear, not for himself I realized, but for me. "You will not be spared my father's wrath if we are caught."

I met his eyes, steely and silver in the morning light. This male had become so precious to me that the thought of leaving him to his father chilled me to my core. If I could help him by staying, I would do it. I lifted to my toes and planted a light kiss on his lips.

"I would rather be damned with you than without."

CHAPTER 25

The dream began the same way it always did. There was the cold rock and the sky full of stars. I felt empty somehow, despite being filled with magic. And slowly the stars winked out as the sky filled with blood.

A sound, like crying or wailing filled my ears. I tried to cover them but found I couldn't move. The sound intensified to a scream, and I realized it was I who was screaming as pain unlike anything I had ever felt raked down my back.

I woke up with a start, sitting up and feeling sweat mingle with tears and fall down my face. Hadrian stirred, reaching for me.

"What is it," he mumbled, pushing himself up on one arm, making the muscles of his chest and shoulder tighten and strain. While normally the sight would thrill me, the aftershocks of the dream made me feel like the skin of my back was on fire.

"A nightmare," I said quietly. Hadrian sat up fully.

"Are you alright?" He asked. It was too dark to see him properly. I lifted my hand to his face, feeling that he was real, and I was here.

Shadows swept out of him and prowled the corners of the room, as if looking for an intruder. Finding none, they retreated, curling around me protectively, sheltering my naked form like a great dog prowling around its master. I ran my fingers through the shadows, feeling warm night-kissed air, and breathed deeply.

Finally, I nodded.

"Yes," I breathed, feeling his shadows surround me with calm and warmth and comfort. Some of them floated up to my face and he batted them away.

"Cursed things," he grumbled. He had explained to me earlier that day, while preparing for another tedious evening of playing our roles for the king, that he controlled the shadows when he willed it, but at other times they acted of their own free will. Perhaps they were an entity of their own that loaned him their power, or maybe they were an extension of his subconscious.

I liked to think of them like a faithful pet, guarding and protecting us, and sometimes teasing and playing. Right now they were in full defense mode.

"I'm fine," I said, mostly to the shadows, which seemed to dissipate a little. Hadrian huffed.

"You clearly have them wrapped around your fingers," he said, watching the shadows curl protectively around my wrists, snaking up my arms and stroking my bare breasts. I laughed, batting them away now too.

"Does it bother you?" I asked, worried that he might resent their attention.

"Not at all," he said, wrapping me in his arms and pulling me down to the bed again. "It shows they have good taste."

I smiled faintly, as his breathing evened and he fell back into sleep.

I couldn't blame him. He had spent the whole day attending meetings, then sparring with the guards and running training drills, then playing politics in the evening. The days were wearing on him.

My day had been spent much less industriously. I wrote to Aurelia, directing the kitchen maid that my letter be sent to Lord Thorn's estate. I helped Mother Vervain with some tinctures while she told me stories about the Seelie Realm before the war, painting pictures with her words of the beauty of the palace, the festivals and celebrations, and the brightness of the stars that blessed the rightful Queen.

"Did you know her?" I asked while crushing dried vermillion in a bowl. She was silent for a moment, looking at me contemplatively as if deciding how much to tell me.

"I did," she said, slowly. "She was a fierce warrior. A powerful Fae. She wanted the best for her people. For our realm."

She looked so sad that I put down the vermillion and went to her, wrapping my arms around her thin frame.

"Thank you, my dear," she said with a sniff. "Now let me show you how you're doing this all wrong."

I smiled at the memory and stroked Hadrian's face

gently, admiring the strong lines of his jaw and chin, and the long dark lashes that framed his eyes.

"Ember," he mumbled, half asleep, but clearly aware that I wasn't.

"Hmm?" I asked, trying to settle into some semblance of calm after the dream.

"Marry me."

I snapped my eyes open. His were still closed, but the corner of his mouth lifted in the ghost of a smile, so I knew he was awake. I sat back up and he groaned, throwing an arm over his face.

"What do you mean?" I asked, heart pounding. Had he really just asked me to marry him? Like, actually marry him? Not pretend?

He pushed himself up, lighting the candle on the table next to his side of the bed, then turned to face me, still propped on one elbow.

"I mean," he said, gazing at me seriously. "Marry me. Be my wife, my partner, my lover." He stroked a finger down my cheek and under my chin, lifting my eyes to his. "Be my mate."

My heart still pounded. I had no words. Hadrian kissed me softly as I sat there completely dumbstruck.

"You don't have to answer now," he conceded, seeing my hesitation and reading it as uncertainty. "I wanted to wait until a better time to ask, but I honestly don't know if there will be one for us." He kissed me again gently. "But I can wait for your answer."

"No," I blurted out, then panicked and amended, "not no, I won't marry you, I mean, no I don't want you to have to wait for an answer. I just…" I paused, still feeling out of my depth and uncertain what to say. I settled on "why?"

"Why?" He repeated, eyebrows raising. I nodded. He frowned. "You don't know?"

I shook my head, and he pressed his lips to mine again. The kiss was claiming, searing. It relayed in it every feeling that he hadn't yet spoken aloud.

"Because," he said quietly, breaking the kiss to speak against my lips, "I have loved you since the moment you first called me a monster. Since the moment you said you'd rather take poison than pretend to marry me." He paused, swallowing some emotion. "If you still feel the same as you did then, a word from you will silence me on this. But I have loved you since the moment I first saw you. Somehow, I just knew."

"Knew what?" I whispered, still bewildered and wondering how my calling him a monster could possibly translate into love, while simultaneously feeling like fireworks were exploding inside me.

"That you are my balance, my equal, my partner," he said, sitting up fully and cupping my face in his hands. "The light to my darkness, life to my death. You are my mate, and I want only you." He gazed down at me, and I could see his love there, like a band of golden light between us. The tug of connection, which had been quiet since our first night together, pulled taught and stretched between our hearts.

"Mates are chosen," I protested. "We have free will. We are not fated by the goddess or by some divine power," I added breathlessly, feeling too much and not enough all at once. "The bond must be chosen willingly."

"I know," he said, shaking his head, "but you feel it too." He motioned between us. "The pull. Whatever that is. I think it's a mating bond."

"You suspected on our first night," I said, a statement more than a question. He nodded.

"I didn't want to scare you if it wasn't true, but I've been prodding at it since that night, testing its boundaries, and I think that's what it is. Seline described her bond with her mate as a physical pull, and that's what I feel for you."

"You asked her?" I said, vaguely realizing I was focusing on the most unimportant parts of what he was saying. He nodded.

"She said she recognized it when she first assessed your spell," he said, stroking my cheek as he explained. "She didn't want to force it on us by revealing it. She doesn't understand how it can be there."

I gave a mental tug on the connection between us. It tugged back. Sinking into my mind the way I did when Seline was trying to break my spell, I prodded its boundaries, feeling for its beginning and its end.

"Ember," he said softly, bringing me back to him, and smiling down at me with such hope and desire and love in his eyes that it made my heart ache, "Even without it, the bond, whatever it is, I would *choose* you. A thousand times. I would willingly bind myself to you every day for the rest of our days, if you let me."

A tear escaped and ran down my cheek. He brushed it away, much like he had done on that night he first kissed me and offered me a beginning. This fierce, strong, kind male chose me. Wanted me. Loved me. If I were truly honest with myself, I wanted him just as much.

"You told me that marriages are rarely happy," I said, pressing my forehead to his.

"Ours will be," he replied matter of factly, brushing

his nose against mine.

"We'll fight and bicker every day," I said, still reeling that this male wanted me as much as I wanted him.

"I look forward to it." Another brush off the nose.

"Yes," I breathed.

"Yes?" He replied, sitting up straighter, bringing me with him.

"Yes," I laughed, another tear escaping as I looked at him and finally voiced what I felt, what I had been feeling for a while now, since even before the forest when I first held him. "I love you and I want you and I choose you too. Yes."

We collided in a tangle of lips and tongues and teeth and bodies, words no longer able to convey our desperation for each other.

In moments I was on his lap and he was in me. I shuddered around him as rolled his hips up to meet mine and teased my lip between his teeth.

"Tell me you want this," he growled, punctuating the question with another thrust of his hips. "Tell me you want me, only me, from now on."

"I want this. You," I breathed, moaning slightly at the feeling of him moving in me, "you are mine."

He rumbled his approval and thrust faster, deeper, lowering his fingers to stroke the place between my legs that wrought so much pleasure. I gasped.

"And you are mine," he said, "only mine. To worship. To adore. To protect. To fuck." He emphasized each word with a hard thrust and a sweep of his fingers, over and over, until I clenched around him, release barreling through me. I cried out and he gripped my hips, nipping at the bud of my nipple as he made sure I felt every wave and crest of pleasure.

"To love," he rumbled against my lips, still thrusting into me, but more gently now, still eliciting sparks of pleasure. He lowered me gently to the bed and I wrapped my legs around his hips as he devoured my mouth, claiming every sound and moan of pleasure as he continued to thrust into me.

"To honor. To revere. To serve. Only you." He thrust in at each word. I stroked down his spine, his backside, his thighs , feeling the strong muscles of his body as they contracted around me. He came, groaning as he spilled himself in me.

We lay like that for a long moment, my legs wrapped around his hips, him still inside me as he kissed me, languidly and lazily as if we had all the time in the world to do this. I shivered as aftershocks still rocked through me, and he finally lifted himself to meet my eyes.

"My mate. My love," he murmured, planting an achingly light kiss on my swollen lips. "My Queen."

CHAPTER 26

Mother Vervain kept shooting me sideways glances as I worked with her the next morning in the kitchens. Whenever I felt her staring, I turned to see her frown and look away. This went on for a good two hours before I was finally brave enough to break the silence.

"What is it, Mother Vervain?" I asked, sighing and putting down the herbs I was grinding. "Tell me what is bothering you."

Mother Vervain, who had been sitting by the fire in her ridiculous numbers of layers and embroidering, of all things, sighed like she alone carried the weight of both realms.

"You've done something," she chastised. I frowned, thinking over my actions that morning to figure out what I'd done wrong. Mother Vervain waved a hand dismissively. "Not this morning, child. I mean there's something different. I just can't figure out what it is."

Hadrian and I had not told anyone about our now very real betrothal, not even Seline. She had looked at us with resigned forbearance as we shared secret smiles over breakfast, and then she had dragged Hadrian away telling him she needed to go stab something. I very much hoped it was not him.

I shrugged noncommittally and returned to my task, trying to ignore Mother Vervain's continued attention.

"You know," she said, still embroidering in front of the hearth. "You remind me of my daughter."

I paused, turning with a smile to the dear old lady.

"I do?" I asked. She nodded sadly, and my smile fell.

"She's gone now," said Mother Vervain, stitching in time with the cracking fire, "but she was a powerful healer. A strong magic wielder. She wove spells that could not be broken, even by the Unseelie King."

I frowned, putting down my herbs and coming to kneel in front of Mother Vervain, taking her hands in mine.

"Was she a noble lady?" I asked. Mother Vervain let out a bark of mirth and smiled, as if amused by some secret joke.

"Yes," she said, "we were quite high up."

"Why are you telling me this?" I asked, studying her ancient face, which was filled with remorse and loss.

"Because, my dear child," said Mother Vervain, patting my hands, then adjusting her layers of shawls more firmly around her shoulders. "When the Unseelie King finally came for her, not even her magic was strong enough to survive him."

Her piercing gaze met mine and my blood chilled.

"Hadrian is not like his father," she continued, adding tiny roses to her design as if we weren't talking about her daughter's demise. "The king made sure of that by taking his mother from him. She was a lovely female," She added, patting my hand again. "And she would have liked you." My heart ached a little at that, wishing I could have met the female who raised such a male.

"But he still wields the same power of death." She looked up, eyes sad. "Life and death must always be kept in balance, but in the end, death claims us all. Be sure you understand what you're getting into with him."

After the warning from Mother Vervain, I felt anxious and uncertain the whole day. I knew Hadrian was not his father, and I trusted him. I wasn't sure what the warning was meant for, other than to put me off balance. Mother Vervain rightfully distrusted the Unseelie court, and I tried to chalk up her warning to an extension of that distrust.

Another unsuccessful afternoon of attempting to unlock my magic passed. Seline had given up and dozed off after the second hour, but I had kept up my assault on the nothingness inside me, trying to find some hole or crack or weakness in the spell that locked up my magic. With no success after an hour, I stopped. I knew I'd be facing the court again tonight, and I needed to not be exhausted for it.

I had chosen a new black gown that night which the seamstress had dropped off earlier, along with a mountain of other clothes. It glittered in the light, and elegant panels of organza fluttered in place of sleeves, making it look like I trailed my own shadows around me. With Hadrian's power on display, we would be a formidable pair.

He arrived, exhausted as usual and covered in mud and melted snow. I squeaked as he reached to kiss me, swishing my skirts out of the way to protect them from his grime, and sending him to bathe. He returned half an hour later, clean and dressed, obsidian crown and spiked pauldrons in place.

I raised a brow at him.

"Are we doing battle tonight?" I asked, as he trekked over to don his usual assortment of weapons.

"Court is always a battle," he quipped. "Sometimes I like to remind the court exactly who they are dealing with."

"Hmm," I hummed, watching him. "Warrior Prince, Prince of Death, when do I get a title?" I joked.

He finished strapping on daggers and swords and turned to me, a glint in his eye.

"How about starting with 'Princess'?" He asked, pulling a large, velvet box from beneath the bed and placing it in my lap. The armor made it impossible to sit next to me on the bed, so he leaned against the bedpost.

"What is it?" I asked warily, smoothing my hand over the velvet case.

"You'll have to open it to find out," he said, grinning like a boy, rather than a male fully past maturity.

I opened the cover and let out a small gasp.

"There is no official crown for the queen, as my father did not marry," Hadrian said, lifting the obsidian circlet from its resting place in the box and holding it in front of me. It was a feminine mirror to his own obsidian spikes, crystals of obsidian pointing sharply up at the front of the circlet and smoothing to finely cut stone toward the back. It caught the light, beautiful and terrible all at once.

"While I would rather adorn you in gold and diamonds," Hadrian said, kneeling before me to place the circlet atop my head, "I felt like this was a better statement for our performance tonight."

I felt an odd twist of joy and sadness at his words. While I knew we still had roles to play as long as the Unseelie King lived, I hadn't thought about how we would have to still act, even though now our betrothal was genuine.

"It's beautiful," I said, meeting his eyes. He frowned.

"What's wrong, my love," he said gently, lifting my chin with his fingers to gaze into my eyes. The bond thrummed between us, and I had to resist the urge to lean into him.

"How long will we have to pretend, do you think?" I asked. "To be the Prince of Death and the Ice Queen, I mean. When will I be able to kiss you in front of court without risking our lives?"

He smiled a little sadly and said, "I don't know. But not forever," he promised, sealing his words with a light kiss on my lips. I leaned my forehead against his and sighed. Mother Vervain's story still had me all twisted up and anxious, but I tried to put it aside for him.

We arrived in the throne room via shadows to find the assembled crowd quiet, standing on either side of the aisle that split the room and led to the spiked throne.

"Ah, my future daughter joins us at last," the king said, beady eyes gleaming down at me. Hadrian still had a hand on my waist from shadow walking, and he quickly dropped it.

"It is time for you to be tested, pet," the king continued, gesturing to a table in front of him on which five identical goblets stood. I moved toward the table, Hadrian behind me.

"Not you, my son," the king said slyly, sending his oily shadows to hold Hadrian in place. "I don't want you helping her."

Cold dread filled me as I walked to the table alone. The five goblets were filled with identical dark red liquid, probably the bitter northern wine the Unseelie preferred. Something felt wrong with them.

"I hear you have the gift of healing," said the king, "and that you saved my son with this gift."

I said nothing, and the king continued.

"To make sure you are worthy to be his bride, I would like to test this gift." He gestured at the goblets in front of me. "One of these is just wine. The other four are poison. You must decide which to drink."

I looked up at the king. He gave away nothing with his beady stare. The raven fluttered down to perch on his shoulder and fixed me with its red eye. I felt a tug of fear in my core from Hadrian.

I took a breath and examined the wine in each goblet, rotating the glasses to examine how the liquid moved. They seemed exactly the same. I put down the last goblet and reached again for the first.

I was a healer. I knew plants and I knew poisons. I carefully sniffed the wine, trying to separate the bitter wine from the poison that might be hidden in the glass. There was a strong additional scent there, slightly musky. Nightshade.

I picked up the second glass and repeated the process. I wrinkled my nose at the sickly scent. Definitely hemlock.

Again and again I smelled the wine, identifying the poisons within. Snakeroot. Oleander. Rosary pea.

"And what is your choice, pet?" The king asked. The nobility around the room whispered and snickered.

"None, your majesty," I said confidently, feeling a wave of relief from Hadrian through our connection.

"None?" Barked the king. "None was not an option."

I smiled faintly. Coldly.

"If I recall correctly, your majesty only said I must choose which to drink, not that I must drink one," I said carefully, injecting as much haughtiness into my voice as I could. I felt Hadrian's approval faintly from the end of the bond.

"All five goblets contain poison," I finished, "so I choose none."

A smattering of applause circulated the room, quickly silenced by the king's growl.

"But we must test your decision," the king said, a new wicked gleam in his eyes. He must have released Hadrian, for he moved next to me to face his father. "If you will not drink yourself, then you must choose who will drink each goblet."

The quiet in the room grew thick with anticipation. This was the entertainment for tonight, I realized. The king would corrupt my soul as he had tried to corrupt Hadrian.

"This seems ill-advised, your majesty," Hadrian said coldly, gesturing to the room at large. "You would sacrifice five loyal subjects for the sake of this game?"

The king smirked.

"Afraid she will choose you, boy?" He asked.

Hadrian opened his mouth to argue, but I stopped him as subtly as possible with a hand on his arm,

"Your majesty, are the Fae to whom I give these goblets bound to drink by blood?" I asked.

"Yes," the king said cruelly, looking around his court. "All but me, of course."

Anxious whispering had broken out around the room, and panic bloomed in me as I tried to figure out how to not kill anyone.

"You may of course choose to drink the wine yourself," the king added. "But you must choose now."

I nodded, lifting the first goblet. I couldn't think of a way out of killing anyone other than sacrificing myself and Hadrian, either through death by poison or by discovery, which left me only one choice. The room stilled. I began to walk toward the Fae along the nearest wall, and as I had hoped I felt a gentle tug. Hadrian was using our connection to guide me, a little to the right. The Fae backed away from me, until I singled out my first victim, forcing him to take the cup.

I knew that what I was about to do would blacken my soul, but I trusted that Hadrian would choose victims that deserved their fate. One by one, Hadrian guided and tugged me around the room, delivering death to five Fae males. Each sneered as he took the goblet but didn't drink, hoping an order from their king may yet save them.

When the five were chosen, I returned to my place in the center of the room. The king vibrated with fury, but commanded, "drink."

All five males shouted in protest as their hands moved without their consent to bring the poisoned wine to their lips. Each choked and spluttered, doing everything they could to resist the magic binding my decision. Something fractured inside me as I realized what I had done.

Five males fell to the ground dead.

"It seems my bride was correct," Hadrian said coldly, taking my hand and squeezing gently despite the onlookers. He must sense the turmoil in me, barely held in check as the weight of what I had done settled upon me.

"Indeed," the king said, looking at me with both interest and wicked intent. "Quite a gift for a Seelie Fae of limited connections. I think we can mold her into a worthy Queen, you and I."

Hadrian nodded once, face unsmiling as we joined the crowd. Several ladies wept as guards came to remove the corpses.

"Why are you all standing around?" The king bellowed.

The crowd moved, music and chatter starting up as Fae skirted the corpses to claim a glass of wine and whisper over what I had done. I felt sick to my stomach, bile rising in my throat as I saw the five males drop over and over in my mind's eye.

"Hold on a little longer," Hadrian rumbled quietly, leaning down so it appeared that he was just brushing the hair off my shoulder.

Several important looking males scrambled around the king, asking questions and demanding things. Hadrian left to sort out the mess my murders had created. Seline, who had glided up to guard me, put a comforting hand on my back.

"It was fast," she whispered, repeating what she had

told Hadrian only days ago.

CHAPTER 27

"Who were they," I croaked after I had finished heaving my guts up. Hadrian crouched next to me in the bathing chamber, holding my hair out of the way and stroking my back as I was sick.

"Two were commanders of the guard who violated their female recruits," he replied, tracing soothing lines down my back as I pictured the men collapsing. I heaved again. "Two more were powerful supporters. Nobles. Both had committed murders on my father's orders."

He handed me a cloth to wipe my mouth and I took it gratefully, still feeling like I might not be done.

"And the last?" I rasped.

"The general of my father's forces," Hadrian replied grimly. "I can't recount his crimes to you, it would take too long. It was a good strategic choice."

I nodded, still feeling sick.

"It doesn't matter how strategic the choices are though," Hadrian rumbled, still stroking my back as I took in shuddering breaths. "Or how evil the males are. It is never so easy to take a life as one might think."

I remembered him saying something to that effect back when I first agreed to this. I had no idea then how right he was. I sat back, leaning my head against the cool tile of the wall. Hadrian didn't move, didn't force me up or make me acknowledge my choices. He sat with me through it as I wrestled with what I had done.

"Is this how it feels for you?" I asked weakly, looking up to meet his eyes. They were dark, their normal gray burned with fury, not at me but for what I had been forced to do.

"Every time," he said.

After I sat for a few minutes without being sick again, Hadrian scooped me up in his arms and headed toward the bath. It was already full of steaming water, scented with lavender and chamomile, calming herbs.

"Did you do this?" I asked weakly as he gently removed the dress, the crown, the dagger strapped to my thigh.

"I haven't known Mother Vervain all these years without picking up a thing or two," he quipped, lifting me into the tub.

I sighed as the hot water engulfed me. A broken, shattered part of me wondered if it would be better just to slip below the surface of the water and never emerge.

"No," Hadrian said sharply, cupping my face so I was forced to meet his eyes, "don't even think it."

"How did you know what I was thinking," I croaked, wondering if I had somehow projected my despair at him through our bond.

"Because I have seen that haunted look and I have felt what you are feeling," he said, lifting my shoulder so he could rub soap over my back. Clearly some of whatever we were feeling could make it down the bond to the other, whether we wanted it to or not. I wondered if that had been true since we had first met, or only since we had recognized what it was.

Hadrian leaned me back against the lip of the tub and studied my face, fury and compassion warring for dominance. I wondered if this is how I had looked to him when our places were swapped after he had been forced to torture those prisoners to death. I lifted a wet hand to cup his face and he turned into it, kissing my palm.

"You had no choice," he rumbled, "but it doesn't make it any easier."

A tear slipped down my cheek. Was I always going to be crying now in front of this male? I brushed it away angrily.

He leaned down and kissed me tenderly. There was no heat in it this time, no wicked promise of pleasure or flame of desire. It was comfort and understanding and compassion and love. I felt like I didn't deserve any of it.

I let him bathe me and dry me and dress me like I was a helpless child. When he tucked me into bed, I pulled him down with me. He held me, telling me stories about his favorite horse when he was a boy, the time he let a toad loose in Mother Vervain's kitchen and she threatened to turn him into one, his first kiss with a noble girl at a midwinter festival, which had gone terribly wrong when his shadows had shoved her into a water trough of their own accord.

I laughed, and then I cried, and he held me through it all.

"At least I know now why they pushed her," he finished, smiling into my temple as his shadows curled around me like a blanket.

"Why?" I asked, almost asleep having wrung myself dry of emotion. He kissed the top of my head and held me a little tighter.

"Because they were waiting for you."

At first I thought that it was the searing pain down my back at the end of the dream that woke me again.

Hadrian cursed, luckily wearing clothes this time as he went to the door. It was pitch black, and I didn't understand who would be knocking so late. I sat up, rubbing my eyes.

Seline was at the door, wearing nightclothes and breathless.

"It's Vanth," she gasped, leaning on the doorframe for support, "we got a message."

I sprang from the bed and rushed over to the door.

"What happened?" I asked, panic rising in me. She shook her head.

"I'm not sure," she said, wringing her hands, "but he asked for Hadrian to come now."

I looked up at Hadrian in panic and he nodded, seizing a belt of daggers and his sword from where he had left them and pulling on boots and cloak.

I hadn't thought about Aurelia in almost two days, and horrifying guilt and anxiety ate at me as I pictured everything that might have happened to her.

Hadrian swept me up in a firm embrace, crushing his lips against mine before disappearing into shadow.

Seline stayed with me as we waited, lighting a fire in the hearth and holding my hand as I sat in tense silence. I wondered if she was as worried for Vanth as I was for Hadrian.

"When my mate died," she said quietly, "I felt it. It was like my heart had stopped beating."

I looked at her, squeezing her hand.

"Why are you telling me this?" I asked.

"Because as long as you feel Hadrian in here," she said, placing her palm on my chest, "he is safe."

An hour passed. Then two. Dawn light began creeping in through the curtains when I felt a sharp tug around my midsection.

"They're back," I said, standing and throwing on a pair of boots.

"What?" Seline asked, following me as I sprinted out into the hall following the tug.

"I can feel him. Kitchens," I replied breathlessly, running down the hall in my nightgown. I pictured all of the awful things that might have happened to Aurelia or Vanth or Hadrian and panic swelled, calmed only by the steady thrum from the bond.

We skidded to a stop at the entrance to the kitchen. Mother Vervain was bustling around in her layers of shawls tending to Vanth, who coughed loudly and wheezed as he tried to speak. He was covered in ash and smoke. When I stepped into the room, Hadrian crushed me to his chest. He also smelled like smoke and looked singed around the edges, and he was covered in blood. I frantically patted him down looking for the source of the injury, but he seemed unharmed when I looked up into his face, confused.

"It's Aurelia," he croaked, pulling me by the hand to the giant table in the middle of the kitchen.

She was there, covered in blood which was oozing from a wound in her side. It had been wrapped haphazardly, as if done while in movement. She was sickly pale in the firefly light of the kitchen, and I let out a cry as I went to her.

"What happened?" I shouted as I tore the bandages from her, needing a clear picture of the injury. My hands shook as I lifted the bandages and saw the damage, a deep gash surrounded by lines of snaking corruption.

Hadrian launched his shadows in a bubble to dampen my anguished cries as I frantically checked Aurelia's pulse. It was thready, but she was still breathing.

"I need aniseed," I said, trying to inject professional calm into my voice. Aurelia was a patient and I was her healer. She needed me to be objective. "And woodsorrel. A paste," I added, shouting instructions to no one in particular. Seline took over tending to Vanth so that Mother Vervain could help me.

"Hadrian, I need you to put pressure here," I said, pointing above the wound as I tried to clean it. It was so deep, and Aurelia's breathing was becoming more shallow with each minute that passed.

"Can you heal her?" Hadrian asked, moving next to me and applying pressure above the wound. He looked exhausted, and I knew his power was waning. "I won't be able to hold back death for long. You have to free your magic now and heal her."

"I don't know how," I snapped in frustration, trying to thread a needle in the dim light. "It was an accident when I did it to you."

"It wasn't an accident," Hadrian insisted, still pressing down as blood continued to weep from the wound. "You willed me to heal, and I did. You didn't even like me then. You love Aurelia. You can do this."

Mother Vervain was on the other side of Aurelia. She took the needle from me and threaded it, motioning for me to take Hadrian's place. Hadrian shifted so I could put my hands over the open wound. trying to keep the blood in Aurelia's body.

"Think of magic as a river inside you, child," she said quietly as she held the paste. "The river is dammed and you must break it to let it flow."

"Feel it here," said Hadrian, placing his bloody palms flat over mine, pushing his power into me as we fought against her death. Sweat had broken out on his forehead and beads of black ash trailed down his face."Pull it into your hands and release it into Aurelia."

I closed my eyes, still feeling for a spark of anything that might be my magic. I felt Hadrian's shadows nearby, warm and comforting, but nothing in the empty place where my magic should be.

"Faster, my dear," came Mother Vervain's worried voice.

"Give her a minute," Hadrian growled.

I shook my head, blocking them both out and trying to concentrate. I tried to picture what I had felt when I healed Hadrian, how desperate I was to close his wound and for him to live. I imagined the wound like a plant growing in reverse, filling myself with the desperation I had felt then and pushing it as deeply into Aurelia as I could.

I pictured her laughing smile when we were children

and she convinced me she could fly. I saw the way she looked at Aspen, and the love that she felt for him. I heard her telling me to guard my left and handing me her dagger. Light blossomed, brightening under my hands.

"Keep pushing," Hadrian encouraged as I pictured her wound closing, her future wedding to Aspen, her blond haired future children sleeping in cradles, then growing and playing with mine. My black haired, gray eyed children.

I gritted my teeth as pain erupted down my back, focusing all of my energy on Aurelia and her future and her life, pulling her desperately back from the darkness. Stars erupted around me, puncturing Hadrian's shadows and driving them back as the light fought for control over Aurelia's life.

Through what seemed like a thick haze, I faintly heard Hadrian shouting for me, Mother Vervain rushing to me with towels, Aurelia lifting a hand to touch something behind me, and such terrible screaming. My screaming, I realized, as I pushed my power into my best friend.

The light died and the room went quiet as I panted and sobbed, great wracking breaths heaving from me as I felt blood and sweat and pain pour down my back.

"Ember," sighed Aurelia weakly from the table. I looked down at her, her face still pale from loss of blood and strain.

"Yes, I'm here," I sobbed, leaning down to kiss her cheek and stroke the hair off her face. I faintly felt something patting my back and Hadrian telling someone to get Nisha and Erebus ready. "I'm here," I sobbed again, "and I'm going to take care of you."

She shook her head gently, smiling faintly.

"No, Em, look," she said, reaching up behind me again. "Em, you have wings."

CHAPTER 28

The next hour or two or possibly day was a blur. I felt completely drained, having poured out all of my power to save Aurelia. I felt myself being jostled as I was moved, and I remember struggling to hold on to Aurelia's hand.

"I've got her. I've got you," came Hadrian's voice from what seemed like a great distance.

I felt us moving in and out of the shadows. Someone held me at all times, sometimes Hadrian, sometimes Seline or Vanth. At one point I felt Hadrian kiss me, whispering that he would be back as soon as he could.

When I woke fully, I recognized my bedroom in my uncle's estate. Outside the window, warm sunlight beamed down, Autumn leaves rustling in the woods beyond. I blinked, sitting up, fighting the wave of nausea that engulfed me, and finding Seline dozing in a chair near my door.

I croaked, trying to speak and finding my throat completely dry. Seline started awake and rushed to me, holding a glass of water up to my lips.

"Thank you," I rasped, pushing the glass from me. "What happened? Where is Hadrian and Aurelia? And my uncle? How are we here?"

Seline smiled, breathing out a relieved sigh. "Asking a thousand questions is a good sign, I think," she said, smiling. "Everyone is safe. Hadrian will be back soon with reinforcements. You've been out for a day and a half."

"What?" I exclaimed, sitting up fighting another wave of nausea and feeling my back ache behind me. Something strange felt like it was stuck on my back, and I reached up to pull it off, stilling when I felt the silky smooth membrane.

I looked at Seline, who nodded and helped me up, guiding me to the mirror. I looked pale and haggard, my hair hanging in messy auburn tangles around two large translucent wings. I turned, examining them from the back. They emerged from my back, about halfway down, where the skin was raw and torn and still bloody. The wings themselves appeared colorless, thin milky veins running over the membranes in symmetrical swoops. The phases of the moon and stars traveled a celestial path around the edges of each wing. I tried to move them and winced. I hurt all over.

I frowned down at my hands, which had glowed so brightly with light as I healed my friend. I felt the warm hum of magic in my sternum filling the void that had once been there.

"I have magic," I whispered, marveling as I pulled the light into my palms again to inspect. A beat hummed in my chest, responding to the magic.

"Hadrian is coming," I said absently, seconds before he stepped out of shadow into my room, causing Seline to jump. He scarcely spared a glance for his sister, striding over to me and kissing me firmly.

"I'll give you two some time," Seline said, backing out of the room quickly. Hadrian nodded absently, looking down at me as Seline left. His lips were on mine again before she had even closed the door, and I threaded my fingers into his soft, dark hair, moaning a little as he kissed me. He moved a hand from my face to my back and I gasped as hot pain sliced through me.

"I'm sorry," he breathed, pressing his forehead to mine and lifting his hands away from my back. "I forgot."

"Me too," I winced, clasping his face and making him kiss me again until the pain subsided. If he could just never stop kissing me, that would be ideal.

Without another word he scooped me up carefully into his arms and moved to the bed. My stomach did a little flip, but he simply sat, stretching out his long legs and gathering me onto his lap. He arranged some pillows around me to keep pressure off my back as best as he could.

"My love," he breathed, forehead touching mine again, his eyes closed as he seemed to whisper a prayer of relief to the goddess. He opened his eyes to meet mine, silver swirling in their gray depths.

"You were magnificent." He pressed his lips to mine in the ghost of a kiss, but pulled back before I could deepen it. I growled, and he laughed.

"We will have time for that later," he promised, nipping my lip and smoothing out the little hurt with his thumb. "There's a lot to talk about before we can get to that."

I sighed mournfully, making him laugh again.

"I suppose we have to talk about these," I said, gesturing behind me to my ravaged back. "And this," I said, pouring magic into my palms and making them glow faintly.

"We do," Hadrian agreed, kissing my nose. "But not yet. I think you and I are missing some key pieces of the story, and we will need some help filling in the gaps." I frowned, but he kissed me again lightly, effectively distracting me from my confusion.

"What we do need to talk about," he said, pulling back again with a little shake of his head, "is our current situation." He gestured to the room at large,

"We are in my uncle's estate," I said, and he nodded with a little smirk.

"Very good," he mocked. I flicked his nose and he wrinkled it at me.

"Where is my uncle?" I asked, accepting that we needed to talk about the specifics before I left the room so I knew which role or act I would be playing.

"He fled when I showed up here with you," Hadrian said, frowning. "When your magic emerged, this was the only place I could think to go that was far enough away that my father wouldn't immediately follow. He can't shadow walk, having never come this far south. You need to have a place in mind when you step into nothing," Hadrian said, gently stroking a finger against the tip of one of the wings. My wings. I shivered.

"Does it tickle?" He asked seriously, as if

contemplating the strategic importance of my wings tickling me.

"A little," I confessed. "They're too sore for anything to tickle really." I wondered what it would feel like when they were healed and whole and he stroked his finger down them again. Warmth pooled low, and he snapped my attention back to him with a little kiss.

"No distractions, not yet," he said, his eyes molten as if his mind had also traveled to the exciting possibilities wings might present us.

"I had to shadow walk everyone as quickly as possible," he continued, taking one of my hands in his and lacing our fingers. "When Aspen saw Aurelia, he accepted my rushed explanations, of course, but your Uncle protested, preparing to go to the king with my betrayal." Hadrian paused, and I nodded. My uncle would betray anyone, including his own son, to advance his position.

"We locked him in his rooms until I could decide what to do about him, but he was gone the next day, along with a small contingent of his staff," Hadrian continued. "The ones who remain are probably loyal, but we can't be sure." I nodded.

"I had to make several jumps to get everyone here safely," he continued, squeezing my hand. "It's why you probably feel so terrible. I had to borrow some of your power to do it."

"You can do that?" I asked in wonder. He shrugged.

"I did, so I suppose yes," he said, frowning. "I just knew I needed to get everyone out, and I pulled on everything I had to do it. I didn't realize some of the power was yours until I felt the glow. I'm sorry, for taking it without your permission." I shook my head, lifting my free hand to his face.

"Never apologize for saving people," I said. "I would gladly give all of myself to help you." He huffed.

"You almost did," he said, chiding himself. "I pulled too much and you collapsed. That's why your memory is probably murky. What do you remember last?"

I frowned, thinking through the haze of soup that made up my memories of the last few days.

"I remember screaming," I said quietly, "and pain," I added looking into his eyes again. He swallowed, looking fierce.

"If I never hear you make that sound again, it will be too soon," he said, pressing a gentle kiss to my lips.

"Mother Vervain had to stop the bleeding while you took care of Aurelia," he continued, shuddering as he remembered the whole horrible ordeal. "Vanth is still coughing. He inhaled a lot of smoke, but Mother Vervain says he will make a full recovery eventually."

"Smoke?" I asked. He nodded. "When I arrived at the border of Lord Thorn's lands, the estate was on fire. Vanth and I got Aurelia out, but she had already been stabbed and left for dead." I tightened my grip on his hand.

"Did you find Thorn?" I asked angrily. "Did he do this to her?"

"I'm not sure," Hadrian replied, mirroring my fury, "We will have to wait for Aurelia to be well enough to tell that story. There was no body."

"Aurelia," I said, sitting up straighter, panic squeezing my heart. "I need to check on her. Is she alright?" I started to wriggle, trying to stand. Hadrian helped me up.

"If you insist, I will take you to her," he said,

catching me under the arms as I swayed slightly, "but I promise she is well. You were able to stop the bleeding, and remove the corruption. Mother Vervain stitched the wound when we arrived, and she is resting as comfortably as can be expected."

"Mother Vervain is here too?" I asked, trying to picture the ancient Seelie female puttering around my uncle's rose gardens, Aspen's rose gardens now, I supposed, wrapped in her layers of shawls. A thought struck me about her that I decided I would examine later. I looked up into Hadrian's face imploringly.

"Please?" I asked. "I just need to see for myself."

Hadrian sighed like a male oppressed and scooped me back into his arms.

"Only if you let me carry you like the delicate blossom you are, my queen," he teased, kicking the door open and striding down the hall as I wrapped my arms around his neck.

"Very well, my king," I replied, and he kissed me soundly, pausing so he didn't run into a wall or a door. I laughed as we broke away.

Aurelia was in a Aspen's room. Seline and Vanth were sitting on the floor outside, chatting quietly, but stood as we approached. They were both in plain clothes I noticed, rather than the spiked armor of their positions.

"My King," Vanth said, his voice still raspy from inhaling smoke. He had a nasty burn stretching down his neck below his shirt and I winced. He bowed, "my Queen."

I glanced at Hadrian at the use of the titles and he mouthed, "later."

"Stand down, Vanth," he said to his friend. "Why don't you both go rest. We will come find you when we are done."

"And let me help you with that burn later," I added. Seline looked at Vanth with concern, but she nodded, dragging Vanth away while he coughed.

Hadrian knocked, and I raised my eyebrows at him.

"What if they're busy?" I whispered, waggling my brows suggestively. Hadrian rolled his eyes.

"Then they'd better unbusy themselves," he said, speaking much louder than necessary. I laughed and shushed him.

"What?" He asked accusingly. "You're heavy."

I glared at him and he grinned as the door opened.

"Aspen!" I cried, throwing my arms around him, which was awkward for all parties involved as Hadrian was still holding me. He pulled me back to adjust his grip on me and Aspen frowned.

"Why are you up?" he asked, shooting an accusatory glare at Hadrian. Clearly the two had not gotten over their initial dislike of each other.

"I tried to stop her," Hadrian lamented. "Please let her see that Aurelia is fine so I can put her down."

Aspen stepped aside and I wriggled out of Hadrian's arms, running to the bed. Aurelia was awake, her face pale and tear streaked, but she smiled weakly and opened her arms as she saw me. I almost threw myself at her before remembering she was injured. And I was injured. I slowed and hugged her gently.

"I was so scared," I whispered, squeezing her a little. She squeezed back.

"Me too," she said. "Thank goodness I was saved by your handsome Prince," she added with a watery smile at Hadrian.

Aspen glowered, and I looked back to see Hadrian

leaning smugly on the door jamb smiling at Aurelia.

"Anytime," he said gallantly, making Aspen frown even more. He looked at Aurelia with none of his former softness or longing, and she could barely meet his eyes.

"What's wrong?" I asked, looking between them with concern. "Have you had a fight?"

"Something like that," Aspen said, giving her a cold stare. And me, I realized belatedly.

"You're angry with me," I said. He nodded.

"At both of us, I'm afraid," said Aurelia in a trembling voice.

"You could have told me," he spat at her, so unlike the cousin that I left behind. "I would have kept your secret. You should have trusted me."

I opened my mouth, unsure how to proceed with Aspen when he was actually angry. His normally jovial personality was gone, replaced by cold fury.

"I'm sorry, Aspen, " I said, going to take his hands. "We couldn't."

"What about you?" He asked angrily. "She told you. She trusted you." Aurelia let out a sob and Aspen turned to storm out. I looked at Hadrian, feeling at a loss.

"I'll go after him," he said quietly, and turned from the room.

I held Aurelia as she cried for a long time.

"What happened," I asked. Aurelia sniffed.

"Well, obviously Thorn didn't buy my loyalty, because he locked me up as soon as I arrived at his estate and made it clear I would not allow him in my bed," she began, settling back into her pillows.

"After two days and multiple attempts to sneak out of my room I realized, I wasn't going to get any useful information if Thorn didn't trust me to be near him.

Vanth and I planned to set the fire as a distraction so I could sneak down to his office and steal his correspondence. I had heard a mention of iron weapons when I first arrived and I wanted to find them."

"I mean, what happened between you and Aspen," I said gently.

"I know that's what you meant," she snapped. Her face crumpled again. "I'm sorry," she sobbed, wiping her face and sitting up a bit. "I don't mean to snap. Just, please let me tell this part first."

"Of course," I said, taking her hands in mine.

"Well," she sniffed, attempting a smile, "the fire got a little out of control, and we had to run. It was supposed to be contained to the kitchens, but it quickly took over the whole house. I didn't even make it to the study, so it was a wasted effort anyway. Thorn intercepted us as we tried to escape. He had packed a huge cache of iron weapons into a wagon and was trying to hitch it. We fought, and..." she trailed off, indicating her wound.

"And he injured you," I added. She nodded, wiping her face again.

"Vanth couldn't go after him because of my injury. Thorn got away. I'm almost certain the dagger used to hurt Hadrian was the same kind he used on me."

"Hadrian can send some guards to hunt him down," I said, feeling for once relieved instead of irritated at Aurelia's recklessness. I knew what Thorn might have done to her if she had stayed locked in her room. "Do you think it was Thorn who sent the assassin after him?"

"I don't know," she said quietly. Tears began to stream down her face again.

"I tried to tell him everything, that I was sorry, that I

knew I hurt him," she continued in a small voice, clearly no longer talking about Thorn. "He was so angry and upset. He didn't believe that I felt nothing for Thorn, that he was just a job." More tears streamed down her face.

"Then he's a fool," I said feelingly. "Anyone can see how much you love him."

She let out another sob and I climbed into the bed with her, holding her until there were no more tears left for her to cry, at least for today.

"He'll come around," I said, stroking her hair, certain that my cousin's love for Aurelia would outlive this hurt.

Once Aurelia had calmed she let me check her wound and fuss over her a bit. As Hadrian had said, the lines of corruption were gone, and neat stitches, neater than mine would have been, closed the wound. A green paste that smelled faintly of mint and thyme covered it. I replaced the bandages.

"I am glad you are healing," I said, bending down and kissing Aurelia on the cheek. "And I know that you are still hurting. I'm here whenever you need me."

"You'll be busy soon I think," she said, reaching up to gently touch my wings. "Tell me how this happened?"

And so I told my best friend everything that had happened in the weeks we had been apart. Despite her own sadness, she was an excellent audience, gasping and asking questions at all the right times.

"And how is it?" she asked, growing pink around the cheeks. "With him, I mean." I blushed.

"It's..." I paused, trying to think of the right word, and remembering what Hadrian had said to me that first night. I smiled. "Perfect."

CHAPTER 29

I awoke the next morning on my stomach, as I couldn't sleep comfortably on my healing back.

The dream that had plagued me since my childhood had haunted me again last night. A sky filled with blood. The agony in my back. The feeling of being both full of magic and hopelessly sad. I had been turning it over and over in my head, and I had a strong feeling I understood the dream now. I would need Mother Vervain to confirm.

I turned my head and saw Hadrian sleeping next to me, face drawn and pale. He must be exhausted after moving nonstop for days and shadow walking back and forth all over the realms.

I reached out and rested my hand on his bare chest, feeling the steady thump of his heart beating beneath.

He stirred and cracked an eye open, scowling when he saw me.

"Why are you awake," he growled, hauling me over to him until I was resting in the crook of his shoulder.

"Breakfast?" I asked, remembering the first morning we had woken up like this. He smiled, eyes still closed against the growing light, and groaned melodramatically.

I laughed, lifting myself up so I could kiss his chest. He hummed agreeably, so I continued my exploration, kissing across his collarbone to the hollow of his throat and just under his jaw. His shadows rose up in greeting and curled happily around me, sending shivers across me as they moved. Hadrian growled.

"You can't be jealous of your own shadows," I laughed. He scowled.

"I can and I am," he rumbled, bending down to kiss me on the lips. His face was scratchy, more stubble than usual covering his jaw after days of neglect. I rubbed my cheek against his, enjoying the delicious scratchy feeling.

"Mmmm," he murmured against my temple. "How are you feeling?"

"Better," I said truthfully. "Less like I've been wrung dry of all my energy."

"Good," he said, sitting up suddenly and pulling me onto his lap. "Because I have plans."

"Plans?" I asked, as he bent his head to kiss just below my jaw, moving slowly down the same path I had followed on him. Heat suffused my core as he kissed lower, and I shifted slightly on his lap, eliciting a growl that I felt all the way down to my toes.

"Not yet," he growled, nipping my lip between his

teeth and sweeping his tongue into my mouth.

At this point, Hadrian had given me many kisses. Soft and hard, tender and claiming. This one was different. It spoke of promises we had yet to make to each other, of a future we might share if we reached for it, of something I couldn't quite put words to, but made me feel like I was home. My toes curled as he kissed me, not breaking away until a knock at the door forced us apart.

"You have got to be joking," he growled at the universe, pausing his hands and mouth and shouting "What is it," angrily at the door. The handle jiggled, but the door stayed locked fast. Hadrian sent his shadows to reinforce it while he resumed his attentions on my neck, my collarbone, and my breasts.

I gasped a little and he quieted me with a kiss.

"Excuse me, my lady, but will you be wanting breakfast?" It was the voice of one of my uncle's household staff. My eyes lit up at the word breakfast, but Hadrian scowled.

"We'll be down in two hours," he shouted.

"Thirty minutes," I corrected, gasping as he flicked his tongue over my nipple.

"An hour," he shouted, sucking my breast into his mouth. I moaned and heard the shuffling feet of the servant beating a hasty retreat.

"You'll scandalize the whole household," I chided, moaning as he repeated the motion.

"Good," he growled, cupping my backside and lifting me so I could feel his hardness beneath me. "Maybe then they'll leave us alone."

Rocking his hips against me, I regretted the layers of fabric between us and hastily began to remove them. I hissed when I pulled my gown over my wings, realizing I was going to have to re-learn how to do many things with my new appendages.

Hadrian helped me get the gown off, tenderly lifting it over the delicate membranes so as not to pull the healing skin. He kissed and sucked my neck when it was off and I groaned.

"I know what I want for breakfast," he growled in my ear, dipping his fingers below my undergarments to the sensitive flesh beneath and growling when he felt the wetness there.

"I can't lie on my back," I panted as he stroked a finger through the dark hair that hid my folds, teasing my entrance before retreating. I clenched, wanting him in me already.

"That, my lady, is easily solved," he said, shifting down until he was lying fully on his back. Pulling my undergarments down, I lifted my legs one at a time so he could remove them and he pushed me up toward his face.

"What are you doing?" I said, putting my hands on his shoulder to stop him, and looking straight down at him from the top of his chest. He gave me that wicked smile.

"Trust me," he rumbled, pushing me up until his mouth was positioned directly under my sensitive flesh.

The first stroke of his tongue had me gasping again, and I reached up and grabbed on to the headboard for support as he swirled his tongue, dipping it inside me and swiping upward. I groaned, tipping my head back as he licked and sucked and teased, pulling my hips down with a firm arm when I began to squirm away at the intensity of it.

"How," I began, barely capable of forming a coherent thought. I looked down, almost coming apart at the sight of his mouth buried against me. He raised a brow at me and I felt him smile as he continued to lick and tease.

I closed my eyes and gave into the sensation, scrabbling at the headboard for purchase whenever he hauled me closer to him. When I came, I had to bite the edge of the board to muffle the sound. I was still quivering when he pulled me back so he could sit up, pressing me down onto him as he entered me in one delicious thrust.

"You were saying?" He asked, capturing my lips as he rocked with me. His kiss was demanding and brutal, as if he didn't really want me to break away to answer him.

"Nothing," I gasped, digging my fingers into his shoulders as we rocked together.

"Hmm." He nibbled my earlobe and whispered into my ear, "do you trust me?"

I nodded, and instantly his shadows rose up between us, wrapping around my wrists and pulling them gently but firmly above my head. He bent, teasing my nipples with his tongue, first the right, then the left, wrapping his hands around my backside and encouraging me to ride him to another orgasm. We came together this time, our cries swallowed by each other in a clashing of teeth and lips and tongues.

The shadows released me and I fell forward onto his chest. Sweat glistened there, but I didn't care, breathing in the supremely male scent of him.

"That was…" I started and stopped, unsure what words I would use to describe what I had just experienced with him.

"Mmhmm," he rumbled, hands still holding my rear as he bent to kiss my cheek. "It was." The shadows curled gently around me as if agreeing, stroking my arms and legs and back.

We lay like that, wrapped in each other and Hadrian's shadows, until the sweat cooled and the sounds of movement outside forced me to admit that it was time to face the new world we were going to forge together.

"What did Vanth mean when he called you his king?" I asked, still collapsed on Hadrian's chest. "And me his queen?"

I lifted my head to see him studying my face. With a gentle kiss, he rolled me off him and onto my side, careful of my tender back.

"I think you know what these mean," he said, barely touching a wing with the tip of his finger. I nodded, frowning.

"You suspected," I said. "Why didn't you tell me?" A bolt of hurt had lodged itself in my heart that he had kept his suspicions from me. He shook his head.

"You were safe from my father as long as the glamour held," he said. "I knew you would try to break it as soon as you knew, and damn the consequences."

"You should have told me," I whispered, trying to let go of the hurt. I knew he had done it to protect me, but I felt like he had lied.

"I should, and I'm sorry," he said, resting his forehead against mine. "More than you know. By the time I realized who you were, I was already so damn in love with you, I couldn't risk losing you."

"When?" I asked in a small voice. He lifted his

forehead.

"The night we made love," he said, reaching up and gently touching a wing again. I shivered. "When you glowed, I saw a shadow of them." A tear rolled down my cheek. He brushed it away and touched his nose to mine.

"You were so beautiful. So radiant. I told myself each day that I would tell you, until it became too big and too difficult." He shook his head, adding in a quiet sad voice, "have I lost you?"

"No, my love," I reassured him, heart aching that he felt he had to ask. I wrapped my arms around his neck and felt his arms and shadows return the embrace. "You will never lose me. Not even if you make me furious every day for the rest of our lives together."

He turned his head into my neck, kissing me there. I felt dampness on my shoulder and lifted his face, wiping the tears away with gentle strokes. I realized we were both dark and broken in ways that we might never be able to fully recover from, but I did not think it would be terrible to make a life with him, even if all we did was glue each other back together and chase away the shadows for eternity.

"I love you," he said, pressing his forehead to mine. "I don't know that I will ever be able to describe how much I love you. But if you let me, I will try every day for however long we have."

"What if it's a thousand years?" I teased, smiling against his lips.

He kissed me gently.

"Then maybe I'll have time to describe it accurately."

I kissed him, tentatively a first as we rebuilt the bridge of trust between us brick by brick, and then deeply when I could no longer stand his hesitant embrace.

For the second time that morning, he showed me in every way he could how much he loved me, worshiping me with his body and his mouth and his soul, until I admitted that I was mostly convinced by his performance.

"So why is Vanth calling you his king," I asked, lying across his chest again in the afterglow of his attentions. He smirked.

"As I am your mate, soon to be husband, and a prince of a realm, that makes me your king."

"What about the Unseelie realm?" I asked, trying to wrap my mind around the political implications of this. "You would be the Seelie and Unseelie King."

"And you would be the Seelie and Unseelie Queen," he confirmed. "Queen of All Fae. The realms would be united under one rule, but this time not through bloodshed or warfare."

I frowned.

"What about our magic?" I asked, thinking about how the division between the realms separated our magic. "When we kill your father, will the divide just fade?" Hadrian shook his head, frowning.

"Truthfully, I'm not sure," he said, placing a kiss on my temple. "Maybe the realms will be fully united. Maybe there will always be a divide. Only the goddess knows." I frowned again, a million other questions jumping to my mind.

"And what role are we to play now? For the Seelie court? The Unseelie court? Are you still the Prince of Death, and I the Ice Queen?"

Hadrian smiled warmly at me and stretched

languorously, again reminding me of that sleek forest cat.

"If you like," he said, giving me a wolfish grin. "But I think I have a better idea."

"And what is that?" I asked as he scooped me up and carried me to the bathing chamber. He smiled.

"I think we should play ourselves."

CHAPTER 30

We bathed together, rinsing the sweat and evidence of our lovemaking from each other's bodies.

"When your back is healed," he growled in my ear under the hot water, "I have *several* ideas about things we might try."

My toes curled, and for one heated moment I thought Hadrian might give in and take me in the shower as well, but he mastered the impulse for the sake of our friends.

I was a little disappointed.

By the time I emerged, I felt like I was finally ready to face my court.

"We can wait, if you want," Hadrian said, standing with me outside the door to the parlor. They were all in there, waiting for us, and my stomach was a mess of nerves knowing I was about to accept a role that I was not totally ready for.

"No," I sighed, meeting his eyes. The familiar flecks of silver brightened as he cupped my face.

He wore casual clothes that one might work in, brown trousers and a white shirt with the sleeves pushed up to his elbows. He looked somehow younger without the mask of the Prince of Death, though he was still far too pale and his shadows still too unnerving to be anything other than Unseelie.

It fit, that we belonged together. He really was my equal, my partner and my balance.

"You are the Queen, and you bow to no one," he said, recalling his advice to me on the first night of our act together.

"Not even to you?" I whispered, pulling comfort from his gaze and his shadows as they wrapped around me tenderly.

He kissed me softly and whispered, "not even to me."

Aurelia sat in a loveseat next to Seline, Vanth standing behind her with his hands on the back of the couch. Aspen leaned against the mantle next to Mother Vervain's chair. She was embroidering in a plush armchair, looking exactly as she had in the kitchens of the Unseelie Palace. The Commander stood to greet me.

"Commander," I said, bowing my head. She smiled, the scarred half of her face contorting with the motion.

"Ember," she said, coming to clasp my hand and Hadrian's forearm. "I think it's possible that I should be the one bowing."

I smiled uncomfortably, realizing we were going to have to address all this right now. I wasn't sure I was ready.

"Right," I said, sitting on one side of the open couch that had been left for us. Hadrian sat next to me, forearms propped on his knees. I looked to Mother Vervain, who sat wrapped in her shawls by the blazing fire, even though it was fairly warm in the Seelie Realm. She was engrossed in her work, something that included tiny flowers and leaves and stars.

"Mother Vervain," I said, smiling and walking over to her. I stilled her hand, her embroidery, a moth flying in a sea of stars, almost complete. She looked down at me and smiled warmly.

"My darling girl," she said, a tear running down her withered cheek.

"It's true?" I asked. She nodded, cupping my face. She had known, had tried to tell me, or at least to lead me to the truth. Another tear trailed down her wrinkled cheek.

"You look just like her," she whispered.

"Like who?" asked Seline, frowning at our exchange.

"Can you please begin the story?" I asked the old female quietly. "I think I know how it ends, but I don't know the beginning." She nodded and I took her hand as I knelt next to her.

"Three hundred years ago, the Unseelie King sought a marriage alliance with the Seelie Queen to solidify his control over the realms," Mother Vervain intoned.

No one said anything, the only sound the crackling of the fireplace as she spoke.

"She refused," Mother Vervain continued, "for he was a cruel male even then, and in retribution the

Unseelie King took the queen prisoner, cutting off her wings so she could not escape, dethroning her and destroying her magic by keeping her wingless in the Unseelie Realm."

She glanced at me and I squeezed her hand, nodding at her to continue.

"But the queen had a daughter, who was left behind after she was taken and became the new queen. She was a fierce warrior, and a strong magic wielder, adept at the old Seelie magics of healing and spell casting. But she was young and untested, and had not been granted the opportunity to learn from her mother's wisdom. For almost three hundred years she waged a bloody, unending war against the Unseelie King to try to retrieve her mother, who all the while remained locked away."

Mother Vervain paused and looked up, meeting the eyes of everyone assembled around the room.

"I do not know all the particulars," she said, standing slowly and releasing my hand, beginning to unwrap her many shawls from her shoulders. "For I was locked away for so long, and I never did see my beloved daughter again."

My heart stopped as she turned. The dress she wore was open in the back, always hidden by layers upon layers of shawls, and now I knew why. Two thick, painful looking scars stretched up her spine where there had once been wings.

I had felt her loss every time I dreamed of her, trapped and alone and captured. My dreams of stars and darkness and pain were her memories, those of the old Seelie Queen. My grandmother.

Why the dream had plagued me, I couldn't say.

Maybe something about the binding glamour that was cast on me. Or, maybe the goddess wanted me to find my destiny, and my mate. I didn't realize what it was about until I had felt my grandmother's pain as the wings ripped from my own back. I might never know, and I sighed, helping my grandmother return to her chair.

"Your daughter also had a daughter," I said, returning to the couch, taking Hadrian's hand. "A daughter that, when she left for the final battle in which she died, she gave to Aspen's aunt."

I turned to Aspen and he blanched.

"My aunt?" he said, confused. "Your mother you mean…" he trailed off, confusion turning to realization as the pieces clicked into place for him.

"My aunt was a handmaiden for the queen," he said, eyes wide as he looked at me.

"So?" asked Vanth, who looked confused about the turn of the conversation. "How does that make Ember the Seelie Queen?"

"Because Aspen's aunt wasn't Ember's true mother," Hadrian said. We had discussed a few theories about this in our shower, and this was what had made the most sense. "The Queen must have entrusted her handmaiden, Aspen's aunt, with her daughter, who she had kept hidden from the Unseelie King, telling her to pass the child off as her own to protect her." His shadows curled around me, as if they could protect me from the loss I would never remember.

"My daughter, the last Seelie Queen, was a healer, and a powerful magic user," my grandmother cut in, nodding thoughtfully as she repeated what she had told me when she said I reminded her of her daughter. "She could have cast a glamour so powerful that none but the babe would be able to break it, and not until she reached her majority."

Hadrian looked at me, squeezing my hand.

"She bound your magic, bound your wings, and gave you up, so that not even my father would be able to find you," he said. "He couldn't recognize you."

I nodded, setting the final piece into place.

"And when she died at the hands of the Unseelie King in battle, Aspen's aunt feared for her life, and mine. She willed me to the only person she thought might be safe from the king's wrath. A noble lady married to an influential but cruel lord, who betrayed her and her sister in the end to win favor with the king."

I turned and looked at Aspen.

"My mother," Aspen finished, shaking his head in disbelief. I smiled sadly, tears pooling in my eyes.

"My love," Hadrian murmured, wrapping his arms around me.

"When did you know?" I asked, turning to face my grandmother. She bowed her head, another tear running down her cheek.

"No glamour cast by my child could be kept from me for long. I knew as soon as Hadrian brought you to me, sick from the fever while crossing the realms," she admitted.

I nodded, not sure how to feel about her deception. Like Hadrian, I knew she loved me deeply, and wanted to protect me. I sighed, deciding to think about it later.

"And who is my father?" I asked, brushing tears from my cheeks. Mother Vervain shook her head.

"I do not know who your father is, my dear, or if he lives," she said sadly. I nodded, feeling the last hope for meeting my birth parents slip away.

"So what now?" Seline asked.

"There's no hiding our rebellion or Ember from my father any longer," Hadrian said.

"If this is all true," Vanth added, frowning at us like he was still not quite sure he believed us, "then the news that the Seelie Queen had been found and that the Prince had betrayed him will reach him in a matter of days. We should be prepared for any offensive he might launch in retaliation."

Hadrian nodded. I felt a twist of fear in my gut. Our forces were scattered and few, and we were outnumbered. How long would it take for the Unseelie King to sweep down with his army and destroy us? I had no idea how to use my power yet, and I wasn't sure how long I would have to learn before having to meet him in battle.

I also thought about the problem of Lord Thorn. If he had been caching iron weapons for the king, where did they come from? The Unseelie King must be trading with the mountain Dwarves, but what could he possibly offer them to make them abandon their natural enmity toward us?

Thorn might right now be with the king, but I knew Hadrian would want to hunt him down. Possibly my uncle too, if he was very unlucky.

"Commander," Hadrian said, turning to face her. She had been a silent audience during the discussion, but she came to life now.

"We need soldiers and weapons," she said, "and Fae who can train the recruits to fight Unseelie magic."

Vanth stood and walked over to me, kneeling and bowing his head.

"My Queen, I offer you my service and my life," he said, looking up at me. "I can help train your soldiers to fight the king's magic."

"And I," said Seline, coming to kneel next to him. "My Queen, I offer you my service and my life."

I smiled down at them, my new friends. Family really. They were all my family now.

Aspen knelt next.

"You have the hospitality of the estate as long as you need," he said, bowing his head. He looked up and smiled faintly, still missing the jovial air he had before all this began. "You have my loyalty, Cousin. I offer you my service and my life."

"We are still cousins then?" I asked, worried that the news of my heritage might have broken something between us.

"Always," he said, glancing at Aurelia before looking away swiftly.

She stood next, joining the half circle that was forming around me. She knelt next to Aspen, who bristled. My heart ached for her.

"You will always have me to guard your left, and to be your knife in the dark," she said. Her golden head bobbed. "My Queen, dearest Ember, I offer you my service and my life."

My eyes pricked with tears as she looked up at me, so sad and broken, but fierce.

"And I will teach you all I know about being a Queen," my grandmother said from her chair. She did not kneel, but I did not wish her to. She was a Queen in her own right, and now the closest connection I would ever have to my birth family. I nodded, a tear sliding down my cheek for the mother I would never know.

"I will need help learning to use my power," I said to the room in general.

Hadrian took his place on the ground. My heart ached as my mate, my balance, my love, knelt before me. He took my hand and kissed it.

"I will help you in any way I can," he said, eyes swirling with silver as he looked at me. "My Queen, you have my service and my life."

I cupped his cheek, another tear sliding down my own.

"And I will lead your forces, if you wish it," said the Commander, coming to kneel before me with the others. "My Queen, you have my service and my life."

I gazed around the room at my friends and family. My heart swelled at their support and hope and loyalty. I would need it, I realized. The last few weeks had been the easy part.

"Well then," I said, steeling my shoulders and straightening my back, heart soaring as I fluttered my wings for the first time.

"Let's go plan a war."

EPILOGUE

The wedding took place on the Winter Solstice, and for once it was a ball I didn't mind attending.

In the four weeks since my magic had emerged, my court had grown to hundreds of supporters and loyal subjects. Many Seelie and Unseelie had fled North, but many had also fled South to swear fealty to me and to Hadrian.

My mate and husband came up behind me as I stood on the terrace of the ballroom at the Seelie palace. Restoration was already underway, but there was still much to be done. The ballroom had been suitably undamaged to host the party, and Aurelia had outdone herself with the decorations, draping every surface in snowdrops and winter jasmine and firefly lights. The place sparkled, and I imagined it might be a little what it had been like before the war raged between the two realms.

Hadrian kissed my neck, resting his hands on my waist and carefully navigating around my wings, which fluttered gently in the winter breeze.

"My love," he murmured into my neck, breathing me in. I closed my eyes, lifting my hand to his face and smiling as he tickled me. He was the dark prince again tonight in all black, and it gave me a thrill to see it.

"Have I told you yet how much I like the dress?" he asked, smiling into my shoulder.

"Hmm, only one or two hundred times," I mused. He rewarded me with a laugh and a little nip on my collarbone.

The dress had been a gift from him, and like everything he chose for me it was utterly perfect. Pale satin draped from the tiny straps that held up the dress, and the whole thing was covered in glittering diamonds that sparkled as I moved. It was heavy, but I didn't care.

He had also chosen a dress that accommodated my wings, which were rather sensitive to touch and temperature now that they were healed. A deep vee in the back of the dress provided them plenty of space to flutter behind me.

The first thing I had done upon learning to fly with them was to take Aurelia flying. She had whooped for joy as we fluttered over the trees, and even though it was a short flight, as I didn't have the strength to fly far yet, I beamed at the joy I was able to give her.

It wasn't enough to lift her out of her despair, but I hoped it was a start.

She and Aspen still hadn't made up. I had cornered

him the day before to try to get him to talk to her, but he shut me down.

"Don't Ember," he said, smile falling as he realized what I wanted to discuss.

"She loves you, Aspen," I said, frustration rising at his stubborn refusal to forgive her and marry her like I knew he really wanted deep down.

"She married another male," he said coldly.

"For the mission!" I replied impatiently.

"I don't care," he shouted back. "She broke my heart."

He stood breathing heavily. I put my hand on his arm.

"I know," I said sadly.

"What's wrong?" asked Hadrian, bringing me back to the present.

"Just thinking about Aurelia and Aspen," I sighed. Turning into his arms, and resting my head on his broad chest. He tucked me under his chin and sighed too.

"They'll find their way back to each other," he said, sounding more confident about it than I felt.

"How do you know?" I asked in a quiet voice, listening to his heart beating in rhythm with mine as he held me close.

"Because we did," he said. "And if we can find each other, then there's hope for them."

We stood there for a long time under the moon and starlight, the sounds of music and laughter and dancing reaching us from inside the ballroom. Hadrian's shadows curled around me, and I let my light out to play with them, creating stars in our own personal galaxy around us.

"Do you want to go back in?" Hadrian murmured

into my hair. I shook my head. Smiling, I looked up at him, meeting his eyes. Silver flooded them as he took me in, growing heated as he focused on my lips.

"Not really," I said, smiling and standing on my toes to kiss him gently. "I have other plans."

"Plans?" He said in mock shock, raising his eyebrows at me, his wicked grin taking over his face.

I grinned back, kissing him more deeply, and taking his hand to lead him to our bedroom.

"Oh, *those* sorts of plans," he said, nipping my earlobe and scooping me up into his arms.

"You know, now that your back is healed I have *several* ideas about things we might try," he added as I laughed, batting his mouth away from my ear. I yelped as he ran the last few stairs to our room, sweeping me into a searing kiss as he put me down at our door.

"Let's try them all," I said, grabbing his lapels and taking him with me as he kissed my face and my neck and my shoulders, worshiping me in the best way he knew how. "I want everything."

The story continues in Book 2 of Queen of All Fae, featuring Aurelia and Aspen in a second-chance romance.

ACKNOWLEDGEMENT

This book was written lightning fast, thanks to a few people who need to be acknowledged.

First, my husband, who put up with me working on this book at all hours of the day and night for a month and a half solid. Without your lead with the kids and your general help with ideas, this book would not have happened. Or it might have, just much more slowly.

Thank you so much to Aurora, my beta reader, for both encouraging me to write, inviting me to her writing group, and reading the book as I wrote it. Your ideas and feedback were invaluable, and I hope you know that part of your soul is imprinted in this work as well!

To Shelly, for reading the book because she is my friend, and then deciding she loved it. I so appreciate your support and time in reading, even though I know you were busy.To my ARC readers who took a chance on an unknown book and author, thank you for believing in me and loving free books. Thank you to Chikovnay from Canva Pro for the beautiful artwork that brought this book to life.

And finally, thank you, dear reader, for taking a chance on me. I hope you loved reading about Hadrian and Ember as much as I enjoyed writing them.

him the day before to try to get him to talk to her, but he shut me down.

"Don't Ember," he said, smile falling as he realized what I wanted to discuss.

"She loves you, Aspen," I said, frustration rising at his stubborn refusal to forgive her and marry her like I knew he really wanted deep down.

"She married another male," he said coldly.

"For the mission!" I replied impatiently.

"I don't care," he shouted back. "She broke my heart."

He stood breathing heavily. I put my hand on his arm.

"I know," I said sadly.

"What's wrong?" asked Hadrian, bringing me back to the present.

"Just thinking about Aurelia and Aspen," I sighed. Turning into his arms, and resting my head on his broad chest. He tucked me under his chin and sighed too.

"They'll find their way back to each other," he said, sounding more confident about it than I felt.

"How do you know?" I asked in a quiet voice, listening to his heart beating in rhythm with mine as he held me close.

"Because we did," he said. "And if we can find each other, then there's hope for them."

We stood there for a long time under the moon and starlight, the sounds of music and laughter and dancing reaching us from inside the ballroom. Hadrian's shadows curled around me, and I let my light out to play with them, creating stars in our own personal galaxy around us.

"Do you want to go back in?" Hadrian murmured

into my hair. I shook my head. Smiling, I looked up at him, meeting his eyes. Silver flooded them as he took me in, growing heated as he focused on my lips.

"Not really," I said, smiling and standing on my toes to kiss him gently. "I have other plans."

"Plans?" He said in mock shock, raising his eyebrows at me, his wicked grin taking over his face.

I grinned back, kissing him more deeply, and taking his hand to lead him to our bedroom.

"Oh, *those* sorts of plans," he said, nipping my earlobe and scooping me up into his arms.

"You know, now that your back is healed I have *several* ideas about things we might try," he added as I laughed, batting his mouth away from my ear. I yelped as he ran the last few stairs to our room, sweeping me into a searing kiss as he put me down at our door.

"Let's try them all," I said, grabbing his lapels and taking him with me as he kissed my face and my neck and my shoulders, worshiping me in the best way he knew how. "I want everything."

The story continues in Book 2 of Queen of All Fae, featuring Aurelia and Aspen in a second-chance romance.

ABOUT THE AUTHOR

Madeleine Eliot

Madeleine Eliot has been writing stories since she was a child. She loves to read in her spare time, especially spicy fantasy romance books, and spend time with her children. Follow her adventures and latest works on Instagram @madeleineeliotwrites

Printed in Great Britain
by Amazon